Rachel Cusk was born in 1967 and is the author of seven novels: *Saving Agnes*, which won the Whitbread First Novel Award, *The Te_____* a Som___ Maug_____ *The Lucky Ones*, which was shortlisted for the Whitbread Novel Award, *In the Fold* and *Arlington Park*, which was shortlisted for the Orange Prize and *The Bradshaw Variations*. Her non-fiction books are *A Life's Work*, *The Last Supper* and *Aftermath*. In 2003 she was chosen as one of Granta's Best of Young Novelists.

RACHEL CUSK

Saving Agnes

ff

faber and faber

First published in 1993
by Picador

This paperback edition first published in 2013 by
Faber and Faber
Bloomsbury House
74–77 Great Russell Street
London WCIB 3DA

Typeset by Intype, London
Printed in England by CPI Group (UK) Ltd, Croydon, CRO 4YY

A CIP record for this book
is available from the British Library

ISBN 978–0–571–27210–5

2 4 6 8 10 9 7 5 3 1

For Sarah Cusk

ACKNOWLEDGEMENTS

My thanks go to Katie Owen at Macmillan,
Jane Bradish-Ellames at Curtis Brown,
to Billie, Mary and Sophie,
and most of all to my family.

FOR SARAH CUSK

Chapter One

THE house, like the party, was subsiding. It didn't lurch or tilt Titanically, crockery and silverware crashing to the floor, women in tight taffeta dresses flung screaming across the room; like the party, it wasn't a large-scale Hollywood affair. As yet the only evidence of its sinking was a crack, a long narrow wound in the sitting-room wall, and Agnes Day felt that it presaged a destiny altogether more menacing.

She stood at the foot of the stairs where a handful of stragglers, having not long ago heroically resisted the two o'clock exodus, now lingered with an air of having in some way been cheated. On the far side of the room, one or two people stood immobile in the landscape of bottles and ashtrays, overturned candles and shattered glass, of wine pools banked by little white hillocks of salt and fringed with crumpled cigarette packets, like contorted statues in an abstract sculpture park. She realised there was no one here she wanted to talk to, no one she could even bear talking to.

'The condemned man ate a hearty breakfast,' said Merlin cheerfully, passing her by as he trawled the room with a large black bin-liner.

Agnes headed for the stairs, where a candle was lying felled in a pool of its own wax on the carpet. Merlin and Nina had, rightly she now admitted, been opposed to her candle scheme; but the house had looked so lovely by candlelight, so aglow with anticipation and promise, that she had forced them to yield. Merlin had submitted gratifyingly swiftly. Nina, less pliant but always with a ready definition of democracy to hand, knew majority rule when she saw it. They had seen it as a whim, Agnes knew; a flimsy, floating thing which scientists might examine under a microscope. But if that were what it was she was full of them, riddled with terminal caprice. She toured her disease like a schizophrenic commuter, trudging back and forth between how things were and how she wanted them to be. The candles belonged to the latter world and it was a place she habitually visited alone. Roaming through the gloaming. she had almost been happy.

Agnes Day paused at the foot of the stairs. Her guests looked wild-eyed and nocturnal, something seen in a nature documentary. Some people in one corner were puncturing beer cans with ball-point pens. A geyser of brown liquid foamed over the curtains. Nina was lounging on a nearby sofa, engaged in conversation.

'Look,' she sighed impatiently. 'Women don't necessarily want men to accept their hideous physical proclivities. We need a secret life. It's part of our autonomy. In fact, I can't think of anything worse than some post-feminist prat fawning over my body hair.'

'Not at all!' cried the recipient of this lecture, apparently undeterred by it. He had something on his upper lip which, on closer inspection, Agnes saw to be a moustache. 'You shouldn't be embarrassed about it! In fact, I think there's nothing more beautiful than a woman with hairy armpits.'

Nina rested her head on two fingers pointed at her temple like a revolver and rolled her eyes at Agnes, who changed course with grim determination and fled up the stairs.

In the bathroom, she peered into the mirror as if trying to see something beyond what was there. Her lipstick had seeped into spiky tendrils around her mouth, clinging like a sea-anemone to the porous surface of her face. Agnes met her own eyes and saw their expression was fearful. She rummaged in the cupboard above the sink and began to draw a new red smile over the flagging grimace already there. Halfway through, her lower lip gleaming like a bloodied crescent moon, she stopped and allowed herself to submit to a wave of despair. What was the point? How, when John had taken all point with him, packing it neatly between a sweater and a book perhaps, could she be expected to care? She looked in the mirror, hoping to compound the tragedy by reading its desolation in her face. Her orphaned lip, however, lent her grieving features an annoyingly comical aspect. She deferred further rumination while carefully drawing in the upper bow.

She emerged a few minutes later to harvest the fruit of her labours. Someone was standing outside, someone she hadn't seen before. The light from the bathroom swung interrogatively over his face as she opened the door and barrelled straight into him, and she saw that look in his eyes as he saw her, the look of surprised appreciation, of suggestion and intent, that speaking glance she had sometimes felt she would do anything for, just to feel again its comforting implication of desire. She apologised and smiled, and somehow a conversation was begun. The slightly distasteful fact that they had met outside the bathroom could be seen as rather humorous, she thought, if presented in the right way. She planned it as she saw him taking every cue faultlessly, like a professional. This is how we met, she would say.

Chapter Two

AGNES and Nina and Merlin met at university; or at least that was what Agnes said. Merlin, prizing information over intrigue, said they met at Oxford. Nina said they met at college. Agnes preferred her own version of events, although not, as might have been imagined, for its lack of bias towards cultural élitism in either quarter. To her, such ellipses contained a world of social possibility which could not be overlooked. So, 'We met at university,' she would say; or, of some fleeting stranger waving to her across a crowded room, 'Oh, just someone I knew at university.' 'When I was at *university*,' she would say, eyes modestly lowered, head tilted slightly forwards, so that her panicked and prurient companion would endure several agonising moments of uncertainty. Was it Hull or Harvard? He (for it was invariably a he) couldn't tell, but now that she'd mentioned it he simply had to know. Was she beautiful *and* brainy? Was his cup about to run over? Almost unable to bear the possibility of disappointment, and unaware that his discomfort was standard procedure, he would somehow stammer: 'Where did you study?' Agnes, with a now quite confident show of shame and humility would murmur, 'Oxford' – low, but not so low as to be in any danger of being misheard – and then would look for a brief moment imploringly into her inquisitor's eye.

Once or twice, when Agnes had left the irresistible bait of her undisclosed place of education hanging tantalisingly in the air, her companion had merely smiled slyly and inquired, 'Oxford or Cambridge?' The admission would take on a very different tone then, and while Agnes was quick to condemn these specimens as offenders against the rules of attraction, she would eventually concede that they must also be the unfortunate living examples of that breed she had often heard spoken about – but whose aversion she had humbly never considered would devolve upon her – who disliked intelligent women.

While none of them, then, could agree on where they met, the plain fact of their mutual liking was less open to dispute. Nina and Agnes had been friends first, and had met in the early weeks of their first year. Nina, freshly emerged from the dustcloud of a genteel Surrey upbringing, was a radical supporter of anything which promised to undermine it; while Agnes naturally gravitated towards things which bore at least a resemblance, however vague, to the small collection of known quantities accumulated during her East Anglian youth. In the event their unlikely convergence was precipitated by Nina's accosting Agnes in a hallway and inviting her to a women's group meeting.

'Women's group?' Agnes had replied suspiciously. 'Well yes, okay. Is that where you all sit around and talk about diets and boyfriends and things?'

At the time Nina had found this jest hilarious, and had had ample opportunity over the subsequent years to ruminate upon the possibility that Agnes might have meant it seriously.

It wasn't long before the arrival of Merlin, a bouncing eleven-stone mathematician, completed their family group and even strengthened their commitment to one another. Many were the times Agnes and Nina concealed their quarrels for his sake, for he doted on them both. Merlin, although quiet and bespectacled, was possessed of the rare ability to make people like him with very little apparent effort on his part. This was possibly owing to a certain air of impartiality, an asocial, asexual calmness in his nature, which never failed to attract those beset by insecurities concerning their own frenetically social and sexual selves; who, it might be added, in those days of identity crises, constituted the great majority of his peers. While Merlin appeared not to mind his involuntary popularity, Agnes and Nina took it upon themselves to protect him from the wasteful wiles of moaners and whingers. They discouraged the distressed individuals regularly to be found taking up tenancy in his room; whisked him away from under the noses of those attempting to waylay him with their problems on his way to the library; and even, upon occasion, salvaged him from the jaws of women who, wounded by less liberated loves, sought to assuage their hurt in the safety of Merlin's enlightened sensibilities.

So Merlin went unscarred, if uninitiated, through the three difficult years of weaning from adolescence; he frolicked untrammelled in Elysian groves of quantum mechanics and chaos, while Nina and Agnes dealt with the hard realities of English literature. They listened patiently, their hands dusty with medieval prose, their foreheads smudged with nineteenth-century hardship, while Merlin spoke sweetly of the frothy surface of time and the vexing disappearance of Schrödinger's cat. It was not, then, without some surprise – and perhaps the smallest quantity of resentment – that as they emerged some years later into the harsh light and noise of a brutal London and anxiously watched Merlin take his first faltering steps, they clearly saw him break into a confident run straight into the arms of a multi-million-pound financial institution, a company car, and a salary for which Elizabeth Bennet would have left Darcy's dinner burning in the oven.

Agnes and Nina listened nervously as Merlin debated the various advantages of living in Chelsea, Hampstead or Kensington, then took to reading the *Hackney Gazette* and the *Acton Observer* in the hope that such publications, if left lying around, might cultivate in him a taste for the distinctive flavour of the more modest boroughs. This practice, however, was short-lived, for as pleasant as the world seemed when reflected in the *Merton Mirror*, it offered little opportunity for gainful employment; although Agnes, it must be said, often spent illicit hours poring over their yellowed pages, lost in the twilit subterrene of out-of-date local intrigue and small-ads; of macabre deeds, petty thievery and sleazy domestic violence, of truth that was stranger indeed than the fiction of bombs, wars and global decay that she observed nightly. She read about a woman who left her husband's corpse rotting on the sofa, claiming she didn't know he was dead; a man who, catching his wife with a man he look to be her lover, shot them both and then shot himself; someone divorcing his wife after discovering she'd been feeding him cat food for the last ten years. 'I was saving him money,' the woman protested. 'I used the extra to buy nylons, a bit of lipstick – you know.'

Agnes imagined them, these borough-dwellers, packed into honeycombed tower-blocks and desolate shopping malls, their territories orbiting round Belgravia and Knightsbridge and Soho like strange satellites round a mysterious sun. She was fascinated by their fearlessness. There were days when she sat until the afternoon died into darkness, her eyes raking the classified pages in search of she knew not what. Models wanted for mail order catalogue. Commis chef required. Earn hundreds from home – own transportation essential.

They ended up living in Highbury; or at least that was what Agnes said. Merlin, taking for his reference the nearest conurbation, said they lived in Finsbury Park. Nina said they lived in the Arsenal. What Nina's claim lacked in glamour it made up for in accuracy: they did indeed live in the Arsenal, a tiny grid of quiet streets possessing an unusually parochial charm for what they all claimed was central London. The Arsenal, however, although dangerously near the borders, was undeniably in Agnes's Highbury, and the two friends were happy to discover they lived in such close proximity. Alas, it was Merlin, insisting as he did on the windswept reaches of Finsbury Park, who dwelt in error; for though it was but half a mile away, this barren region of concrete and cast-iron, of clotting traffic and petrol-heavy air, of desolate pavements overrun with skulking dogs and whirling litter cyclones, of filthy strings of shops selling only what nobody wanted to buy, was – and on this Agnes insisted – a world apart.

The house belonged to Merlin's uncle Dan, but Merlin's preferment displayed scant consciousness of the time-honoured rituals of heirloom and inheritance. Dan deserted the property like a precipitant rat at the first sign of listing, when rumours of the street's subsidence were still but rumours. The council had agreed to purchase the house at the end of a two-year period – by which time, they assured him with what appeared to be complacency, it was certain to be uninhabitable – and Dan was partially comforted to find in Merlin a tenant prepared to pay handsomely for the pleasure of witnessing the property's decline. The proximity of the Arsenal football ground went some way towards recompensing Merlin for his pains, and although the value of this bonus had been calculated without his incumbent flatmates in mind, they at least were relieved that he seemed to have abandoned his dreams of security guards and private swimming pools.

What it lacked in elegant accoutrements the house made up for in symbolic value, for it was, after all, their first. Like its occupants, 14 Elwood Street was detached from its neighbours. Merlin claimed there was an exiled Cameroonian prince living in disgrace next door; but while Agnes and Nina had seen for themselves the broken windows, overflowing bins and constant stream of unsavoury visitors that paid testimony to the latter part of this statement, they had no evidence as to the veracity of the former.

Once Merlin had started his job, Agnes and Nina spent their days scrubbing and sweeping and purging like symbiotic housewives. Within a fortnight, however, Nina found a job on a local newspaper, which shifting of the household's employment ratio meant that home improvements were relegated to weekends. While the democratic process exempted Agnes from days of lonesome toil, it did not see fit to replace this occupation with any more productive form of employment. She spent days wandering the streets of her unfamiliar home, and was eventually driven to go into different newsagents, buying three papers a day just so that she could talk to someone. On one of these social forays she encountered her next-door neighbour, the erstwhile prince of the Cameroons, rooting in his own rubbish bin as if in the hope of scavenging something that he, as a monarchist spendthrift, might have tossed away half finished.

'Morning!' Agnes called out, driven by pity and desperation to an attempt at human kindness.

The man looked up and stared at her. Presently, he grinned and indicated a battered lime-green Cortina parked outside the house.

'Joy ride?' he said. 'Me and you?'

'No thank you,' said Agnes smartly as she walked on, chilled by this untimely encounter with derangement.

'Fuck you!' she suddenly heard him shout behind her.

She quickened her pace tearfully as the cry wheeled in the air like a vulture, blocking out the sun. *Fuuh-kyooo*.

Agnes liked to believe there was some good to be gleaned from every situation, however bad it might seem, but when she had been working for a month at *Diplomat's Week* magazine she realised the higher purpose of the benevolent universe was taking a little longer than usual to reveal itself.

She had been employed, for reasons she was not yet able to ascertain, as assistant editor of this illustrious weekly, but soon came to feel that she was not so much assisting as getting in the way. The pain of this suspicion would become particularly acute when, sitting in her overheated office, she would find herself transfixed by the arthritic motion of the clock on the wall, and, forgetting for a moment that her imprisonment was owed to an act of will rather than one of international terrorism, would become tearful at the thought that perhaps the rest of her adult life was to be wished away thus.

A hostage, then, only to fortune, and determined from the start swiftly to make good her escape, Agnes saw little point in absorbing herself in the dull round of tasks which befell her, and still less in cultivating meaningful relationships with her guards. The editor, Jean, was a grim and tight-lipped woman, whose all-encompassing role as high priestess of form and slave to detail meant that Agnes was ever within spitting distance of her wrath; a proximity made more terrible by the fact of Jean's having devised an office system either so complex or so irrational that only she could understand it. The blame for Agnes's complete failure to grasp any one of its labyrinthian tenets could therefore have been apportioned to one of several quarters, but her inferior position in a hierarchy which seemed to her to be riddled with the same predestined injustices as that of her family, rendered her wholly accountable.

'Don't buck the system, Barbara!' Jean would cry as Agnes was discovered performing emergency surgery on a filing cabinet so full that it appeared to be vomiting sheaves of paper. Barbara was the name of Agnes's predecessor, whose ghost evidently still walked for Jean.

'I was only trying to help!' Agnes would rejoin; but Jean, who wore the look of one doing things for the war effort, had long since formed the opinion that there was a saboteur in their midst and was not to be fooled by any such protestations of innocence.

Conspiratorial solace soon appeared in the form of Jean's personal assistant, Greta, who returned from holiday just as Agnes was beginning to wonder if she would ever return to waking life. Greta was certainly personal, to the point of rudeness, with her employer, but Agnes was cheered to see that there was someone who was of even less assistance than herself. On first encountering her, Agnes had been somewhat alarmed by Greta's transatlantic accent and air-hostess smile, but she soon learned that Greta had a curious allure, an ability to arouse unlikely behaviour in those around her, which lent her a strange and devilish beauty.

'This city is bizarre,' she sighed when arriving in the office one morning. 'I was crossing the road over there when some guy in a truck drinking a can of beer stopped at the lights and just spat a whole mouthful all over me.'

The beer stain adorning the front of her jacket bore witness to her story and she waited, doe-eyed and credulous, for an explanation, while Agnes and Jean assured her that such occurrences were far from commonplace; which admission seemed only to baffle her further.

'The guy in the truck?' she said finally. 'He kind of reminded me of my boyfriend back home.'

Greta was a Ukrainian Canadian, and if a marriage between these two cultures seemed unlikely, their brief encounter in the form of Greta was unregrettable. She had come to London six months earlier, and despite finding the city to be drab, tedious and inhospitable in the extreme, saw no reason why she should leave. In addition to her unconventional style of dress – she favoured garish colours and dressed as if in preparation for a carnival or costume ball: clownish stripes combined with military epaulets, Elizabethan ruffs with rakish ponchos – Greta's voluptuous beauty and unsuspecting nature invited much attention, most of it, as far as Agnes could see, unwelcome.

'I'm on a diet,' she announced one lunchtime.

'Why?' queried Agnes, amazed that she should contemplate such an activity when her life already seemed to be in constant peril.

'Oh, some guy came up to me in the street last night and said I was a fat cow,' said Greta cheerfully. 'He suggested I might try and lose some weight.'

As if it were infectious, Agnes too began to discover the discomfort of strangers, but the weightiness for her of such encounters could not be so easily lost. She began to attract the attentions of the mad, the vagrant and those down on their luck in a manner she hoped was no relation to recognition. Once a soft touch for these ragged moralists who inveigled her into sparing them her change, Agnes began to cross the road, begging for some change in her circumstances. She witnessed her expulsion from the civilised world daily as she completed the arduous journey to the misleadingly named Finchley Central, where the offices of *Diplomat's Week* clung to the city's edge like a penitent cliff-top suicide, hoping against hope that someone, anyone remotely sane, would stay on the train beyond Highgate; but by the time they reached Camden Town the majority of those whom she could not picture stealing her wallet had long since disembarked, and as the train blasted through the topsoil into the charmless overground world of East Finchley the last feverish, pulsating remnants of the mad morning rush were gone.

Until that moment Agnes usually managed to sustain the appearance of a thrusting young professional running on a tight schedule; but then someone switched on the lights, pulled off the mask, revealed the pretender for exactly who she was. Women fanned themselves and fainted in the aisles in dismay; men in tight tailcoats stood up, red-faced, and waved their programmes demanding redress. For she was none other than Agnes Day: sub-editor, suburbanite, failure *extraordinaire*.

Chapter Three

AGNES Day was her real name, but this seemed to surprise no one other than herself. For her own part, she could not conjure up a single plausible reason why anyone should want to inflict a name such as that upon an innocent person. Agnes had, in fact, been the name of her father's mother; and while most of the time she chose to overlook the rather pedestrian logic this coincidence implied, in moments of fear at the world's cruelty she was forced to concede that to have inherited little from this lady other than her appellatory misfortune constituted something of a lucky escape.

As a child Agnes had been imaginative – a word often used to explain the character of a compulsive liar – and had enjoyed frequent changes of identity which, as far as she could see, it would have cost the small group of people who counted as her world in those days little to honour. A few times, in truth, they had attempted to humour her delightful precocities, their faces taut at first with suppressed smiles and later with irritation, but the rapid turnover of transmogrification often left them standing.

'Bathsheba, could you pass the salt?' her father would politely inquire.

'*Boadicea!*' Agnes would cry; which exhortation would usually rend from her less indulgent mother a plea along the lines of 'Oh, for God's sake, Agnes!' Agnes would then be forced again to correct the form of her address, and would inevitably be rewarded with a stinging backside and the liberty to retire to her room as soon as she liked.

As Agnes approached puberty her identity crisis, escaping the contemptuous adolescent pruning of all things childish, grew, along with the other nascent buds of her evolving world-view, from a whimsical fantasy into an issue of earth-shattering importance. A rejection of all things outlandish in favour of the ephemeral trappings of peer conformity was only natural, and although she soon lost her taste for elaborate nomenclature, her desperate need for acceptability outpaced it. Seeing the Dominiques, Gemmas and Antoinettes at school become more beautiful, clever and confident than the rest, and seeing also that she had not accompanied them in this transformation, merely confirmed what she already knew to be true – that what would have been success by any other name was fast becoming failure by her own.

The adult world being impervious to the tender-hearted miseries of youth, and assuming that identity was a more or less fixed matter whose flaws were the responsibility of no one other than their owner, Agnes knew that hers would be a solitary struggle. Wishing to spare those who did not really deserve any more careful consideration than they had shown in naming her, and secretly fearful of straying too far from the terms on which her worldly existence so far had seemed to depend, she chose her own middle name, Grace. Even her elders in all their irrational mystery could not object to such a choice, as they themselves had selected the name from all the thousands which had haunted her mother's bulging belly like wispy little-girl ghosts, as runner-up.

Why Grace, superior as she so evidently was, had not won this early contest Agnes could not imagine; but her battle for reinstatement second time around looked set for victory. To Agnes's dumbfoundment her parents did not object to her plan, and even humoured her so far as to suggest measures for its smoother implementation. Her mother advised that she try the name at home first to see if she liked it, and Agnes, always glad of an opportunity to disguise apprehension with obedience, made a fine show of reluctant agreement.

For a while, then, Grace was an honoured guest in their house, a favoured foster-child who emanated sunshine and laughter wherever she went. Her pronouncements were solemnly heard, her opinions sought out, her health and happiness the priority of the household. Only her brother, the more prosaically named Tom, continued to refer to Agnes in a manner not entirely respectful to the dead.

'Let's say Agnes,' he would declare as the family were bowed for grace before supper; or, if Grace declined to join him in a game of cards, 'Don't put on those airs and Agneses with me' would be his scornful riposte. Tom missed Agnes and had little time for her double, but would certainly not have shared this information with either of them.

Inevitably, as the days wore on, it fell to Grace's lot to do the share of household chores which had been Agnes's, and which had been temporarily forestalled while her arrival was still a novelty. There was also a portion of ill-humour and reprimand to be claimed, and it surprised Grace to discover that it was indistinguishable from that which had befallen Agnes. Gradually Grace began to feel disenchanted with her new home, especially when she contemplated in the mirror the toll it was taking on her looks. She was not the ravishing creature of fantasy she once had been, and nor did she inspire the love and admiration she once had known. She began, in short, to consider taking her leave; and although the change was so gradual as almost to elude their notice, the family one day realised that Agnes was with them once more.

Their joy at this discovery did not console their prodigal daughter. Agnes was convinced that Grace had been driven away by her family's ill-treatment – not to mention their incurable tendency to call her Agnes – and under such circumstances she could ill afford any pleasure at their very evident relief to have her back with them. Tom's cunning wordplay, however, remained, and enjoyed frequent airings in a context which Agnes could only later begin to see, with a controllable quantity of grief, as family humour.

It would have surprised them, no doubt, to learn that some part of Agnes had been irretrievably lost through this episode;

and though it would never have occurred to her to blame them, she sometimes wondered why the proliferation of selves she would have liked to be and lives she would have liked to live remained locked inside her, prisoners of utmost secrecy and shame. And while it taught her that reality meant failure, ugliness and self-contempt, it also instilled in her the belief that the good in her was but fiction. As she grew older and encountered the approbation of friends and lovers, this fiction became ever more elaborate, until she feared that one day she would crumble beneath the weight of her deception and lose all that she most valued. Once Agnes had mourned Grace, but eventually she came to loathe and fear her; for she had taken everything that she once loved in herself, every particle of hope and optimism and beauty, and made it false. Agnes did not create Grace: it was Grace who created Agnes, slapped her together with the dross and scraps she did not want herself. Agnes saw her sometimes, the model on the cover of a magazine, the byline on a witty news feature, the laughing glamorous figure in a red sports car driven by an adoring boyfriend. I wish it were me! she would think. It should have been me.

Chapter Four

AGNES Day painted her face and starved herself; she shaved her legs and plucked her eyebrows and scrubbed the gravelly flesh on her thighs with a mitt of similar texture. She moisturised here and desiccated there, purged her skin of odour and oil and then force-fed it with creams and sprays, as if hoping that one day it would give off of its own accord the exotic fragrance and softness which were now but briefly borrowed. Occasionally, she would bleach the rather unsightly shadow of dark hairs that fell across her upper lip, a process which, albeit temporarily, necessitated that she sport an ebullient white cream moustache over the meagre but offending dark one. Sometimes it seemed to her as if her body were in a constant state of revolt, maliciously engendering odour and ugliness, coarse hair sprouting through every pore, flesh puckering here and sagging there. She was vigilant and artful in stemming protuberance and decay, but subversion was all around. Only recently she had discovered a horrifyingly virulent crop of dark hairs on the backs of her marbled – or, as Romantic poets would perhaps rather, marble – thighs. The fact that this discovery had come only days after she read of a similar complaint in a women's magazine was, she thought, a sublime if unsettling coincidence. The magazine had suggested waxing or electrolysis as the most efficacious remedy, but to Agnes these things were redolent of mystery and pain, and were more easily applied, in her mind, to the writing of great poetry than to the backs of the legs.

Contrary to appearances, Agnes would have liked nothing better than to be natural, for she regarded this incessant pruning and weeding as burdensome. She did not see it as her womanly business to pluck and purge and preen; rather, it was with the aim of securing for herself what nature omitted generously to bestow that she occupied herself thus. She regarded Nina's bare face and downy legs with more envy than contempt and, with a degree of humility which would have surprised no one more than herself had she been aware of it, strove not to please others but merely not to disgust them.

So it was that Agnes, knowing herself to be a fake, and being fatally attracted to the unforgiving expert sex, spent her days in mortal fear of discovery. Guiltily she hid the tools of her loathsome trade; filled with self-hatred, she left her bed, on those sparse but nonetheless harrowing occasions when there was someone sharing it, to scrub from her the unnatural stench of the night's activities. She would meet her own eyes in the mirror and would see them fill with tears as they contemplated the red and blotchy character of their surrounds. Before she numbly set about superimposing with artifice the glowing and satisfied visage the evening had somehow failed to supply, she sometimes felt the hatred almost reaching down and dissolving her fear. Something wild and indecipherable had taken hold: for had she been discovered then, bare and trembling in the cold bathroom, all the acrimony in the world would have been but confirmation. She derived a strange comfort from knowing she was as naked as the truth.

Few, then, would have perceived that Agnes Day felt less vanity than guilt as she readied herself for an assignation in central Islington. Her destination was the stranger encountered by the bathroom door, and the brief memory she had of his quiet and critical bearing informed her that her preparations would require exceptional assiduity if he was also to become her destiny. She met the glance of her bare face like that of a stranger and eyed her naked body with the indifference of a bored husband blunted by years of custom. Robed and daubed, however, she recognised herself once more, and scrutinised her reflection front, side and back as if in preparation for attack.

She wore her hair long, a trick intended to clear up any queries as to her gender. As a child she had often been mistaken for a boy, and although now she felt she possessed sufficient evidence to refute any such claims, the memory of those who once doubted lingered uncomfortably at the back of her mind.

As it was still light Agnes walked the distance, crossing Highbury Fields just as the sun raked over the soft pastel sky and disappeared, leaving it scarred with violet welts. Boys kicked balls and wheeled aimlessly on bikes, their cries fluttering up through the trees like fugitive birds, their shadows long and skinny as poles.

'All right, darlin'?' someone shouted to her.

A row of teenagers sat on a bench like crows on a telegraph wire, blowing artless clouds of smoke from summer cigarettes through their gappy, grinning mouths. Agnes passed behind a tree and used her temporary occlusion to tug at her skirt, wishing it were not so short. She felt suddenly vulgar with her cardboard face and gashed bleeding mouth, shown up by the delicate evening, the whisper of twilight, the soft texture of leaf and sky. Her perfume clawed at the translucent scent of flowers and grass until she felt almost nauseous.

She passed through the park and regained the thundering roadside. A lorry roared by her with a hot rush of diesel. The sudden commotion was deafening. She stood on the concrete pavement in terror. People looked at her as they shoved past, some with annoyance, others, the men, with a kind of sneering admiration. She thought of him waiting for her, and for a moment the whole predictable chute of their putative future opened out there on the roadside: a saga of love and loss, a lightning cruise around places she had seen before. At that moment she would have stayed there, paralysed, until dogs cocked their legs against her; but the oddity of her predicament soon forced itself upon her, and she began to walk. Perhaps, after all, he could save her. Perhaps he would.

He was late, but Agnes had learned not to mind that; indeed, she expected nothing less. She sat at a table out of sight of the door but perfectly angled by a window which afforded a view of the street, so that she would receive information of his arrival early enough to be able to greet it with studied indifference. Outside night had fallen, and she found her gaze wandering into the darkened street, where a decrepit neon sign over the launderette opposite read WE CLEAN CURTAINS AND LOVERS. She got on well enough with anticipation. In her view, the experience of things before they happened generally provided the most pleasing version of events. It occurred to her that believing in anticipation was not unlike believing in God, another of her covert vices. It was the same drift of soul and mind towards perfection, and to Agnes the thought of perceiving the world without this dimension was to see only shadows and not the things which cast them.

There had been times, of course, when she had gambled all and lost, when she had thought her heart would surely break with disappointment that reality had not exceeded – or even matched – her imaginings. Nina, whose belief in the concrete was almost architectural, had often advised her to expect less; the reasoning being that what she did receive would thus seem like more. Agnes considered that now, as her malicious watch told her he was fifteen minutes late. She tried to imagine him coming in, flopping down uncouthly opposite her, drinking tepid vats of stinking beer until she thought his gut would explode; then belching, perhaps, a hand on her knee.

So successful were the effects of this unpleasant hallucination that she began to feel rather sick. She closed her eyes and it was then that she suddenly felt the elusive breath of him beside her, the warm, clean smell of him, the soft expensive touch of his coat against her arm. He bent over and planted a smooth kiss on her forehead, tender as a blessing. The practised air with which this gesture was accomplished did not entirely pass her by. She was glad he knew what to do. She had been foolish to underestimate him. He was, as she had seen when first they met, a professional. That, she hoped, was something they had in common, for a start.

Chapter Five

ONCE Agnes had been in love and since then she had just been in pain. The men she knew now drifted in and out of her life like ships in a harbour; some staying for a brief, inebriated night of rest and recuperation, others weighing anchor for weeks. She examined every new face for augurs of past prosperity, but her Golden Age had never been revived. Such traffic as she encountered, however, intermittent though it was, kept her a slave to hope; although she didn't know whether her renaissance would take the form of a resurgence of old joys or the onset of new ones, she was confident salvation was at hand.

Having recognised love once, she thought she would know it again, but resemblances are cruel: grinning skulls behind painted masks, deceiving the eye to fool the heart with empty promises. She had seen John's face in other faces, had pursued him on filthy pavements in the rain and then stopped, duped and foolish, her chest pounding wildly with disappointment. Then she would feel herself take wing, plunging and diving and wondering if she might not find more happiness up there among the birds and rooftops. But the pain of it dragged round after her like a ball and chain; and while she was her own jailer, he held the key. Without him she could not contrive to escape from herself. He had made her what she was and then he had left her. She was a house with no occupant, a church with no religion. She had never known loneliness until she'd had company.

*

Agnes's father was a tall man. Like most children Agnes had had her adoption fantasies, but as she grew older she learned to accept her own considerable height as a natural gift; and later still to seek a man who could see eye to eye with her on such matters.

Consequently she was rather mystified when, at a party in her first term at university, she found herself accosted by an unquestionably handsome, but equally indubitably diminutive, stranger.

'I've seen you around the place,' he said, smiling calmly at her in a manner which hinted that he did not find anything in her stature to suggest the conquest might be somewhat over his head. 'My name's John. Some of my friends think we look alike.'

She did not, then or afterwards, point out the obvious dissimilarity between them. He found her in the dining hall the next day and asked her to meet him later that evening. For the next two weeks he visited her constantly, and when he found her out even left notes adorned with small drawings apparently etched by his own hand.

Agnes took her dilemma to Nina, who, she was assured, had seen it all before. Every man had a short man inside him, Nina explained, but those whose shortness took a physical form felt that a world of injustices had been heaped upon them for which they must be compensated. Consequently, the short man would make it his mission to have everything he felt his deficit precluded. Look, for example, at how many of the world's richest men were short.

Agnes, feeling that this seminar, elegant though it was, had little relevance to her original query, took it upon herself to mention that the deficit in question was a matter merely of an inch, two at the most, and surely did not, therefore, merit such suspicions of megalomania. Nina advised her not to be deceived, but nevertheless hastened towards her point. The spoils just mentioned, she explained, were but the preliminaries, the foothills of the short man's Himalaya. For what, after all, was the only thing in whose procurement the short man

22

would realistically be disadvantaged? What did the tall man automatically lay claim to, the laws of nature and attraction admitting him entrance, on which his shorter companion had no purchase? The answer? Tall women. And what did every short man want? A woman taller than him. The fame and fortune, Nina added, were merely the currency by which such an accessory could, according to male logic, be bought.

But what of those who failed to complete this arduous course? Agnes asked. The man in question seemed even shorter of cash than he was of limb. Pity them not, said Nina, for they have long since given in to hubris and despair; which description made Agnes feel that perhaps she had more in common with him than she'd thought and should look again.

She began to anticipate his visits, and had trouble sleeping at night. Before long, she found it difficult to think of anything other than him. Soon she found she could not eat, and she grew thin. Her physical metamorphosis, however, could not be wholly explained by her loss of appetite.

'You've shrunk,' he said one day, as they were walking in the park.

She made reference to the biological findings which claimed the effects of vertical growth were irreversible.

'You have!' he insisted. 'Look, measure yourself against me.'

She did, and did it again before a critical audience when they returned home. All were agreed upon this rarest of phenomena. She had, it seemed, grown smaller. At the time she had marvelled at this evidence of the force of his personality. Through sheer love, it seemed, he had made her his perfect match. It did not occur to her to wonder why, if this were indeed so, he had not succeeded instead in making himself taller.

Greta, whose logic hit the mark with the spectacular arbitrariness of someone jumping off a building and surviving at the cost of those below, took a more succinct view when Agnes related this story, some years later, in the offices of *Diplomat's Week*. 'There's nothing in the whole world more depressing than sitting next to a guy whose thighs are smaller than yours,' she said, nodding sagely.

People used to take them for brother and sister in a manner Agnes found morally reprehensible. For her, it was more like looking into a mirror and being greeted with a reflection of herself that she liked. He instructed her not just in the art of love, but in the gentler, narcissistic skills of self-acceptance.

'You're like a black hole,' he said when he left. 'You consume me.'

Chapter Six

'I hate Sundays,' said Nina, her entire body appearing to go limp with exhaustion at her aversion. 'They were obviously designed by someone who thought stimulation was a row of closed off-licences and a feature-length episode of *Songs of Praise*.'

'But isn't that the point?' Agnes shifted back into the shade. 'I mean, for some people Sunday is the most interesting day of the week.'

Their garden was no Eden, but at least it got the sun and was the uniform khaki colour which generally passed for green in London. Agnes and Nina sat on two deckchairs Merlin had found in the cellar. Bloated flies straying from next door's garbage-infested garden revolved around their heads, droning against a monotonous bass-line of traffic from the Blackstock Road.

'Name one.'

'The Archbishop of Canterbury.'

'Name another one.'

'Look, all I'm saying is that maybe – well, maybe you feel that way because there's something missing from your life.'

'Jesus Christ,' said Nina from behind the shield of her newspaper. She was angry, but for reasons unconnected with Agnes's position on the decline of Christian beliefs in the western world. 'Are you telling me that *I've* got a problem because I don't want to spend half my weekend dancing round an altar with a bunch of God-squad maniacs or filching money off innocent people for the bloody Seventh Day Adventists, or even hanging out with a load of lapsed Catholics whingeing on about the bloody meaning of life for that matter?'

Agnes groped for her sunglasses. Her white face felt porous and blasted in the sunlight. In this grim square of atrophied horticulture she felt like no living thing.

'I mean, *are* you?' Nina persisted.

An explosion of exhaust from the road just then caused them both to jump. Agnes felt an acrid tide of sweat prickle over her. Her heart was beating fiercely.

'Not necessarily,' she said.

Agnes and Nina had had company the night before. While neither guest had specifically confirmed their reservation, Nina had been either confident or peremptory enough to warn her housemates of her putative night of passion several days in advance. Agnes, forced by her indirect nature to run the gauntlet of suspense in such matters, had been unable to make a similar promise. She did not suppose, in any case, that the presence of an additional love-interest would be cause for conflict. A discreet form of apartheid was normally employed on such occasions which kept things from taking on the aspect of a production-line. The trouble had started when, the next morning, these carefully segregated individuals had succeeded in encountering one another in the kitchen and had revealed themselves to be old friends from college. Despite their mutual surprise at the unexpected nature and location of their reunion, they immediately formulated a plan.

'Do you come here often?' one of them was heard to ask the other as they left together to find breakfast.

Agnes had consoled herself with the thought that any doubts which might have been lingering in her own lover's mind from the night before would, at least, have been partly compensated for by the events of the morning after.

'Just as long as we've got that straight,' snapped Nina.

Agnes picked up the business section of the Sunday papers and applied herself to learning the art of mergers.

Rumour had it that as a child Agnes had once been discovered walking with her eyes shut and one arm outstretched beside her.

'Agnes, what on earth are you doing?' her mother had cried nervously. They were on a family walk, and their bewilderment as they stopped and stared had eddied uncomfortably through the reassuring crunch of wellington boots on frosty grass and the caws of winter birds.

'I'm holding hands with God,' Agnes had loudly declared before drifting imperviously ahead to leave them standing, a group of sudden strangers huddled in the pale bowl of field and sky like people waiting for a bus.

At the time they might not have known whether to laugh or cry, but later, large and boisterous in the pagan glowing hub of the kitchen, their confidence in their own grasp of what was essentially what regrouped and sent gales of hilarity whooping up the chimney stacks. Agnes, small and sulky, had sent her own thoughts with them, martyred orbs of saintly passion which found better company amidst the glittering spheres of the heavens than amongst the rabble of her earthly station. *Lord, give me the strength to deal with these infidels*, she would implore before retiring to read her *Lives of the Saints* in which her namesake, worryingly rouged and buxom, appeared to be struggling beneath the weight of the large sheep in her arms.

Later Agnes denied the truth of this anecdote with almost as much fervour as she had given it life. Her protests inevitably ensured its endurance in family folklore, and it continued to provoke a hilarity with every repetition which her own more deliberate attempts at humour could somehow never match. At such times the possibility of Agnes experiencing some sense of relief that the tip, rather than the underlying iceberg, of her spiritual life had been made public was cold comfort indeed.

She was proud of her beliefs, and with the confidence which often accompanies such convictions looked forward patiently to the time when her family would be made to pay for their good humour in this life with the cold flame of perdition in the next. The last laugh, she was sure, would be hers. Nevertheless, their certain punishment did not make hers any easier to bear; and she hid from them the full extent of her love, creeping off to converse in solitude with the Almighty. Such concealments were in fact superfluous. Her mother had often paused by the bedroom door at the sound of Agnes weeping and had judiciously let her alone, surmising that her daughter's tender age and burgeoning affections had doubt-lessly led her to nurture unfulfilled passions for some reassur-ingly untouchable icon of popular culture. Had she known all passion was being spent in contemplation of a naked man nailed to two sticks of wood she would probably have made some effort to intervene. Uninformed, however, her con-clusion that it was all hormonal was in any case accurate enough.

At university Agnes reclaimed herself as a Catholic, an ethnic minority which, she decided, had undergone enough per-secution in the past to make allegiance to it defensible. While no match for the children of Israel on this score, she was surprised to discover that Catholicism held a peculiar attrac-tion for her peers. Agnostics and atheists alike confessed that if they were ever to surrender their religious bachelorhood, their thoughts would in all probability turn lightly to the Vatican.

'But why?' said Agnes with ill-concealed amazement, con-fusing herself and all her dubious charms with those of the creed whose acolytes had murdered and martyred in liberal quantities to spread the good news.

The reasons, it appeared, were twofold. On the one hand were the attractions of ritual, of incense and jewel-encrusted robes, of transubstantive cannibalism and the horror film of crucifixion. On the other were subtler individual perversions like sin and guilt. The former seemed to function as a kind of spiritual scenery; the latter were the regions wherein unfolded the real drama. It had been some years since Agnes's own idolatry had faded to a kind of grudging, habitual affection; and there lay within the ripe ground for proselytism she had discovered amongst her peers a golden opportunity to resuscitate the honeymoon period of her youth. Strangely uninfected by their enthusiasm, however, Agnes began to experience instead the contagion of doubt. The public purchase of her private world rendered her disaffected with it. Her goods appeared soiled with handling. She – if not her sins – was no longer original.

The feminist lobby, meanwhile, questioning her on the subject of her beliefs with mingled fascination and dismay, unwittingly extinguished the final, guttering flame of belief. The Catholic Church was sexist, hierarchical, capitalist and corrupt! they cried. It put an embargo on women's sexual freedom and forced them to stay at home and have babies. You don't abide by the rules, they argued. Why do you bother? Agnes, who in truth had been practising certain deceptions, saw that she could not claim to have done so in the spirit of subversion and civil disobedience, her acceptance of spiritual authority being voluntary rather than enforced. She had, she supposed, just hoped that He wouldn't notice; that He wouldn't come home unexpectedly in the middle of the day to find her in a tangle of rumpled bedclothes and milkman's limbs. She had cheated, but in doing so had assumed that the very fact of her bothering to believe that that was what she was doing would absolve her of it.

Eventually she surrendered outwardly to the forces of agnosticism, but there was some corner of her that would remain forever faithful. Contemplating a lovely sunset, for example, or a summer field full of flowers, tears would well in her eyes for the beauty of it all and her heart would instinctively rise in praise. There was also, it must be said, a subtle worm of fear wandering vagrant through the unlocked

29

passages of her mind. She had been told He would come like a thief in the night, and at night she prayed.

'Almost a full house last night,' remarked Merlin later in the kitchen. 'If the rest of the world were not so immune to my charms it could have been a hat-trick.'

'Well, don't blame me,' said Nina sharply. 'I told all of you last Wednesday that Jack was coming over. I wasn't to know the place would end up like the bloody Friends Meeting House.'

'Oh, it wasn't a criticism,' said Merlin mildly. 'More of a cry for help.'

They were watching Merlin make lunch. Outside, a low grey blanket of cloud had long since covered up the sun.

'Look, Nina, I'm sorry,' blurted out Agnes finally. 'I didn't ask him to come back. He just sort of – did.'

'Nasty man!' pounced Nina. 'Poor little Agnes.'

'That's not what I mean!' rejoined Agnes. People always misunderstood her. 'It wasn't like that.'

It really hadn't been like that, although her memories of that particular stage in the evening were akin to a blanketed criminal's recollections of being bustled from police van to courtroom.

'Oh, come on,' said Nina. 'It's not as if his reputation didn't precede him. You must have known he wasn't there to admire the upholstery.' She picked up a magazine and began leafing indifferently through it. 'I don't know where you get off on all this helplessness, Agnes. It's such an act.'

'What do you mean?' Agnes considered the alternatives being offered up for elucidation and opted for the lesser of two evils. 'What has he got a reputation for?'

'It's obviously not much of a reputation,' said Merlin kindly. He cast a meaningful glance at Nina.

'Shut up, Merlin,' snapped Nina, ignoring it.

'Tell me,' said Agnes.

Nina sighed reluctantly, surrendering responsibility for the pain she was about to inflict.

'He's a bit of a womaniser, that's all. I thought you knew that.'

Agnes, who did not readily identify herself with the species on which her suitor was so widely supposed to prey, had, while being vaguely aware of his rumoured skills, not thought herself a likely medium for their application. The idea that he should judge her fit to be womanised, as it were, struck her now as more complimentary than degrading.

'Yes, I suppose I did,' she said after a while.

There was silence in the kitchen. Merlin watched her nervously. Nina shook her head in disbelief.

'Don't tell me!' she said exasperatedly. 'You think he'll be different with you, is that it?'

'I don't think that,' replied Agnes truthfully; she did not, in fact, know what she thought.

'Why?' Nina raged, it being too late to divert the passage of her rhetoric. 'Why do women always think they can change men? They go straight for the bloody animals and they try to tame them! It perpetuates myths of masculinity. It suggests ill-treatment is attractive. Why should we let them just bloody get away with it?'

She lit a cigarette and inhaled angrily. Agnes watched her mouth, waiting for the smoke to reappear like a papal vote. She felt the exhalation was necessary as a token of forgiveness, a thin white curl of acquiescence to counter the suck of disapproval.

'What am I saying?' Nina laughed and out it came in mirthful puffs. 'Look at that travesty of manhood, for God's sake. Merlin, what have we done to you?'

Merlin smoothed his apron primly.

'I'm like Agnes,' he said. 'I've had manhood thrust upon me.'

'Your way is just as bad,' cried Agnes, going on the offensive while Nina's guard was down. 'It's almost like you want men to be animals so they won't threaten you on your own terms. That's just another form of control. In fact—' she risked, 'in fact, it's sexist.'

To her annoyance, Nina started to laugh.

'It is!' Agnes insisted. She was stepp'd so far in the blood of her own betrayal as to make retraction impossible. 'You can spend your whole life running away because you're afraid of being hurt. I just want to judge people on how they behave towards me, not on how they might have behaved in the past.'

Although she was speaking so sincerely as almost to convince herself, the pain of Nina's recent revelation was beginning to nag at her like a tooth emerging from its anaesthetic. There had been times when her heart had felt as if it would snap beneath the weight of her lovers' lovers, their stale laughter and dead kisses, their ghostly lips and pale bodies slipping paper-thin into the tiny hot space between flesh and living flesh. She loathed the smug self-containment of the past, and usually saw no alternative but to smash it open like a piggy-bank and trample on its mystery. She had frightened even herself with such murderousness and was no stranger to the horror that came after it. She was alive with the subtleties of endgames.

'That,' said Nina matter-of-factly, 'is why you are always disappointed and I am usually pleasantly surprised.'

Nina barred herself in her room for the rest of the afternoon, leaving Agnes little choice but to pick up her end of the ill-feeling and carry it around like some ugly and burdensome object. She resented such an occupation being foisted upon her but knew not how to free herself from it, pinned as she already was beneath the fallen beam of the oncoming week's drudgery. Nina was working upstairs and her typewriter filled the house with staccato machine-gun fire.

Agnes wandered disconsolately into the sitting-room, where Merlin was lying prone on the sofa watching television. He took his hours of leisure – and perhaps also, by implication, those of work – more seriously than she herself did. He held a can of beer in one hand and dangled the other over the carpet, as if trailing it in water from the side of a boat.

32

'You executive types,' she said, observing him. 'You just don't know how to relax.'

'I'm a zen economist,' said Merlin. 'I go where the mood takes me. Come over here and watch Bette Davis being romanced in Rio.'

Agnes perched uncomfortably on the arm of the sofa. On the screen, Bette leaned nonchalantly on a balcony overlooking a monochrome sea while her lover pleaded with her elegant back.

'Moods!' exhorted Agnes presently. 'I go where other people's moods take me. I do, Merlin,' she insisted, although as yet he had not denied it. 'I mean, *I* never upset people. I don't think I even know how to.'

'What?'

'I said, I don't know how to upset people.'

'Oh.' Merlin put down his beer can and folded his arms patiently behind his head. 'I'm sure Nina would teach you. She's a bit hard up for cash at the moment.'

'Very funny.'

'Look, it'll blow over.' His eyes pulled reluctantly away from the screen and settled on her. 'Nina gets angry. It's her way of releasing tension. She'll get over it.'

'I shouldn't have brought him home,' said Agnes. Now that she had Merlin's full attention she could afford to indulge her confessional instincts, although such remorseful forays were strictly reserved for those who could be relied on to offer absolution rather than concurrence.

'I thought we'd already established that he broke and entered.' Merlin was evidently aiming for levity.

'I should have made other arrangements,' continued Agnes. 'Maybe I should go and apologise. It was all my fault.'

'No, it wasn't.' He was reliable as a slot machine where saving Agnes was concerned. 'This isn't a bloody Middle Eastern bombing, you know – we can't all claim responsibility. Anyway, I told you, she'll get over it. Nina brings home a lot of guys. You only think you do.'

'What's that supposed to mean?' Agnes was horrified. The

33

implications were mushrooming. Were her actions so transparent, her assumptions so unfounded? Had she been misinformed?

'It means you have a sensitive soul,' said Merlin firmly. 'Now stop torturing yourself and give me some details.'

'What kind of details?' said Agnes suspiciously.

'Well, what's he like? When are you seeing him again? That kind of thing.'

'I don't know when I'm seeing him again. He said he'd phone.' She was embarrassed by her deficiency of whispered promises and heated troths. 'Anyway, you all seem to know far more about him than I do.'

It came out sounding more stand-offish than she'd meant it to. Merlin shrugged, giving up, and turned back to the television. Sometimes, she wanted to say, sometimes when I tell the truth it feels like I'm lying.

Agnes lay in bed waiting for the telephone to ring, believing as she did that the former event would precipitate the latter. Her faith, though gritty, was, she knew, ill-founded, attempting as it did to harness the perversity of the universe and make consistency where there was essentially none. By taking upon herself the task of second-guessing ill-fortune, she was in fact violating the creed of her anti-faith, which, if its principles were to be understood, would presumably visit her only at her own inconvenience. The fact that she was aware of this loophole merely served to deepen the complexity of her plight; but Agnes was full of such grim closets of superstition, cobwebbed enclosures of small expectations which should have housed just deserts. She would have loved to have recourse to the protection, implore the help, and seek the intercession of the official bodies, but for her the proper channels were strewn with past disappointments and offered easy passage only for the penitent. In the past Agnes had asked and had not been given; or at least not been given what she'd asked for. It had occurred to her that within the nature of her petitions, which generally lay outside the realm of the common good, there might be concealed the reason for their speedy return to sender, redress unknown; and with the dubious workings of divine intervention thus under investigation, it seemed only natural that she should try to take things into her own more reliable hands.

The telephone was for Agnes a symbol of pure, unsolicited intention, containing none of the ambiguity of other more complex forms of encounter; but her loathing was, of course, an equal match for her love. As a tool of common communication, she accepted the telephone with the normal technological indifference of the age. It was in its role as ambassador to the affairs of the heart that her feelings about it became more political. Days when she was expecting a call stretched out before her like empty motorways, banked on either side with anticipation and dread. In the early, optimistic hours she would be as attentive to it as a mother with a child; never out of earshot, constantly checking that it had not met with a misplaced receiver or other mishap, anxious if anyone else picked it up for too long. But as the dark of evening swept in she would grow fractious and impatient with its intractability. It would become ugly to her with its cyclops eye and distended curly arm. She would implore, plead and cajole; and then it would be war.

It was usually about then that she would begin to indulge in the witchery of her pagan rites, baiting it with long baths and loud music over which its cries, if there were any, would barely be heard. Often it would respond with cruel tricks: calls for other people, wrong numbers, and so on. Agnes, cresting the wave of expectation, would bear down on these innocent bystanders with the full weight of her disappointment, dashing them with her hopes and disposing of them with scarce civility. As the night wore on she would become morose and despondent, and would retire to bed, vigilant even in sleep lest it should call for her.

Sometimes, of course, the call would come before the drama had even got under way; better still, it would occasionally even surprise her and come unexpectedly of its own volition. Had she compared the joy of these occasions with the grief of their remission, she might have found their emotional expenditure did not tally; but for Agnes the intervention of fact was enough, a blessed relief from the pyrotechnics of speculation that she sometimes felt she would burst in the effort to contain. Like a secret drinker, she would view her emotional binges the next morning through a hangover of guilt and self-loathing. At these times she inhabited a world more private than confession, and it followed that to confess would have been unthinkable. When the errant caller casually achieved too late what he had so dramatically failed to perform some twenty-four hours earlier, Agnes would accept with admirable indifference the vague apologies handed over as gracelessly as wilted flowers.

'Oh,' she would say, her night of despair now tame as a kitten. 'Did you say you would call? I completely forgot.'

It came as some surprise, then, that as Agnes lay in her bed signing over her soul to the Mephistopheles of the telecommunications network, all at once she heard the distinct sound of the telephone ringing. She sat up in bed, her heart beating as if she had heard the cry of a wolf from her log cabin. The shrill bell repeated itself unashamedly, twice, thrice. It seemed somehow to be saying her name. Before she could swing her legs over the bed, however, she heard the soft patter of Nina's feet on the stairs. She lay back for the second she knew it would take him to ask for her. A murmur and a low laugh. More murmuring, and then the sound of Nina bounding up the stairs to Agnes's room. Agnes's heart bounded with her. The door opened tentatively.

'I'm awake!' she cried impatiently.

Nina crept to her bedside and sat down in a manner which did not suggest the desired urgency.

'He called,' she said.

Agnes's heart was sinking.

'Who?'

'Jack, of course.'

Even in the darkness, Agnes could hear Nina smiling to herself. You too? she thought. *You?*

Nina lay down and Agnes, unbecomingly wrapped in her duvet like a giant caterpillar, shuffled over to make room for her.

'Hey.' Nina raised herself up on an elbow. 'I'm sorry about before. I didn't mean to bite your head off. I was just a bit on edge.'

'Animal lovers of the world, unite,' said Agnes nastily; but Nina, her conscience cleared, appeared to have gone to sleep without catching the snipe. The taste of it stayed in her mouth, undigested. What good were they, these slashes and parries, when all she wanted was the birthright of damsels in distress? There came a point when one tired of things hard-won. To be favoured, now that was something else; to be so privileged as to sleep, as now Nina slept beside her, with a face innocent of artifice. Agnes looked at her as a lover might and saw that her superiority lay in the very quality of being effortless. Fortune attended her in sleep unasked, while Agnes's fate snored wildly in cold cream and curlers. Like two laboratory experiments, they had started at the same point that morning: yet already Nina had results, secret catalysts which made nature seem like magic. She had taken the scenic route, while Agnes ploughed hopelessly forward over dry reaches of tree-less desert, sand-blind and lonely, knowing nothing but the straightness of her own line.

Chapter Seven

FIVE days was a long time at *Diplomat's Week*. Agnes, who had once thought days existed merely for identification purposes, temporal name-tags to facilitate social confluence, came to know each one as a prisoner does her jailers. Of course Monday was the worst, a jack-booted Nazi of a day; people did suicidal things on Mondays, like start diets and watch documentaries. Fear of Monday also tended to ruin Sunday, an invasion which Agnes resented deeply. Moreover, it made her suspicious of Tuesday; a day whose unrelenting tedium was deceptively camouflaged by the mere fact of its not being Monday. Wednesday, on the other hand, was touch and go, delicately balanced between the memory of the last weekend and the thought of the weekend to come. Wednesday was a plateau and dangerous things could happen on plateaux. For example, one could forget one was in prison at all. Thursday was Agnes's favourite, a day dedicated to pure anticipation. By then she was on the home stretch, sprinting in glorious slow-motion towards the distant flutter of Friday's finishing line; which, however, when reached, often felt to her like nothing but a *memento mori* of the next incarceration.

'What's the time?' asked Agnes.

'Eleven o'clock,' said Greta. 'Almost lunchtime.'

He had called on Tuesday. Agnes's hopes had been beaten to a pulp by then, but she managed somehow to manufacture a tone of mild surprise at the promptness of his overture, as if she had not spent the past two days dreaming of whispered midnight conversations, gravel against her window in the moonlight, desperate unexpected callers at the door and mysterious floral deliveries. They arranged to meet; and with the certainty of happiness now firmly embedded in her heart, Agnes was amazed at the transformative light it shed on things which had previously seemed unbearable. She ceased to balk at the slow passing of time, knowing as she now did that it would terminate in her future assignation. She proof-read the details of the Tongan High Commissioner's ambassadorial career with admiration and joy. She speculated with Greta on the tragic demise of Jean's love life in the manner of one who pitied but could not empathise. Their prearrangement assuaged all memory of pain. In moments of doubt she could call on it and it would run to her side, faithful as a dog. Moreover, like a good exam result it confirmed both future and past; for she had in the past few days endured several private flashes of an agony too raw to be acknowledged, as memories of her performance in the sweaty arena of their intimacy jumped out at her unbidden. His call permitted this testing hour, which she had all but blanked out, to be received back into history: she had passed; she was normal. She could now squirm and smile secretively with valid pleasure at the memory.

'So have you guys done it?' said Greta, colliding in mid-air with the winged passage of Agnes's thoughts.

'Yes.' Agnes considered the addition of 'of course', but settled for 'We have, actually.'

'Wow.' Greta bit vociferously into an apple. 'That was quick.'

Nina had once told her that if ever she felt her fancy turning to unhealthy devotion, she should imagine the object of her worship in the fifth form at a school disco: aged sixteen or thereabouts, skin crawling with adolescent pustulence, odorous and sweating and heaving himself drunkenly across the dance floor. Such a picture was bound to demote her demigod from the heaven realm to the human, or perhaps even lower, and was designed to relieve her from the discomforts of excessive admiration.

Such practices may have allowed Nina to become the cool and distant lover she was purported to be, but Agnes, although sensing an imminent need for such stringent measures, was not by nature an iconoclast. She had tried to imagine a time when she might have found him charmless and had only been able to picture him young and lovely in a distant corner; aloof from the malodorous crowds, desperate to get away and sit beneath the moon, writing poetry perhaps. Such trains of thought, furthermore, inevitably led to the contemplation of her own ungainly youth, which, had she shared its details with her lover, she felt sure would have had the effect on him which Nina's suggestion had designed.

John had used to solicit tales of her adolescent embarrassments with glee. He had loved all her uglinesses and seemed to delight in the evidence they gave of her humanity. Once, when she had fallen over and cut her knee, he had watched her pick off the scab and had taken the crusty flap of skin from her hand. Agnes, who had thought she was removing the hideous excrescence unobserved, cried out in protest and shame. To her horror, and later wonderment, he held it up in the air for a moment and then put it in his mouth.

'There,' he said, smiling and swallowing calmly. 'Now I know what you taste like.'

'What shall I wear?' said Agnes, standing dolefully before her wardrobe.

'Where?'

Nina lay down on the bed and kicked off her shoes. One landed in the bin and the other hit the wall, leaving a small black mark.

'Yes.'

Agnes ran her hand along the rail where jackets and shirts hung like obedient ghosts, like escorts.

'You don't say "yes".' Nina screwed up her face. 'You say "to the cinema" or something.'

Agnes took out a jacket and held it up. It hung elegantly from the scrawny neck of the coat-hanger, svelte and poised. It looked better without her.

'I'm going to the cinema with Jack, actually,' Nina continued. She stretched her legs into the air and twiddled her bare feet on their joints like flesh-coloured periscopes. 'Tomorrow. You know what he said when I suggested it? He said, "Oh, great, we can sit in the back row and snog." Can you believe that? It was so funny.'

Agnes replaced the jacket and it eyed her with disdain. She did not want to look glamorous. He would think she was trying too hard, although in reality it would be equally laborious for her to appear unadorned. There was little that taxed her art more than having to imitate nature.

'I mean, I thought he was really gormless when I first met him but now I realise he's just – well, honest. He doesn't go in for behaviour. He just says what he wants. That way, everyone knows where they stand. I feel like he's undermining my preconceived stereotypes all the time, which is quite a challenge.' She yawned. 'Especially since I didn't think I had any.'

'What shall I wear?' said Agnes. Her voice was now tinged with panic. Nina looked up.

'Oh, for God's sake,' she said frostily. 'Just wear anything. He won't even notice.'

They had gone to the Science Museum once. Exhibition Road on a rainy Sunday afternoon evoked childhoods not spent there, a sort of displaced nostalgia for tea and cakes and nanny in the schoolroom. At times like these, wet leaves from Kensington Park clinging to her shoes like beggars' hands, the smell of bonfires besieging her nostrils, Agnes felt the force of a cultural memory take hold of her that was not her own. They had had tea and cakes in the small East Anglian town where she had grown up, but they had come from Sainsbury's in packages and had made her feel sick in a way she was sure the steaming scone of yore wouldn't have. Such disappointments were the fault of the Victorians, she thought, looking at diminutive knickerbockers in the V & A. Her strange regressive longings were always firmly rooted in that age, while other historical daydreams were enacted via the persona of an adult male in doublet and hose.

Some time later, John suggested they move on to Science and Technology. Although just across the road, this edifice of concrete and plate glass was a world apart. Wandering the pale-floored forecourt studded with sculptural confections of plastic and steel like invaders from another planet, Agnes felt somewhat alien herself. The room was packed with self-possessed children dressed in primary colours.

'This is crap,' said one small blond specimen, pressing buttons and twiddling knobs with expert indifference while lights flashed and vast plastic molecules spun. Agnes was relieved they had not visited Natural History, where similar lights flashed in ominous patterns of invasion over diagrams of prostrate female thighs and pubic jungles.

'Agnes!'

John was examining a dimly lit booth on the far side of the room. As she approached, she saw he was seated in front of a large pane of glass and he motioned with his hand for her to sit in the vacant chair on the other side. She sat down opposite him. In the dark glass she could see her own reflection.

'Watch this,' he said softly.

Her own reflection suddenly melted, to be replaced by his face grinning at her through the glass.

'How did you do that?' she queried.

'Light,' he replied. 'The button on your right adjusts the light.'

He turned it again and her own face reappeared. It was odd to see them occupying the same space, their heads floating disembodied in and out of the dark, under and over each other like symbiotic beings, like split personalities.

'Now watch this.'

He loved to surprise her, to entertain her with his mastery. She would, he knew, never think to press the buttons herself. That was one of the reasons why he loved her. She let him show her things.

'What are you doing?' she said.

All at once, she saw there was something wrong with her face. The eyes weren't hers. John began to laugh behind the glass. Her mouth seemed to be laughing with him. Her jaw suddenly appeared to have become unusually square.

'Stop it!'

Her mouth moved again. Part of her was still there, but altered, like the face of a long-lost relative. The other part was John. He was in her eyes, across her forehead, around her chin. He was sitting in her head, rubbing his hands together gleefully. He had somehow found the space between them and he had rented it out like an apartment.

'You see?' he said. 'Do you see how wonderful this is? This is what our children would look like.'

Chapter Eight

WHEN she was younger Agnes had wanted to be a boy, a fact which, like a South African passport or an inherited income, she had since expended much energy in concealing lest it expel her from the warm embrace of her ideological family. Now the world of men seemed distant and barbaric, but Agnes was unnerved to find that sometimes, observing from her hill-top the shaking spears and strange customs of this rival tribe, she was besieged by sensations of longing and familiarity. In the face of such uncompromising anthropological perspectives in her own camp as Nina's (who, when questioned on the problematic issue of cohabitation between the species, had replied: 'Why would a panda suddenly go off and live with a giraffe?'), Agnes feared that, unable to conform to the specifications of either side, she would be deserted by both. The deep-seatedness of her anxiety was revealed to her once in a dream, when she had found herself in possession of a giant penis like an elephant's trunk and was forced to bundle it up beneath her skirt like a dark and terrible secret and walk around in mortal fear of its discovery.

Her early ejection from the masculine world was remembered not as a gradual drifting away on a soft cloud of burgeoning femininity, but rather as a hideous eruption of deformities accompanied by a simultaneous rejection from the society of her brother Tom and his friends. If in the latter case this shunning had been precipitated by hazy boyish visions of

Agnes, laden with sanitary towels, slowing down their cycling trips and becoming a cumbersome camper, Agnes was never told of it. Early manifestations of more tangible changes, however, had been volubly noted and were still uncomfortably memorable. Once, while at the swimming pool, Agnes had executed a graceful dive and had emerged to see Tom's face contorted not with congratulation but disgust.

'Yuk!' he cried. 'You've got hair underneath your arms!'

Much of what followed proceeded along similar lines, with subsequent developments being acknowledged only when they were found to be repulsive.

'Time we bought you some deodorant,' her mother would say, sniffing the air as Agnes embraced her on her return home from school.

'Can't you get her a bra?' her father would inquire as Agnes lunged, T-shirted, over a tennis court.

Agnes, who had long since started patrolling her body for acts of hormonal terrorism, had already requested funding for security devices and had been turned down on the grounds that she had not yet officially reached puberty. Knowing from those heavyweights at school who had graduated early from childhood that legitimacy could be attained at the cost of a little bloodshed, Agnes finally committed the felony of false menstruation; a transgression which, while considerably taxing her imagination, allowed her to jump the queue undetected without any of the disadvantages she had heard about in corridors and common-rooms. Her deception, however, carried with it its own punishment. As time wore on, fact did not appear to be catching up with fiction. For two years Agnes existed in a torment of guilt and anxiety. She toiled beneath the burden of a double conceit as she tried to find ways of disposing of the stockpile of monstrous surgical swabs which her mother, regular as clockwork, placed in discreet paper bags in her room. She grew confused by the hybrid growth of both the lie and the abnormality it concealed, and on one occasion even indulged her fantasy so far as to ask her mother is she might change to Tampax. Her justification may have been honest – they were, she reasoned, easier to get rid of – but it gained her little moral or material ground. Indeed, it seemed even to retard her cause, for her mother had become shocked and flustered at the suggestion and had begun to babble in the most distressing manner about penetration, which led to a long discussion concerning intimate details of what she and Daddy did together when they were on their own. Already fully informed and disgusted on this score, Agnes found her situation becoming more complex as she was expected to feign innocence on top of the worldliness she had long been forced to pretend.

Her joy, then, when at the age of fifteen the indubitable proof of her femininity finally arrived, was intensely private and tinged with remorse. Even when daubing and stemming with the best of them, Agnes felt that she had not done it properly. The redness of her own blood, official though it was, could not begin to compensate for all she had suffered.

As she grew older Agnes realised, somewhat to her dismay, that really she had little to complain about with respect to her childhood. While her parents had claimed from the start that this was the case, their concomitant conviction that Agnes's adolescent dissatisfactions were nothing but the offspring of her melodramatic and rather lachrymose disposition was less justifiably held. The pain Agnes had felt within the tastefully papered walls of her family home was, she now knew, partly the product of her ignorance of the injustices of which the larger world outside them was capable. Nina, for example, had been brought up in a mock-Tudor villa in East Sheen, where all her friends called her mother 'Margo'. But the subtler dramas of country living, with its cruel provincial ways, its sniping observations and censorious unwritten laws which bound young aspiring souls like the feet of Japanese women, could, Agnes later found, compete with the most scarred of childhoods. At university she was surprised to discover that a background such as her own was almost *de rigueur*: the régimes of the middle classes, she learned, ranked side by side with those of small Central American countries in terms of the abuses they perpetrated. But bashing the bourgeoisie required a certain distance from them; and having always judged herself fortunate in possessing two kind parents, she was understandably reluctant, not to mention afraid, to orphan herself so precipitantly. As time wore on she was glad of her reticence, for during the ensuing three years most of those who had so scornfully kicked over the traces of their past were driven either by penury or maturity to uncover them again. By then, even Nina herself was calling her mother Margo.

It was only later that Agnes came to suspect she might have deprived herself of a necessary kind of exorcism by declining to follow her peers through this rite of passage. Hers was a life of small hurts, she realised, rather than gross abuses; but nevertheless it began to disturb her that, even thus embarked as she now was upon her adult life, she could still be ambushed by pain at things which should have been long forgotten. Incidents from her youth would sometimes surface unbidden in her mind like creatures from a murky swamp, and she would relive them with a freshness unsullied by the passing of time.

'You're off-loading childhood guilt,' said Merlin comfortingly. He had grown up in a women's commune in Hampstead and had an easy grasp of this sort of vocabulary, presumably the residue of a childhood which had not required off-loading. 'It's perfectly natural.'

Agnes, worked up by his kindness into a spirit of confession, told him about a time when, at the age of about twelve, she had persuaded her brother Tom to stage his own death beneath one of the highest windows of their house. She had covered him in tomato ketchup and left him lying in a flowerbed while she ran to get her mother, who had, for some reason which eluded her at the time, become completely hysterical and, having elicited a confession from the treacherous Tom, had chased Agnes around the house with an egg-flipper. Merlin's expression was one of uncertainty.

'That *is* weird,' he said. Seeing the devastation on Agnes's face, he added: 'The bit about the egg-flipper, I mean.'

John had loved that story, Agnes remembered. She had told him a lot of things she would never tell anyone else, things that lurked in the pit of her mind smothered in a furry mould of guilt. He had hoarded these rancid pieces of her past and would occasionally bring them out and gleefully examine them.

'What did you think she would do?' he had asked, eyes glinting with an enjoyment which bordered on malevolence. 'Your mother, I mean. What did you think her reaction would be?'

Agnes thought about it for a while. She saw her brother's small body curled up amongst the hydrangeas, the ketchup lurid in the sun.

'I thought she would think it was funny,' she said.

Chapter Nine

AGNES and he met religiously twice a week, although
Agnes was beginning to experience heretical feelings of
frustration at the formality of their arrangement. The unerring
symmetry of Wednesday and Saturday oppressed her like a
dentist's appointment, and was equally as far from the passionate spontaneity she longed for. He would drive her home with
a kind of reined-in intensity, his face set, his beautiful hands
veined and strangely articulate on the steering wheel; but if at
first she had thought this exercise to be a prelude to other
transports of delight, she soon learned not to expect them.
Sometimes he would come in, locking the car and following
her to her room wordless as a shadow. Other times he would
keep the engine running, looking at her like a taxi driver
awaiting his fare while she talked too much and too loud to
cover her embarrassment. At these times she often wondered
if she should be doing something – if there was something
everyone else did at times like these to force the moment to
a resolution – but he was silent and left her no clues. Sometimes she felt as if they were both wrapped in cellophane, their
mouths formless as melted wax.

They whiled away afternoons in art galleries or parks, evenings in bars and restaurants. Often he would arrive late,
making her wait for an hour or more. At first she wondered
if he was putting her devotion to the test and she sympathised
with his uncertainty accordingly; but he always seemed mildly

surprised to see her there waiting, as if they had met by coincidence. On Saturdays they would go back to her house – always her house; his, which she had never seen, was somewhere in south London. The next morning he would return there without delay, mysterious and alone like an alien to its planet. Later she would try to find evidence that he had been in her room, and was often surprised to discover she couldn't even remember anything he had said. She thought about John frequently and realised she could recall almost every word he had ever spoken to her. The less conventional order in which they had done things – restaurants for breakfast, the park at night – sometimes interfaced in her mind with the current course of events like a shadow. She did not entertain such recollections in the spirit of comparison: they floated disembodied and glittering like stars above the wheel of her fortune, detached recollections of a thing met by chance, like a banknote found in a gutter.

'I feel as if I'm in control of a relationship for the first time,' she told Nina.

Stay with me, she had said one night; a Wednesday night when he had come in but then seemed inclined to leave. Don't leave me on my own. To her amazement he had stayed, as if he didn't care what he did, and had slept beside her all night. John would never have done that. If John had wanted to leave Agnes could have slit her wrists and it wouldn't have stopped him. She had felt almost uncomfortable with his obedience and had slept little that night, unable to enjoy a thing so devoid of the pleasure of his desire, so single-handedly orchestrated by herself. His presence felt like a loan rather than a gift.

'I mean,' she said, 'it's what men have been getting for years, isn't it? Passivity, obedience, servitude.'

'Right.' Nina didn't look so sure.

'Well, maybe he's the ideal feminist man, then.'

It had come to the point where she almost felt like she was using him, for, try as she might to force upon him the gift of her affection, he did not seem to want it. She supposed they were having an affair, a tiny, delectable confection. The thought that she might love him, might try and live off his unnourishing presence, almost amounted to a social gaffe. It would be like falling in love with a kitchen appliance. She laughed nervously, thinking of something.

'He's a bimbo!' she cried.

Nina lit a cigarette and stared into the middle distance.

The first time he had come back to her house they had sat on her bed reading the next day's papers, bought in advance in Leicester Square. Wishing she could procure more immediate aspects of tomorrow's news with such ease, Agnes feigned deep involvement with a leader on the Middle East crisis while trying to deal with a crisis of her own. Why wasn't he doing anything? If he didn't want to make use of the strategic location she had offered him, why was he here? She shifted on the bed portentously and yawned, but even with all her defences down he seemed unwilling to attack. Initiation had never been one of Agnes's strong points, and its meaning for her was double-pronged. A rare moment of identification with the male sex, strangely unrelated to the envoy beside her, came upon her as she launched into a long and rambling monologue about how many things she had to do in the morning, followed by a clumsy sort of half-hug, and found it had not been the conflagratory spark to his tinder she had hoped for. He seemed willing enough to respond in kind, but his simple mirroring of her actions reminded her uncomfortably of an annoying game her brother Tom used to play when they were children.

'Mum, he's copying me!' she would cry, running to find her mother.

'Mum, he's copying me!' Tom would echo, running and laughing behind her.

Eventually she threw caution to the winds, switching off the light and removing his clothing in a manner she wished had seemed less matter-of-fact. She simply could not see how else they would get out of the situation without severe shame to them both. As it was, all available embarrassment was at least under her control. Filled with guilt and self-disgust she pursued her course, until finally he seemed to get the right idea; and now that they were rolling around together quite happily she didn't have the heart to mention contraception. Having seemingly forced him into it, it seemed impolite, not to mention ridiculous, then to fight him off on the grounds she didn't want to get pregnant.

'Why?' said Nina the next morning, horrified by Agnes's story. 'Why? You don't *have* to do it, you know. You can say no.'

'He didn't ask,' replied Agnes shamefully. 'I started it. I didn't know what else to do.'

'Well—' Even Nina seemed stumped by this one. 'Well, why didn't you just ask him to leave? You're mad,' she concluded confidently, sighing and walking off in disgust.

In fact, they never did get round to discussing contraception, for reasons which had made themselves apparent on that first night and which Agnes would not have disclosed to Nina even at the price of salvaging some self-respect. To her surprise and horror, while she had drawn an unforeseen amount of pleasure from their congress, he had seemed, in her limited understanding, to have none. When they made love, the first night, the last night, and all the nights in between, in all of those languid and sweaty exchanges on which Agnes swiftly developed a frightening and unrestrained dependence, he never came. At first she thought he had; like a thief in the night, as it were, quiet and unobserved. Later, however, with the space between her legs feeling strangely empty and dry, the inevitable convergence of logic and biology forced the truth upon her. He would keep going until she wanted him to stop and then he would turn over silently, everything in his demeanour discouraging concerned conversational sallies of the encounter-group variety, and would go to sleep.

Thinking his failure to be directly descended from a deficiency in her own attractiveness, Agnes had not expected, after that night, to see him again. But then he had called the next week at the usual time as if nothing – or indeed something

– had happened, and the occurrence had repeated itself. Gradually Agnes got used to it. Soon, it seemed like nothing out of the ordinary; indeed, it became exceptional, for the peculiar sacrifice he offered up for her nightly removed the obstacle of his desire and left her free to love him unrestrainedly. Being with him was like being alone, like being with oneself as another person.

The pattern of their confluence emerged and her days arranged themselves around it like petals on a stalk. The fact that really she knew nothing about him, that when he was not with her he would disappear, his phone ringing unanswered in a house she had never seen, that sometimes she wondered if he even knew who she was, ceased to matter. He arranged his attractions behind bullet-proof glass. He bore as little scrutiny of his depths as a reflecting surface. He obsessed at close quarters and then disappeared, leaving a crater his company had never filled, a space he had uncovered, not caused.

The fact that even in their most private hour, in the secret interchange between the darkness of their bodies, that even in that moment of abandon he had given her nothing of himself, impressed upon her in some half-formed way the idea that he was cleverer than she. She would think about it sometimes after he had gone; about how he left her tired and empty when she had thought at the time it was he who was giving and she receiving. She wondered how he did it. His mysteries were auto-destructive. Like a mirror he gave her back nothing but what was already there; smash it and he would be gone, her fist too clumsy, her eye too slow to see what was behind it before it obliterated itself like a Christmas cracker, leaving her with nothing but a rearranged face and a few years of bad luck.

Chapter Ten

FEMINISM had discovered Agnes in her first year at university and, recognising in her the potential for prime, dissenting flesh, had been prepared to fight long and hard for her soul. While Agnes's resistance had been what might be called textbook, her capitulation was less so. Attending the women's group to which Nina had invited her, she had become so terrified by their proselytising and their promises of bondage that, when asked for her opinion, she had thrown them the first scrap of meat she could lay her hands on.

'I like having doors opened for me!' she had cried, scarcely believing the words – which she had heard reverberate around the counties of her youth and had thought, even then, absurd – had come from her mouth.

Thankfully this missile, being old and ubiquitous by design, was shot down with consummate ease by her companions, who became quite friendly in their relief that she had not mounted a stauncher defence. The door to cultural emancipation had been firmly opened and Agnes found that, try as she might, it would not shut.

What none of these genial campaigners knew was that Agnes had lived most of her life in constant fear and loathing of her own sex. The convent school where she had grown up had been red in tooth and claw with female cruelty; and when her new friends spoke of the women's community, Agnes was beset by images of hooded nuns, ungodly punishments and peer-group persecution. Unspeakable things had gone on there, things which she had thrown into a cauldron of grief and terror in her heart and which now bubbled like a noxious soup of carping, taunting, bitching, menstruating femininity. The taste of it still rose in her throat like bile. Eventually she could talk of male oppression as freely as anybody; but in those days the cheerful indifference of men and their unemotional talk, although later a source of grief and frustration, was something of a relief.

Agnes bought feminism because she was afraid of women; and, as with so many things in her life, when she was driven by her sense of what ought to be it was some time before truth eventually caught her up.

The first thing she perceived about feminism was that it allowed women to be fat and ugly. As if such qualities were infectious, Agnes secretly put this idea to one side. Like aspirin, she found ideologies hard to swallow whole. Indeed, her mother had often railed at her for what she called her 'pick and mix' attitude to religion. Agnes's God floated on a soft cloud of love and forgiveness and was far too busy trying to justify famines and earthquakes to care whether Agnes told lies or used contraceptives. Along the same lines, she selected equality and freedom from domestic servitude from her new creed, and disdained the promise of liberation from the trappings of the feminine stereotype.

'If we're truly free, then we're free to wear make-up,' she told Nina, who for some reason did not seem impressed by such logic.

Agnes was not particularly enamoured of the feminine stereotype: it just so happened that it offered a convenient and effective means of disguise. She created herself daily, and did not want to know – or others to know, for that matter – what murky truths lay beneath her finery. That by disguising these smaller truths she was merely uncovering several larger ones was clear only to those who threatened to address the defect of her superficiality; but what to them was a disorder, was to Agnes the very thing that kept chaos at bay. Feminism was for her a war of words, a catalogue of social injustices that were as interesting but as unrelated to her as a history book. She saw in its medicines no cure, merely a placebo of self-acceptance that could aid only those with a less intimate knowledge of the rules of deception than herself.

'Your understanding of the relationship between form and content needs work,' wrote her tutor at the bottom of an essay, but Agnes saw in such comments no clues; only a vast sea wall beyond whose forbidding stone a boiling ocean crashed and foamed like a rabid dog.

Later, Agnes found easier ways of justifying self-adornment. By exploiting the currency of their social acceptability, she argued, women could precipitate change from the heart of the patriarchal establishment. She shared this opinion with her parents when she went home one weekend.

'Chaps are more likely to listen to a pretty girl,' mumbled her father, nodding his agreement behind a newspaper.

'You look amazing,' said John, watching her undress in the shuttered light. 'You look like a stork.'

It was ninety-eight degrees in the dark. The white sheets were limp with sweat. They were in Seville, with the sounds of mopeds and laughter from cafés making waves through the thick air. They were melting in Seville. It seemed to Agnes they were dying in Seville.

'Thanks a lot,' she said, turning from him. Her pique fizzled and blunted itself in the heat.

'Don't.' John sat up in bed. 'Don't move. Let me look at you.'

She turned around, the bars of light from the shutters appearing to swim over her naked body like eels. Once his fascination had disturbed her, but now she had come to know, if not to understand it. She knew she could rely on it if all else failed.

'Why do you love me?' he marvelled, shaking his head. 'I see other men looking at you. You're so much better than me. What do you see in me?'

He said things like that sometimes. He said they were his rape fantasies. Agnes, not understanding, was frightened of such allegations of superiority. She perceived within them intimations of incompatibility and hence desertion, little land-mines of truth in a desert of lies. He pulled her down on top of him.

'Why?' he whispered. His white teeth shone in the dark like a crescent moon.

'Because,' said Agnes.

Her body felt like it was melting into his. She clung to the moment. A second skin, irremovable.

'Agnes? It's Tom.'

'Oh!' Agnes disengaged the telephone cord from where it had wound itself round a table leg and sat down. 'How are you?'

'Well, this phone box stinks of piss but apart from that I'm okay.' The tinny roar of traffic drowned his voice.

'Where are you?'

'Outside your house. Can I come in?'

A minute later her brother stood on the doorstep. He looked too big for it. Tom had always had the dubious ability to make his surroundings appear exiguous and rather shoddy.

'Nice suit,' said Agnes.

'Savile Row.' He flicked at his shoulder. 'Hand made. The ladies love it.'

He grinned and negotiated the doorway by lowering his head exaggeratedly.

'My sister the cave-dweller,' he said, strolling into the sitting-room. He looked around. 'Nice place. Good ventilation too,' he added, running his fingers over the crack in the wall.

'Where did you think I'd be?' Agnes inquired. 'In a card-board box under Waterloo Bridge?'

'I'll admit you've always been a bit prolier-than-thou,' replied Tom, 'but I think that would be stretching it.'

Such power struggles tended to characterise the early stages of their meetings. While the exaggeration of their differences had long since been employed as a method of partly ameliorating them, Agnes had begun to nurture an unspoken anxiety of late that on one of these ice-breaking occasions she would discover Tom had actually become the person he caricatured so expertly.

'Do you want something to drink?' she said.

'Great.' He grinned. 'I'll have some champagne.'

Agnes was astounded.

'We don't have any,' she replied.

Tom rummaged in his bag and produced a bottle with a flourish.

'You do now,' he said.

'You shouldn't have,' she murmured penitently.

'I didn't,' he replied. 'I had to go and see someone in Finsbury Park on business. That's why I'm up here. He gave it to me.'

Having ascertained the spirit of the occasion, Agnes went to the kitchen in search of two matching glasses. She opened cupboards aimlessly, unable suddenly to remember what she was looking for. Tom's impromptu visits often disturbed her in this way. This was not so much the fault of their differences – in Agnes's environment Tom often took on the aspect of one who recognised nothing within it, coming as he did from an element of corporate largesse – as of a sense she had of two worlds colliding which hitherto had been kept apart. It made her unsure of how to behave.

Back in the sitting-room, Merlin had just come home. Agnes emerged from the kitchen to see Tom slapping him on the back in the jovial pantomime of manhood he always employed with Agnes's friends, and possibly even with his own. Merlin, visibly shaken by the blow, took to the sofa.

'Look what Tom brought.' Agnes waved the bottle in front of him. 'Do you want some?'

'Yes please,' said Merlin politely, recovering his spirits. 'That's very generous of you, Tom.'

Agnes fled to the kitchen for another glass.

'Don't mention it,' said Tom behind her. 'Actually, do mention it. Mention it often.'

When she returned, Tom was easing the cork from the bottle with his large thumbs. Merlin cringed. Agnes, confident that Tom's removal of the cork would be consistent with his general demeanour – a smooth pop and fizz as opposed to a loud racing-driver's bang and a foaming geyser – remained calm.

'Hey presto.' He put the cork on the table and began pouring champagne into the glasses.

'You've done that before,' said Merlin.

'All in a day's work,' replied Tom. He was a management consultant in the City, and, Agnes reflected, was probably being truthful.

'How's work?' she inquired.

'Fine.' He leaned back into the sofa, his legs firmly spread in a V emanating from his crotch. Agnes looked away, obscurely embarrassed. 'I'm on a job for a publishing firm, actually, which might interest you.'

'Oh, really?' said Agnes brightly. She was unaccustomed to talking shop, and was prepared now to enjoy its new intimations of adulthood. 'What are you doing for them?'

'Usual sort of thing. Getting rid of dead wood, tightening things up. It's not difficult, seeing as they've got three people doing one person's job. We're slimming down editorial at the moment.'

'Oh.' Agnes felt rather cold. 'So what happens to the other two?'

Merlin shifted on the sofa, perhaps made uncomfortable by the prospect, albeit theoretical, of brother reducing sister.

'Sacked.' Tom elaborated his succinct reply with a throat-cutting gesture.

'But – but what are they supposed to do? What's to become of them?'

She fixed him with a glance intended to mortify him. He looked back at her for a minute and then stared into mid-air, as if considering the problem for the first time.

'Oh dear,' he said finally. 'They'll all probably kill themselves, won't they?' He sighed exaggeratedly. 'Don't be so soft, Agnes. They'll get other jobs, of course. Better ones, hopefully. It's not my problem.'

'No!' she cried. 'But it's theirs! They might have – *circumstances*. For all you know, they might have five children each and sick relatives to look after!'

Merlin guffawed delightedly.

'Christ.' Tom clasped his forehead. 'Look, they could have enough dying aunts to hold a wheelchair rally for all I care. It still doesn't make sense to keep them on.'

'Sense!' shrieked Agnes. 'How does it make sense to sacrifice innocent people on the – on the altar of capitalist greed? And even if it does make sense to you, why does that make it right?'

'I never said it did. You said that.'

'But don't you *care*?'

'No.' He grinned infuriatingly. 'That is what you wanted me to say, isn't it? I'm an unprincipled capitalist pig. I drink the blood of unemployed people.'

'I think I'll leave you guys to it,' said Merlin, getting up to leave. 'Nice to have seen you, Tom.'

'Bye, Merlin.' Tom raised his hand in farewell. 'I mean, oink.'

Merlin laughed as he retreated up the stairs. Agnes glowered after him. They all banded together in the end, she thought.

Had Agnes had a sister, she might have found that feelings of sisterhood came to her more easily; as it was, such emotions were left to her imagination. Her early needy conjectures had sculpted only a more perfect version of herself in their quest for female companionship, and while at first Agnes had been content to trail around adoringly after her demigoddess, her later suspicions that in Grace she had created a monster were perhaps a more accurate simulation of sibling rivalry than she realised.

Agnes's wistful longings for sisterly love had been if anything intensified by her years in the convent. Although the word 'sister' underwent temporary etymological corruption – denoting as it did those creatures of habit who glided like phantoms down dark corridors – the dormitories aflame with cruel whispers and classrooms echoing with malice served only to drive thoughts of gentle love and cheering loyalty deep into her heart like a stake. Agnes's imaginary sister, who looked something like Doris Day, was not required to vanquish these uniformed imposters; she just smiled and sang as she lay beside Agnes in the dark, remembering the time they tried on their mother's lipstick, the time they dressed up in her clothes, the countless times they played house and baked cakes and talked about the boy who worked in the village shop. Tom, who had been the most pliant of playmates, had at first indulged in these unliberated fantasies with her; but their differences, she soon learned, went beyond his inability to sustain any sort of credible interest in the boy at the village shop. The sweet, secretive mystery of the feminine continued to dog Agnes like her own shadow. Whipping round to capture it in the mirror with a glance, she would be met only with her own eyes, which were brown and plain as daylight.

Apparently there had been a little girl, or so her mother told her, before Agnes; a little sleeping, dreaming coil whose heart beat in a warm ocean of blood. A curled pearl who smiled and sang, a tiny white angel, too good for life. She had come out to see the world, with its dust and glare and noise and men in white masks, and had closed her eyes. She had flown away and never come back. She had to make room for you, her mother told her kindly. She was too tiny for life, too delicate. Agnes held her like a feather in the palm of her hand. Agnes, with her big bawling mouth and her destiny gnarled and heavy as a tree trunk, had chased her away.

Chapter Eleven

UNDER ground, Agnes felt the world was stripped down to its bare essentials. Her lover, in a rare and uncomfortable moment of loquacity, confessed that he rarely took the underground and only then to see how the other half lived. Later it became plain to Agnes that he drove his car to keep that distinction alive, but at the time she was strangely relieved to hear him express an opinion so different from her own. He seemed so indistinct to her sometimes, flimsy as a ghost on the treadmill of his deepest moments. They came back to her in the full moon of her loneliness, the odd things he said, little islands of identity marooned in an inscrutable ocean. The memory of them sustained her on the long journey until the next sighting of land.

Agnes boarded the train and headed for an empty seat in the middle of the carriage, but was beaten to it by a woman laden down with plastic bags, who elbowed her out of the way with the expertise of one who has had to fight to get what she wanted in life. Agnes, who didn't even know what she wanted, conceded the territory with an awkward twist of her body, as if she had never intended to sit there in the first place. People stared. She edged her way back into the space by the doors and hung on to one of the straps dangling from the ceiling.

'Sorry,' she said, half-inclining her head to the person behind her. She had leaned into him with the pull of the train as it left the station, although she did feel it wasn't entirely her fault. He was standing rather closer than was necessary.

He did not acknowledge her apology and she turned away, her gaze loosely focused on her concave reflection in the door. She looked dwarfish and squat. Walking down the street sometimes, she would catch sight of herself in a shop window and her heart would plummet and rise with mingled horror and love. Beneath the tumultuous act of self-recognition, however, she never stopped experiencing a sense of relief that she was there at all. Merlin had once told her that if she looked in a mirror whilst travelling at a high enough speed her reflection would disappear; but at present the events in her life had not achieved the velocity required even to resemble progress.

Agnes shifted nervously. The motion of the train had again pressed her against the man behind. The hard edge of his briefcase was knocking against the back of her thighs. She shifted again, this time more ostentatiously to show her irritation. The briefcase lodged itself more firmly, right underneath her buttocks. She glanced nervously at the other passengers and then turned round in an attempt to catch his eye, but in the vice of bodies clamped around them she could not do so without further aggravating her plight. A sudden shift in pressure, however, allowed her room to look down at the offending briefcase. She went rigid with horror. No! It couldn't be! She averted her eyes and stared fixedly ahead. Blood burned in her cheeks. It couldn't be! Looking around again, this time with stiff deliberation, she saw that it was true. There was no briefcase: just a monstrous bulge of blue pinstripe, an accusatory cloth-covered protuberance proclaiming her most secret and shameful places.

With as violent a thrust of her body as their confinement would allow, Agnes attempted to escape her tormentor without alerting those in the carriage to the nature of his affront. Her heart was pounding. She had heard of such things before; of girls emerging from crowded trains, the backs of their legs splattered with semen. She felt quite faint with nausea. In the carriage, it was impossible to move. The rocking train seemed

63

lewdly to be exacerbating the situation. She wondered if she should broadcast her violation to those around her; but although she knew her only alternative was to suffer in silence, the compromise which such a declaration to a carriage full of strangers would force upon her seemed at that moment worse than that which she was currently enduring. She thought of what Nina would say if ever she discovered that Agnes had aided the enemy, had become the very handmaiden of Satan himself, by passing over an opportunity to fell a Goliath by exposing him in flagrant indelicacy. This proved a more effective spur, and, impelled by fear of such an accusation, she managed to twist her body round so that she was looking him in the face.

Surprisingly, his features were exhibiting a terror which uncannily resembled her own. He was sweating profusely and began to shake. Really, it was hard to tell who was threatening whom. She looked down at his trousers and saw they had regained their proper shape. His eyes followed hers shamefully. She opened her mouth, about to speak. There, she wanted to say. You have put down your weapon. Like this, we have no quarrel with each other. The train drew into a station and in the sudden bustle she was swept away from him. He put his hands in his pockets and disembarked without looking back at her.

The carriage filled up again with people. Looking around, Agnes felt suddenly angered by their slavish submission to silence: strangers passing one another by, while in their minds a thousand babbling mouths spoke of sadness, of worry, of loneliness. Why couldn't they all just sit down and talk about it? Why couldn't she lean over, touch the arm of a stranger, ask them what they thought of love? If they could not do it here, deep beneath the city, circulating like plasma around this strange subterrane – if they could not talk of the heart here in the heart – then where?

Run to ground by the trains, Agnes took shelter on the buses. The overground journey to Finchley Central was far more laborious, entailing at least three changes of vehicle, but it seemed a fair exchange for the less pressurised form of human commerce it afforded.

Like most children Agnes had once thought transport the central focus of any outing, regarding A and B as two unrelated points of departure and arrival between which, however, was to be found the real fun. In those days cars had seemed an inferior means of conveyance; like Christmas, they cordoned off the family into a compression chamber of solitude, which isolation seemed to render its members fractious and ill-behaved. Moreover, they emphasised the tiresome power structures which already characterised the hierarchy of their home.

'Don't distract your father!' their mother would call from the realm of adult responsibility in the front seat, with its flashing control panel and ominous wheel.

'Mum, he's hurting me!' Agnes would yell from the hotbed of insurrection behind, as they were carried off against their will.

Trains had seemed then to afford a greater degree of equality and, as they proffered their tickets to the inspector with unwarranted nervousness, to bind them together in the face of uniformed authority as if they were attempting an illegal border crossing or smuggling contraband. The presence of strangers, too, ensured their enjoyment of one another's company in a manner somewhat foreign to their own hearth.

'Really, darling?' said their mother as Agnes entertained her with a thoughtful monologue on why Jessica-at-school's birthday party had been so superior to her own, while their father guffawed benevolently at a story of Tom's involving a dead rat he had put in another boy's desk.

'Kids,' they would say, shrugging hilariously at their companions in the carriage.

Now Agnes disdained the trains, and found she enjoyed the bustle of the roadside, despite their congested and tortuous progress along it. 'Hold on tight!' warned the conductor as the open-ended 19 careered around a corner and Agnes did so, warmed by the thought that this man, who didn't even know her, nevertheless did not want to see her flung through the cavity in the vehicle's side and mauled between tyre and tarmac.

She examined her fellow passengers in this spirit of benevolence and felt cheered by their differences. Women in saris and monkish robes, through which their long chattering hands protruded with the jangle of bracelets and the flash of rings, sat beside truculent boys with indolent eyes and fluffy nether lips, thighs splayed and arms folded like adolescent pashas in garish track-suits. In front of her, two vast West Indian women were packed into one narrow seat, merging and spreading into the aisle beyond like a mountain range. Agnes looked at the palm trees and orange groves depicted in the fabric of their ebullient head-dresses and wondered, guiltily, at their wilful disenfranchisement from such splendour. Picking out from the crowd a few of her fellow-natives, the women with tired faces and straggling perms, the men with ill-fitting suits and threadbare heads, shoes the grey of shopping malls, pigeon-chested and pot-bellied, her wonder doubled. Could *they* not go at least? she thought. Could they not sample for a while the lapping oceans and languorous palms, the chirping forests and somnambulant lakes and sweetly choiring minarets? Whatever deprivation they found there could be no worse than that of this concrete island with its poisonous drizzle, its sewer-lakes, its banshee road-drills and filthy streets. Could they not get together and solve each other's problems?

Agnes seemed to hear, as if from around her, dissenting voices which appeared to take exception to her vast cultural exchange programme. Condescending! they cried. Racist! Her thoughts short-circuited with self-doubt. It was so hard sometimes, having to think for oneself. A loud blare of horns from the surrounding traffic seemed to chorus their disapproval. A stream of cars backed up and ground to a halt on the road ahead. She got off the bus and walked.

Chapter Twelve

ON Monday morning Greta arrived later than usual at the office. Agnes was sitting alone proof-reading the details of the embassy of St Martin and the Grenadines, and had been transported in spirit if not in body to a palm-fringed beach on which she and her lover sat while a warm ocean fawned at their feet like an affectionate cat.

'Is there anyone in there?' whispered Greta volubly, while occluding herself behind the doorframe.

'The coast is clear,' said Agnes.

'Good.' Greta bounded with more agility than grace on to Agnes's desk. She produced a paper bag from which she extracted a cake that looked like a road accident. 'Sorry to leave you in it. I got tied up.'

Agnes leaned back in her chair and looked at Greta's shoes, which were high-heeled and festooned with a bondage of straps and laces.

'I met this guy on my way here,' continued Greta between bites. 'I was going to be on time for once, too.' She yawned, displaying mashed vistas of jam and cream. 'We met in the tube station, so I knew it was destiny. You can't ignore things like that. Anyway, I showed him my ticket and we just sort of got talking. He was really nice.'

'Why did you show him your ticket?' Agnes wondered if she had missed something. It was a suspicion she often entertained about herself.

'What? Oh, I get you. He works for them, you know, the tube people. He's the guy you show your ticket to. He was really nice,' she repeated, shaking her head and smiling. 'We had a good time together.'

'So—' Agnes hesitated before requesting further elucidation. Greta's details tended to obscure rather than clarify. 'So what exactly did you do?' she asked finally, overcome by curiosity.

'We went for a ride.'

'You mean you just went off with him in his car? But you don't know anything about him! He could be anybody!'

'I told you,' said Greta calmly. 'He works on the tube. He had one of those neat tickets where you can go anywhere you want without paying. So we just rode the trains together for a while.'

'How far did you go?' asked Agnes, with some anxiety.

'Northwood.'

'Do you want some coffee?'

'Sure.' Greta smiled. 'That would be nice.'

Making coffee, Anges grew increasingly troubled. The mysteries of social intercourse had never seemed to elude her so completely. Beside Greta's chance meetings, her own encounters seemed both laboured and conservative. Did not everyone ponder, observe and ruminate before electing a mate? Or perhaps she was blind to it; perhaps the world around her crackled with fusion and fission, while she blundered with every step through electric fields of sexual activity, secret currents of attraction! How else had they come about, the infinite pairings on which the world had depended through all its ages? Had it been left to her, she thought glumly, Adam and Eve would even now remain absorbed in the round of art galleries and cinema trips which her romantic protocol judged the fit testing ground for love.

Within a very few minutes, however, her mind had found reassurance in the further contemplation of Greta's predicament. What matter was there for envy, after all, in the attentions of those not encountered by recommendation or reference? She had been right to disapprove. Agnes did not condone social separatism, but nor did she attempt to subvert it. While largely ignorant of those details which distinguished one echelon from another, she was growing increasingly expert in the machinations of that underworld which underpinned them all. The subtle propinquity of this realm, mingling as it did with the city's pattern, was almost disarming. One could be blind to its close mystery, and yet be ambushed by its missionaries on every corner. Their individual plights concealed their numbers. Agnes pitied their predicament but remained disabused of their innocence. They had nothing to lose, and therefore would stop at nothing. She must take it upon herself to salvage Greta from the clutches of despots and dissemblers. She must set her on a course where malicious chance could not intervene. She would invite her to a dinner party.

'What are you doing on Saturday?' she said as she went back into the office.

'Nothing,' Greta replied. 'Unless you can make me a better offer.'

The first time Agnes kissed a boy she was thirteen. There had probably been other kisses before then, pecks on the cheek and such, little moth-like eruptions of schoolroom fantasies; but her first proper kiss occurred when she was invited to a party at a large house owned by a local farmer, where the surrounding gentry landed, bomb-like, for frequent such festivities, with explosive consequences.

Agnes, understandably nervous in the face of such a mountainous social opportunity, deliberated long and hard over the choice of the outfit in which she would most expeditiously scale its heights. In the end, fear had made her suggestible; and she had worn an old dress of her mother's, a boned black affair with breastplates like ice-cream cones which projected an unsubstantiated pertness, and which, she was assured, had smoothed many a path to social congress in its time. Once arrived, however, Agnes speedily understood that that time had long since passed. She grew uncomfortable as her attire drew an excess of wry, comical glances, and a noticeable deficiency of admiring ones. Some of the boys, wearing their fathers' dinner jackets, seemed equally uncomfortable; but it was the others, the ones with the arrogant, laughing mouths, the tall ones who tossed their lank hair out of their eyes and smoked cigarettes, whom Agnes watched. Her heart sank as groups of girls with long curly hair and cloud-like dresses came into the room, laughing and smoking cigarettes with mouths which were more delicate but just as arrogant.

Made polite by desperation, she had allowed herself to become engaged in conversation with a tall, spotty boy who believed her when she lied about her age. He was with a friend, one of those boys whom Agnes had so liked the look of, and who seemed to be looking at her. Agnes ignored the spotty boy and instead giggled and jabbered at his friend. The friend stared at her, his hands in his pockets.

'That dress makes you look fat,' he said finally, sauntering off.

Left with the tall spotty one, Agnes allowed herself to be drawn outside and comforted. She recoiled at the feeling of his tongue in her mouth. It seemed rather unhygienic. Their teeth knocked together as they kissed.

'Don't,' she said, as his hand crept under her skirt and attempted to inveigle itself into her knickers.

Her father, come to collect her at midnight, had caught them thus intertwined and had observed a tense silence on the way home. Agnes had spent the next few days in an orgy of alternating guilt and self-congratulation, and had worn polo-neck sweaters for two weeks in the height of summer to hide the lovebite which swelled painful as a boil on her neck.

'You know guys?' said Greta.

'I suppose so,' Agnes replied.

'Well, they say dumb things, right? Like this friend of mine, okay, her boyfriend says to her that she's got a really big butt. All the time, like she really wants to talk about it, right? I mean, change the fucking record.'

'And does she?'

'Does she what?'

'Have a big – you know.'

Greta leaned back in her chair and thought about it.

'I guess,' she said.

Once, in a tone of mild surprise, her lover had told her that her shoulders were actually quite tiny, as if someone had just accused them of the opposite. Surprised by his attention to her detail, she had allowed herself to be warmed and flattered by his compliment; if compliment it was. Over the next few days, catching sight of her reflection with a renewed increase of zeal, she was surprised to notice that her shoulders, far from receding, appeared to be growing larger with every glance. At first she assumed that their bulkiness was directly attributable to her own magnified interest in them; but eventually, trying on without success one of the close-fitting jackets which she now plucked eagerly from every shop rail she passed, she was forced to admit a more pedestrian and disturbing truth. Her shoulders were not tiny; in fact, by some standards, they could be judged quite broad. His comment, which for some time had been casting its bright and attentive beam around her troubled mind, became all at once rather menacing. It circled her like the fin of a shark, hinting at a black and malicious force beneath.

'What really gets me,' Greta concluded, 'is that it's kind of like they think they're trying to get on our level. Like they're being kind of friendly, you know? I mean, they think we really *think* about that stuff.'

Agnes's dinner party on Saturday was an unremitting failure. Her Brylcreamed and blazered guests, selected as if from a line-up for their suitability as companions for Greta, had seemed to detect something untoward in their gathering and had remained diffident and ill-at-ease. Agnes had spent the early part of the evening luring their interest with Greta's forthcoming attractions; but as the night wore on, it became apparent that Greta would have to be taken off the bill of fare.

'I can't believe she didn't come!' fumed Agnes as she and Nina were clearing up. 'After all the trouble I went to – all the effort I made!' She clattered plates noisily in the sink. 'It was for *her*. I wanted her to meet nice people. Is there anything wrong with that? I just wanted her make some friends.'

'She'd have had more chance at a bloody outpatients' Christmas party,' said Nina. 'I don't know where you found that bunch of bank clerks.'

'They weren't that bad! Anyway, it doesn't make it right. She should at least have phoned to make an excuse. Maybe – maybe something's happened to her. Maybe she's been hurt.'

Nina cackled. 'Grievous bodily harm has never looked so good,' she said.

'How can you say that?' cried Agnes furiously.

'Okay, but it's still a bit suspect. It's like you're trying to control her.' Nina began putting things away. 'You're not her mother, you know. You can't relive things through her. You just have to get on with your life and let other people get on with theirs.'

A loud knock on the door just then inflamed Agnes's heart with hope at her own defence. Nina ran to open it. It was Jack.

'How's it going?' he said as Nina hustled him past the kitchen and into her room. A few minutes later, Agnes heard muffled whispers and giggles escaping from beneath the door. She continued clearing up in a desultory way and then decided to phone her lover. She let it ring for several minutes but there was no answer. She wondered where he was.

The next day, Greta appeared on Agnes's doorstep clutching a bottle of wine.

'You must be really pissed,' she said penitently.

Agnes stared at her, uncomprehending.

'About last night,' elaborated Greta. 'I'm really sorry.'

'Oh.' Agnes stood back to let her in. 'What happened to you?'

'Well,' Greta flopped down in an armchair and threw up her hands despairingly. 'I was all set to go, right? I bought the wine, I changed my clothes, and then I thought, well, I'll have a little nap, right? It was still pretty early, so I just lay down on the bed and closed my eyes. Next thing I know, I wake up and it's eight o'clock!'

She slapped her forehead and gazed at Agnes in entreaty.

'You could still have made it,' observed Agnes stiffly. 'No one even got here until eight thirty. Failing that, you could have phoned. I was worried about you. All of us,' she added, resorting to numbers, 'were worried about you.'

'Eight in the *morning*!' wailed Greta pitifully. 'I slept all night. In fact, I was halfway here before I realised anything was wrong – it was dark when I left, you see, but then it started to get light. It was kind of weird.' She grinned. 'I was totally freaked.'

Chapter Thirteen

AGNES walked to the tube station every morning. In the first few weeks of her employment she had undergone this journey in a haze induced by the unaccustomed earliness of the hour, but now that she was used to it it had become almost enjoyable. It was a free space, a few liberated minutes of prologue in which she could regard the forthcoming day with unbridled optimism. This optimism was rarely borne out in the dreary dawn of activity at *Diplomat's Week*, but Agnes's early ruminations gave her the strength to endure at least some of its hours. She found it hard to renounce her faith, however unfounded, in the ultimate, inexorable improvement of things.

As she emerged from her house into a particularly iridescent eight o'clock mist, the tincture of sky and air recalled in her the memory of similar auroral practices from long ago. As a child, she had often used to wake early – sometimes six or seven o'clock – and had become acquainted with the quiet hours, before the rest of the world awoke, like a new and secret friend. She would open her curtains and rejoice at the newborn blueness of the sky, the lawns wet and golden with dew, the great trees shaggy with leaves and hung with choiring birds. It seemed to her then as if she had woken into the world of castles and fairy tales in which she had found sleep the night before; and she would run lightly downstairs in her bare feet, struggling with the locks on the front door until they released her into the magic beyond. She knew she had discovered a region grimly disbarred by the adult world with its fortresses and fastenings, and she would run out into it, cavorting on the wet lawn in her nightdress. In autumn she would dance in a whirl of leaves; in winter, she would put on boots and forge small tracks beside the spiky delicate imprints of birds.

Agnes thought of her small pagan self all the way to the tube station. She remembered the feeling of clean air against her body, naked beneath its nightdress. So far was she now from nature, she realised then, that she didn't even know what month it was; and as she perused Gillespie Road for clues, there was to be seen neither tree nor flower to help her.

She stopped at the news-stand on the corner to buy a paper. Normally she did not do so, preferring to daydream her way to Finchley Central, but she had often pitied the withered old man who perched in the kiosk as one of the few whose job was possibly less rewarding than her own.

'Fank you, fank you,' he was saying as strangers grabbed newspapers and thrust jangling coins into his outstretched hand. Agnes gave him her money and awaited his reply, but he turned away and began fumbling with the neat stacks of cigarettes behind him instead. She reddened, her heart lurching with rejection, and buried her embarrassment in the front page.

It was late September, it seemed, the very glorious and glowing nub of autumn. She could scarcely believe that summer had sickened, died, and been buried without her even noticing. Looking around, there was little evidence now of mellow fruitfulness. She longed suddenly for the lost seasons of her youth, whose verdant memory had not been withered by time. She had surely been more alive then; had felt cold winters and hot summers, had rejoiced in the ebullience of spring. An old taste of innocence and freedom rose salty in her mouth and was gone. The bare pavements and monotonous skies of her exile echoed everywhere the stark chords of disenfranchisement, and in the thrall of its hideous music she was suddenly hit by a terror so large and black she thought it would surely crush her.

The crack in the wall was getting bigger. It had begun to slope off to the left, wiggling crazily like a mountain path on a road map. Sometimes they could hear scratching and rustling sounds coming from within, and Agnes wondered if strange creatures might begin to squeeze out from between its jaws. Nina said it was mice. Merlin said it was sediment.

'Shouldn't we get something done?' Agnes asked him one night.

'No point,' he replied, biting into a crescent moon of pizza. 'The council are going to knock it down anyway. We'll be long gone by the time the walls cave in.'

'Where are we going to go?' She sipped red wine and focused her mind on this future dilemma from the comfort of her armchair.

'Dunno. I might buy a house, I suppose.'

'Oh.'

Agnes, whose thoughts had been running more along the lines of the three of them with sleeping bags cosily bedding down in deserted shopping malls, was at a loss for words. The singularity of both his personal pronoun and his affluent future made her feel apprehensive. After a while, she said: 'Merlin, do you get depressed at the thought of working? For ever, I mean.'

'Not really.' He put down his plate, now adorned with bare, smiling pizza crusts, and picked up his glass. 'It depends what you mean. Do I find working in itself depressing – enough, say, to give it up and find an alternative way of life; or do I find the notion of eternity depressing, the idea that the only thing separating me from my own funeral is a load of paycheques. They're two different things.'

'Whatever,' said Agnes irritably. 'The first one.'

'Do I find work innately depressing?' Merlin sat back and rubbed his stomach. He had become rather pompous since he

76

had started this job, she thought. That was what happened to men. Once they started wearing suits, they began to get their personalities off the peg too. 'No, not really. I mean, it depends on whether you have anything you'd rather be doing.'

'Well, everyone does, surely?' said Agnes impatiently. 'Everyone would rather go to the beach or watch a movie than sit in an office, wouldn't they?'

'To a point, yes. But day in and day out, I don't know. It's easier if you're rich, probably. You can cater to your own boredom thresholds.'

'But rich people go on working, even when they can't possibly spend all the money they've made.' Agnes wondered why she never met people like the ones she referred to so often in her arguments. 'I would never do that.'

'That's why you're not rich,' said Merlin. 'For rich people, money is the most interesting thing in the world. They enjoy making it. For everyone else – well, it's a means to an end, I suppose. A way of eating and buying what you need and having a holiday. And a way of passing time.'

'That's it!' Agnes shrieked, banging the table top so that a wave of wine from Merlin's glass slopped over the rim into a blood-coloured puddle. 'That's exactly what I mean! Passing time – don't you find that depressing? I mean, if all we're doing is trying to pass time, why don't we just kill ourselves?'

When she was younger, that sort of comment would have aroused groans and sighs from Agnes's family. She was so melodramatic, they would complain. Why did she have to get so worked up about everything? Merlin smiled.

'Absolutely,' he said. 'Why don't we? Come on, Agnes – you hate your job. Why don't you kill yourself?'

'Well.' Agnes considered the question, which had been pronounced more in the spirit of intellectual debate than active encouragement. 'I suppose I believe that things will get better. If I knew I had to do this for ever, it would be different.'

'Exactly,' said Merlin. 'And that's the pleasure principle. Things are more valuable if they're rare. Just imagine if you had to go to the cinema for ever or lie on a beach all day for the rest of your life. Imagine if we spent all our time on holiday and then went to work for two weeks a year. Work would be the high point of our lives. That would be awful.'

'Maybe,' conceded Agnes, although secretly she thought she could bear it.

'I once heard someone on the radio being asked what he would take with him if he had to spend the rest of his life alone on a desert island,' Merlin said presently. 'A beautiful island, mind you, with palm trees and stuff, but nothing else. You know what he said?'

'What?'

'He said he would take a gun. To shoot himself with, that is.'

'That's really dumb,' said Greta when Agnes told her Merlin's story. 'Why didn't he just take a plane with him to get him off the goddamned island?'

Her lover hadn't called now for two weeks. Agnes knew that the reasons underlying his lapse would not, if known, be likely to reveal anything in her favour, and she clung to the mercy of his silence as well as, more obstinately, to the hope of its interruption.

Tom called to say that he was going to visit their parents in East Anglia on Saturday, and as her only weekend plans thus far had been to spend it fending off all arrangements lest her lover should call and want to see her, she agreed in a fit of pique, as Friday brought the unsullied vacancy of the ensuing two days perilously near, to accompany him.

Tom drew up outside her house in a car as handsome and glossy-flanked as a racehorse, and as he bore her off within it, Agnes lived out with vicarious satisfaction the thought of her lover calling to be told she had gone away. It occurred to her then that her pleasure at the idea of his doing so was of a really rather secondary variety, and furthermore that he might share some of it on receiving news of her departure.

She looked out of the window. The city clung interminably

to the roadside, grey and elastic as old chewing gum. They drove through parts of London she had never even heard of, battered strings of shops and houses nestling in motorway intersections or beside underpasses, festering round tatty overground stations with foreign-sounding names. They passed vast tower-blocks festooned with washing lines, purple sheets fluttering in the breeze like flags. Agnes wondered what one had to do to end up behind one of their slit-eyed apertures.

'Awful, isn't it?' said Tom, putting his foot down on the accelerator. 'Poor sods.'

Their parents were waiting for them at the end of the smooth gravel drive which wound its way to the front of the house, feigning involvement with the herbaceous borders. They liked to present an active image of country life. At the sound of the car, they looked up and waved distractedly, trowels in hand.

'Keep digging, slaves!' yelled Tom out of the window. 'You've got half an hour to grow lunch.'

Agnes got out of the car. After months of concrete and tarmac the green of their garden was hallucinogenic. Giant trees posed along the drive like old movie actresses, their gnarled and hysterical limbs dripping with red and gold curls of leaves. The lawns rolled and billowed out beneath them, the manicured stretches of their garden giving way to the rougher fields beyond. Her parents' small farmhouse lounged comfortably amidst this splendour. It had large windows fringed with frenchified shutters, coquettish as false eyelashes. Agnes thought of those captives of the tower, their lives grim and phallic and seasonless beside all this fecundity, and for a moment she burned with shame.

'Your problem, Agnes,' Nina had once said to her, 'is that you don't want to be like everyone else. You want everyone else to be like you.'

'Agnes, you're not eating,' said her mother when they sat down to lunch. 'What's the matter? Don't you feel well?'

Agnes was forced by her words to recall several past occasions when, by disdaining nourishment, she had drawn similar polite inquiries.

'Nothing's the matter!' she would retort, aged seventeen and passionate. 'I just don't think we should all be stuffing ourselves when people in the Third World are starving, that's all.'

'Don't be ridiculous,' her mother would say, nervous at the sudden intrusion of several emaciated, hungry-eyed nomads in her beige-carpeted dining-room. 'Honestly, what a waste.'

'Why don't you send them your leftovers?' Tom would opine. 'Cold carrots and congealed gravy. Yum, yum.'

At that point Agnes would stand up.

'I hate you all!' she would cry, bursting into tears and leaving the room. As she slammed the door, a wave of badly suppressed laughter would gather and break ignominiously over her furious head.

'I'm fine, Mum,' she said now, staring into a swamp of green vegetables and gravy in which pieces of beef sported and swam. 'I think I'm a bit car-sick, that's all.'

'Well,' replied her mother. 'At least it's not all that business about starving children any more.'

Agnes, ruminating on her youthful protests, felt amazed that she should ever have dared to care so passionately. Now the wanting, begging world frightened her. It occurred to her that these days she seemed to care about little other than herself.

'Don't let her fool you.' Tom spoke with his mouth full. 'We passed within a mile of some poor people on the way down. Agnes is on hunger strike.'

'She does look awfully thin,' said her mother to no one in particular. She raised her voice a few decibels for the benefit of Agnes's father, whose hearing defect was no less severe for being wilful. 'Don't you think she looks thin, Alex?'

'Appetites like birds,' came the mumbled reply. 'The lot of them.'

'I like a nice red,' Tom said, raising his wine-glass to Agnes.

'If she's in a skirt,' Agnes witheringly replied.

'Children!' their mother breathed uncertainly. She appeared to require reassurance that these strange, rather good-looking young professionals who had come from London for lunch were in fact her offspring. 'Honestly,' she sighed, bearing off their half-finished plates. 'What a waste. And with so many people in the world starving.'

After lunch they walked the dogs, Duke and Duchess, titles bestowed on them, Agnes hoped, more in the spirit of anarchy than aspiration. Tom, when he had heard what they were to be called, had suggested they call them Muck and Brass instead.

'Whatever can you be thinking of?' their mother had cried aghast. 'Imagine calling a dog Muck!'

'Why don't we call them Simon and Garfunkel,' said Agnes, who, aged twelve, had just purchased her first album.

'We'll end up calling them Belt and Braces at this rate,' interjected her father to the bemusement of them all. In his younger days he had been known to enjoy the occasional joke, but had since retreated from the front line for reasons which his daughter expressed more succinctly and volubly than he ever could when she claimed that nobody understood her.

The dogs were old now and resembled ambulant barrels as they trotted heavily over the meadow. Tom chucked a stick far ahead of them and they lumbered after it.

'You love it, don't you?' said Agnes as they walked.

'Love what?'

'All this.'

She swept a regal hand airily over their surroundings. Tom pursed his lips and looked at his boots, which were kicking up a fine spray of recent rainwater from the grass as he walked.

'Don't you?'

'Of course. It's home, isn't it?'

'But?'

Agnes considered her next comment. It disturbed her to realise that she had become distanced from her egalitarian plans for society. It had begun to occur to her since they had arrived that she quite possibly might never attain for herself the standard of living to which her upbringing had accustomed her. The world of work had surprised and dismayed her with its terms. It did not seem to respond to the methods by which she had hitherto always achieved success. There might come a time, all too soon, when she herself would need to be saved from the perdition of economic failure.

'But it's not fair. It's not fair that we should have all of this when other people have nothing.'

'Ha!' Tom turned abruptly on his heel and continued walking. Agnes had to run to catch up with him. 'So what do you suggest? What would make you feel better about it? How about, say, we sell the house and put Mum and Dad in a council flat?'

'Don't be childish,' retorted Agnes. 'You know that's not what I mean.'

'Explain to me, then. Tell me what you mean. I've always wanted to know what people mean when they say things like that.'

He smiled and shook his head in a manner which Agnes found most infuriating, and to which her immediate reaction was to cry and stamp her feet with frustration. Knowing, however, that such a response would do nothing to advance her cause, she groped for something more ingenious.

'Why do you have to be so aggressive about it? I'm entitled to my point of view.'

'Oh, sorry,' said Tom gleefully. 'I forgot. Human rights. So, Ag, tell me the point of your bloody view.'

Agnes had not intended to precipitate an ideological exchange of such ferocity, and felt now that she was somewhat out of her depth. Admittedly, Tom himself was being insufferably shallow, but his graphic illustration of the effects of her causes had unsettled her, for in truth she would not have wished tower-blocks or penury upon anyone. She was passionate, of that she was sure: her emotions on viewing certain television documentaries were reassuringly genuine. But when it came to whiting her own sepulchre, things became rather unclear. None of her family, now that she came to think of it, had ever seemed remotely threatened by her plans to vanquish them. Her colourful polemic had always been taken as a spicy sauce of dissent to flavour the bland taste of conformity. Indeed, she sometimes felt they almost expected it of her. Perhaps it gave them pleasure to watch her capitulate at the altar of élitism and ingest the fruits of capitalist exploitation.

'You just don't want other people to have what you can't get,' Tom was saying. 'You don't really care about the poor or the homeless. It's your fear of failure that's behind it. If nobody wins, you can't lose.'

'What do you call winning?' Agnes rejoined, inflamed anew. 'Sitting around and making money out of other people's misfortune, like you? What about people who actually *do* care about things, who reject a system they didn't choose in the first place? Are they losers just because they refuse to play the game?'

'Don't talk to me about caring! You're the one who wants to turf her own parents out of their home, remember? I'll tell you what I care about – I care about them.' He pointed towards the house but his gesture also encompassed the dogs, who, splayed on their sides in the long grass and breathing heavily, bore a poignant enough resemblance to their masters to further his cause. 'They've worked all their lives for this. How do you think they feel when you throw it back in their faces just to make yourself feel better? I feel sorry for you.'

'Watch out, Tom,' sneered Agnes. 'You're becoming a bleeding heart.'

'Actually, it's your *brain* I'm worried about. Your precious brain, with all those years of private – ' he emphasised the word – '*private* education that have gone into it.' Tom had always nursed a sizeable chip on his shoulder about Agnes's superior academic prowess, but would not have seen this as any reason to identify with her protagonists. 'Well, it's rotted with self-pity, if you ask me. You've overfed it with your precious socialism and your bloody feminism so it's got fat and lazy. You've given it so many excuses that it's stopped working, along with all your leftie feminist friends.'

'Nothing that a good screw wouldn't cure, is that it?'

Agnes herself was impressed by the fluent delivery of this masterful stroke. She wished Nina could have been there to witness it. Tom, being a staunch defender of family values, visibly blanched at the slight to his sister, before realising that she herself had delivered it.

'That's about the measure of it,' he said. 'If you could ever hang on to a man long enough for him to give you one.'

With this he began walking back to the house, perhaps realising that his descent into the realm of the personal would in all probability render certain of his own regions vulnerable to attack.

'Talking about brains,' Agnes yelled after him. 'Whatever happened to yours? Do you think we should send out a search party?'

The next day, they drove back to London in silence.

'What would you like to eat most in the whole world?' said Agnes.

She and John were starving in India, and Agnes was torturing them both with her imagination. The fan above their bed turned slowly, stirring a soup of hot air and flies.

John leaned over and kissed her warm and fragile neck.

'You,' he said.

Chapter Fourteen

GRETA'S mother called the office every week long-distance from a remote farm in Saskatchewan, where, Agnes imagined, large crows perched on telegraph wires which looped crazily over lonely acres of prairie. Greta would talk to her for what seemed like hours, murmuring inaudibly into a receiver already insulated by her cupped hand, as if her mother were a spy or a secret lover. One day, however, the call came when Greta was out of the office for the afternoon; and Agnes took it with a prurience provoked as much by this suggestion of mystery as by the aspect of miracle she had formerly noted.

'I want to speak to Greta Sankowitz,' enunciated a woman's voice carefully over a sudden static squall.

'She's not in the office at the moment, I'm afraid,' replied Agnes. As her mind traversed the vast distances over which they were conversing, she wondered if she should take this opportunity to make one or two observances in the spirit of human commerce; ask about the weather in Saskatchewan or life on the farm, for example, in exchange for news of Finchley Central.

'Excuse me?' said the voice after a pause.

'Yes, I'm still here.'

'Who is this speaking?'

The woman sounded frightened. She spoke slowly, as if mistrustful of foreigners or telephones. Agnes felt guilty that

she should be contributing to anyone's feelings of technological alienation, and decided to clarify the situation.

'My name's Agnes,' she said. 'I'm a friend of Greta's. We
work together, actually. Greta won't be back until tomorrow,
but I'll tell her then that you called.'

There was another pause. Waves of static crashed against
the receiver and Agnes wondered if the woman had been
cut off. She had an image of Mrs Sankowitz, tumescent and
clutching a shopping basket, orbiting untethered in hyperspace
like a giant loosed zeppelin. After a minute or two the woman
spoke again. She sounded almost catatonic with terror.

'Yes? I'm trying to speak to Greta Sankowitz.'

When Agnes related this occurrence to Greta the next morning, embarrassment at the memory led her to embellish her
narrative with hazardous technological incidents, as if Greta
should be protected from the knowledge that two people so
closely connected to her had completely failed to communicate
with each other in her absence.

'It was a terrible line,' she said generously. 'She sounded so
far away.'

'Oh, she always sounds like that,' said Greta.

'Don't you miss your family?' Agnes inquired.

'Sure.'

'What are they like?'

'Oh, pretty normal, I guess. My mom is really cool. She's
had it kind of rough. My dad's a son of a bitch.'

'What about your siblings?' said Agnes, swerving away
from a head-on collision with unpleasantness.

'My what?'

'Your brothers and sisters.'

'Oh, yeah. You really want to know about all this?'

Agnes nodded.

'Well, there's my brother Clary, he's in the army. He's kind
of a fascist enforcer type. I guess he takes after my dad. Then
– let's see – then there's my sister Joanne, she married this real
sleaze called Douglas. They moved to Ohio. Then there's
Lynette – she's divorced and now she sings in this nightclub in

Montreal. She's really neat. Then there's my sister Samantha, she married this guy called Steve. They're cute but sort of weird.'

'What do you mean?'

'Well.' Greta rolled her eyes. 'Samantha – she's my sister – she used to be really pretty, okay? She was the best out of all of us, really. Anyway, Steve lived in our town and he was the best-looking guy. So the two of them start dating, and when they were eighteen they got married. So, all is well. Anyway, they bought this farm and everything was fine until they started getting fat.'

'Both of them?'

'Yeah, that was the thing. These two gorgeous people. At first everyone just said, well, they're in love, they're happy – you know, some folks like to live a little round the middle when they settle down. But it kept happening, a bit more and a bit more. I guess they both just love to eat. After a couple of years they looked like a pair of giant slugs.'

'But that's awful!' said Agnes, aghast. 'What happened to them?'

'Nothing.' Greta shrugged. 'They're real happy together. They just got fat, I guess. What about yours, anyway?'

'My family?'

'Yeah. No, your frilly drawers.' Greta grinned. 'Dumbo.'

There was a time somewhere in the past when her parents had stopped being parents and she and Tom had ceased to be children. While it was hard to say which metamorphosis had precipitated which, or indeed if they were merely coincidental, it was still harder to locate the moment when the change had actually taken place, for there was within it no aspect of violent severance. It was more of a reversal of roles than a disassociation from them. There had been a time when Agnes's parents were in charge, and they had worried, commanded, and spoken in hushed tones accordingly. Now their mystery was somehow no longer intact. Now Agnes and Tom worried and advised, and even, occasionally, criticised their parents' behaviour.

While unable exactly to date this turn of events, Agnes aligned it in her mind with the period when, in some way she was never able to define but which she recalled with ineffable sadness, things had, for want of a better explanation, ceased to be real to her. Unlike the murky exchanges of adulthood, this moment – and it happened, literally, in a moment, nothing more – still retained a clarity which allowed its details to be summoned up at any time.

She had been walking down a street in the provincial town where her convent school lodged like a malignant tumour, passing the hour of parole before study by wandering, in the company of two or three other uniformed girls, along the shop-fronted pavements in the hope of glimpsing within these bright glass-plated spheres the promise of a future as yet unimaginable, though undoubtedly seductive. Normally on these excursions they purchased nothing that could so effectively liberate them from their imprisonment, but rather things that confirmed it: coloured pencils, ink-pens with flowered cases, logo-bearing rubbers; things which put a fatal insignia of identity on the nightmare of school, and which suggested it was not just a fleeting and horrible dream. She had, at the moment in question, been neither happy nor particularly unhappy. It was a grey afternoon in March, still light beneath a low cloudy sky. She walked beside a girl called Christine Poole, while the other two walked behind. She didn't know what it was they were talking about, although the fact that they must have been talking impressed her now as amazing; even then, at the age of thirteen, when she knew so little about the world, she had been pronouncing and articulating.

In any case, what she did remember was that they had paused on the edge of the pavement to cross the busy road, and there, in a grey and unremarkable town-centre, watching for gaps in the traffic, she had suddenly felt her mind disengage and float away from it all. It was most unexpected. She had become frightened, sensing that something irrevocable had taken place, and had forced herself to speak in an attempt to recover her sense of there-ness.

'I don't feel as if I'm here,' she had said to Christine Poole; and she remembered very clearly what had happened next. First of all, she realised her voice sounded distant, as if she were listening instead of speaking. Secondly, Christine had looked at her as if she were mad. These two events now seemed to have characterised much of her later life.

It was, then, with the onset of what she now termed 'aloofness' that she identified her parents' regression. Two further incidents from that period stuck in her mind confirming her suspicions. The first was brief, and concerned her mother in much the same way as a snapshot taken unawares in a secret moment. Agnes was hunting for an old jumper which she suspected her mother might have secreted to the laundry basket, or worse, to the dustbin, and failing to locate it, had gone to attempt negotiations for its rescue. She had called her mother's name, and, receiving no response, had begun searching one by one the rooms of their house. Agnes's certainty that her quarry had such limited possibilities for escape did not, in her mind, make any matter for leniency. She had finally tracked her mother down to the small room off the kitchen where the laundry was done and had begun a furious address on the subject of her lost jumper.

Her mother, whose back had been turned, turned around to face her; not in the manner of one surprised, but with that same quality of aloofness which Agnes had begun recently to detect in herself. The picture she had, and which still came back to her so clearly, was that of her mother's face in the moment before she had seemed to engage with the intrusion. She had looked dreamy, certainly; but there was also a split second in which Agnes was uncomfortably aware that her mother didn't recognise her.

The second incident concerned her father, and was far spicier and more horrific that the first. During more or less the same period, Agnes's father had begun to breed rabbits. He kept them in a shed beyond the vegetable patch and was

unfailingly dutiful and tender in his ministrations to this nascent colony. Agnes early on became fascinated by these small
creatures with their glowing eyes, and would often accompany
her father to the hutches; although once she had seen a large
rat lying nonchalantly along a beam in the shed, and had
postponed her visits while dreams of its long, rubbery tail had
haunted her sleep. One night, her father had trudged off by
the light of a gas lantern to perform his caretaking duties, and
had come rushing back a few minutes later in a state of great
excitement.

'It's Ed McBain!' he had cried. 'She's having babies!'

In his fondness for the creatures, her father had named them
all after his favourite writers of detective stories; although the
genre, unfortunately as it turned out, had not allowed for
much variety in terms of gender.

Agnes alone felt compelled by this news to trail after her
father in the rain out to the rabbit hutches, and the two of
them settled themselves on overturned apple crates, with the
lantern suspended overhead from the erstwhile perch of the
hideous rat. At first there was little to see within the straw-
lined hutch. The mother-to-be crouched at the far end, her
body quivering. Agnes could see the red points of her eyes,
which in the sepia light seemed to her to be infused with a
strangely devilish intent.

'Here they come!' whispered her father excitedly. 'Look –
just there. Can you see it?'

Agnes looked in time to see a peculiarly pink-fleshed ball
drop into the straw beside the mother rabbit. It squirmed,
tiny and myopic.

'It doesn't have any fur!' she cried.

'It's not supposed to,' reassured her father. 'That comes
later. Look, there's another one.'

The tiny flesh-balls were dropping every few minutes into
the straw, where they began to move and unfurl pinkly like
foetal fists. Agnes and her father sat in wondering silence,
while the gas lamp hissed above them and the smell of straw
suffused their nostrils with its dust. Agnes knew there was a
miracle at hand.

'What's she doing now, Dad?' she asked.

The rabbit had, apparently, finished her labours and was snuffling about the new-born bundles with her whiskered snout.

'I think she's cleaning them,' her father replied.

The rabbit looked up as he spoke. She seemed disconcertingly to be staring at them. Agnes felt strangely uncomfortable beneath her eyes. Then, as they watched, the rabbit turned back to her progeny and took one in her mouth.

'Dad?' said Agnes. 'Dad?'

He did not reply. They sat there in silence as the tiny back legs disappeared into the rabbit's mouth and – unmistakably! – she swallowed.

'Oh my God,' said Agnes, as the rabbit bent her head and took another bundle between her small teeth. The baby rabbit wriggled as it disappeared into the cavity. 'Dad, we've got to do something! We have to do something!'

Neither of them looked at the other as the rabbit swallowed. She appeared to be growing fatter as they watched. She ate a third baby and a fourth. Her eyes grew dreamy.

'Dad, why don't you do something?' Agnes cried. She stood up and faced her father as tears began to form in her eyes. Her father sat still, hunched disconsolately on his apple crate.

'What can I do?' he said. 'It's nature's course.'

'You can take her out of the hutch – you can stop her! Look, there's only three left!'

Her father shrugged impotently.

'She probably didn't have the nutrients to support them,' he said. He began to sound rather cross. 'It happens sometimes. It's the survival of the fittest. We can't interfere, Agnes.'

Agnes stared at him in disbelief. She was not afraid of his anger. She knew that he was wrong. Turning back to the hutch, she saw the last of the tiny rabbits disappear. Tears began pouring down her cheeks. She felt sick. The mother sat sluggishly in the hutch, her belly inflated and obscene. Agnes couldn't believe that her father – an adult, a maker of decisions, a protector and punisher – had been so weak. She heard him stand up behind her and she turned around. His face was ashen. Then before she could say a word, he bolted out of the shed and into the garden, from where she could hear the sound of retching.

'Who's your best friend?' Agnes asked her mother.

They were in the car on a rainy Monday morning, on the way to school. Agnes's knees, which were blue and bony, protruded from beneath the hem of her darker blue skirt. She thought there would never be anything other than this: driven through the rain, her skirt too short, school waiting like a fate worse than death.

'Your father,' said her mother, changing gear. 'Daddy is my best friend.'

'Oh, Mum! He doesn't count.' Agnes felt wounded. No one ever took her questions seriously. 'Who's your *real* best friend?'

Like most people, Agnes had once toyed with the idea of ending her life before it had really begun, and at times it struck her how much subsequent failure she might have saved herself had she but been able to count teenage suicide as one of her early successes.

Her plans for ending it all had progressed to a respectably advanced stage, but what surprised her now was not so much her failure to bring them to a triumphant, albeit fatal, fruition, as the fearlessness with which, faced by certain of life's problems, she had lighted on self-slaughter as the most effective means of solving them. This was perhaps the fault of nothing but the mere thirteen or so years which she had by then accrued; an interlude brief enough still to qualify as a trial period, a sort of fourteen-day satisfaction clause during which time commitments could be reneged upon and life handed back unsoiled.

While her opinion of the quality of her existence might not

have been substantially altered by the events of the subsequent years, their almost redoubled number made them that much more resistant to attack. In moments of despair she would occasionally drift off to sleep thinking of how pleasant it would be never again to wake up, but come morning the memory of *Diplomat's Week*'s unedited pages or the imminent recurrence of her rent demand would send her careering back into consciousness with an admonishing jolt.

At thirteen, however, such concerns were unimaginable; and while the thought that one day the world might find her indispensable had often crossed her mind, the gloomy trajectory of the intervening period seemed then too high a price to pay for the brighter epoch that lay beyond it. Her belief in the charms of the distant future was unshakeable, but the unanaesthetised slowness with which formative years tend to pass made nothing but the immediate continuance of her own misery seem inevitable. The adult world was dream-like, and her own grasp of it myopic; and although later it did occur to her that, had she glimpsed then the life which actually awaited her, she might have flung herself without delay from her dormitory's perilous window, at the time it was this very element of uncertainty which caused her hand to falter.

It was the Lent term at school, a time of freezing beds, endemic viruses, and abstention from all but the trading of insult and abuse, which knew neither seasons nor abatement. Agnes had by now spent two years observing the business of persecution, and during her apprenticeship had had ample opportunity to ruminate upon the implications of what she understood to be its cyclical nature. The preceding term had seen no fewer than three heads hunted – one of whom had been bought out by her parents in the preliminary stages and was now enjoying life at a co-educational non-denominational establishment at three counties' remove, while the other two were to be found, broken-spirited, loitering together as if joined by the hip in the corridors outside the music rooms which encountered the least traffic of any in the school – and with the climate so bullish, Agnes had returned for the new term with the dread certainty of higher quotas and increased efficiency.

Her fears were realised within days as, entering her room one evening, she found a group of six board representatives seated jury-like on her bed, while Christine Poole read to them, in a voice so full of menace and mockery that a uniformed future seemed at that moment both glittering and assured, several extracts from Agnes's diary which directly concerned, and, albeit less directly, maligned those present.

Agnes had long since been driven by solitude to keeping a diary, and had for some time been nurturing an anxiety that, should this intimate tract ever fall into the wrong hands, it would precipitate exactly such a scene as she was now enduring. At first she had tried to enforce neutrality in her seamless ramblings, interspersing what loaded moments there were with liberal quantities of daily trivia and nonsense; but although her hand had trembled with presentiment as she wrote, her lack of other confidantes had, when compounded by habit, made the outpouring of her rage and misery uncontainable.

The discovery of a self-signed death-warrant was so sensationally superior to the usual paltry findings of the investigation room that Agnes almost achieved a form of celebrity with it; but her punishment was correspondingly dramatic, and before long she found herself longing for the Siberian exile of her early days. Her friends' terror campaign was a Mafia-style affair, whose bravado and lawlessness any cowed schoolchild might have found breathtaking to observe. Although occasionally – when, for example, precious objects would disappear ·from other girls' rooms, to be discovered hoarded beneath Agnes's bed – the hand of a subtler strategist was betrayed, generally the nightly dumpings of the contents of the kitchen bins over her sheets or the crude graffiti listing her defects with which the blackboards would greet her on her daily arrival in class reassured her that it was only a matter of time before such artless tactics drew the attention of the proper authorities, and with it their own demise.

Several weeks had passed before Agnes, confident that she had been the victim of a bureaucratic oversight, took the impressive list of her woes to her form-mistress. She had deliberated long and hard over whether such a course of action would merely exacerbate her problems; but she was now in fear of her life, for having recently discovered that her expensive winter coat, while hanging in her wardrobe, had come to grief in a manner which, involving as it did the meticulous and time-consuming application of sharp scissors to heavy cloth, could not be easily passed off as accidental, her mother's righteous and considerable fury promised to erupt over the horizon and vanquish her exhausted spirits at any moment.

Her form-mistress listened to Agnes's tale with tight lips and disbelieving eyes. Seeing her audience thus moved, Agnes allowed herself to weep rather copiously as she blurted out the range of her peers' transgressions, and was gratified to see the emotions of her confessor's face progress from sympathy to full-blown anger and enraged shakes of the head.

'What can I do?' Agnes finally cried, preparing to launch her full weight into the open arms which at any moment would surely be offered her.

'Have a bit of backbone, for goodness' sake!' the woman had exploded. 'Look at you – you're pathetic! I've never seen anything so feeble in my life! Don't you ever think about how lucky you are? There are children your age who can't even *go* to school – why don't you think about them instead of yourself? Hmm?'

Agnes did; and instead of admitting that in fact she quite envied them, took herself off to a secluded corner of the chapel garden to consider her options, which were looking decidedly limited since the removal from them of adult intervention. Death, she soon realised, was the only solution; and with not a moment to be wasted, she succeeded in inveigling herself into the sick bay that very afternoon, where, cunningly distracting the ancient and bumbling nun charged with administering three hundred girls with potentially lethal drugs by alerting her to the presence of a fictitious mouse, she managed to secrete into her pocket an almost full bottle of aspirin.

At first she could scarcely contain her excitement at what she had done, and was so overjoyed by her successful subterfuge that she delayed the implementation of her plan for a day or two. On the second evening, a visit from Christine Poole reminded her of her purpose; but as she was deliberating over the time and place in which she would most like her lifeless form to be discovered, with the maximum horror, guilt and tragic effect for all concerned, she began to feel a strange tickling in her throat. Half an hour later the sensation had grown distinctly uncomfortable. She drank some water and found she could barely swallow. Unable to face the thought of returning to the sick-bay, she removed two aspirin from the bottle, swallowed them, and went straight to bed. In the morning her head felt pounding and feverish. Her throat was by now inflamed. Again she was forced to dig into her supply, and continued to do so during the day. By evening, the bottle was worryingly depleted; although as she tried to go down to supper and found herself falling, disorientated, back on to the bed, it did occur to her that nature might have taken things into its own hands, thus temporarily shelving the problem.

She was discovered in this pitiful state by one of the kinder nuns, who called a doctor, and by morning she was diagnosed as having contracted glandular fever. Her parents were notified and she was whisked from the convent's fiendish portals with scarcely a backward glance. Her mother, noting Agnes's wan appearance, could have been forgiven for thinking that its causes were more viral than psychological; but the six weeks she insisted her daughter take off school, during which time she ministered to her with loaded trays and maternal affection, nonetheless were sufficient to avert a fatality either way. Agnes returned to school to find another girl occupying her unenviable place; and although she was not brave enough to intervene in her defence, she liked to think that her obviously reluctant participation in that persecution with which by now, after all, she was so familiar, along with the occasional sympathetic glances she offered her when other eyes were turned, did not go unnoticed.

Later, when she met John, she would sometimes be over-whelmed with relief that she had not taken her leave of life so peremptorily. One night, with an excess of intimacy, she had told him of her suicide *manqué*, in the hope that he would share her loving interpretation of destiny's mysterious inter-vention. To her surprise, he had seemed barely moved by the thought of how close he had come to losing her.

'Everyone does that, don't they?' he said, as if surprised that she should mention something so commonplace.

'Did you?'

'Oh, I expect so. Or thought about it, anyway.'

She had felt almost disappointed by his response. It sug-gested that her emotional register was in some way incompat-ible with his. How, if this was how he felt, would she ever encourage him to scale the heights of passionate love which ascended within her with every passing moment? After swap-ping suicide stories so casually, what was there left to live for?

Chapter Fifteen

HAVING always been advised to take the rough with the smooth Agnes did so; but found in her hands the two so successfully blent as to form a dull and coarse texture that bore little resemblance to either of its originators. She fondled her experiences too much, played with the past until it was dog-eared and tattered; its purer moments sullied by the oily press of palms, its horrors soft and elastic. Then, like movie-star monsters, her recollections would sometimes come back from the dead with a thrilling lurch, wringing out unplied reservoirs of sensation from places that had been thought drained.

She began to grow suspicious of the future. There had been a time when she had thought that by forecasting its events she would therefore control them: she could never be surprised, for her mind was always in wartime, a busy operations room in which possibilities snaked like rivers over maps of foreign places. Now, looking back on the reality her dreams had become, she felt foolish for having thought herself forearmed. There was an inexorability to disappointment. It lived on, like something radioactive. It contaminated things. She began to think of herself as existing only in the present tense, a conduit through which the future flowed to become the past.

She met her lover by chance in the street and they went for a drink in a pub that was too hot and crowded. She found herself sweating and babbling while he watched her, gaunt

98

and quiet. Afterwards he left her on the road, his tail-lights glowing in mercurial retreat as he roared away. As she walked home her heart leapt at every shadow and barking dog. She soon broke her vow not to call him and gorged herself on his answering machine for two weeks with a hunger she did not attempt to control. It became something necessary, the reassuring click and hum, the sound of his voice trapped like an echo, like a ghost. When he picked up the phone himself one day she almost hung up in terror. To her surprise, he was kind and did not object to the idea of seeing her.

'Let's go somewhere,' she said, emboldened. 'Let's get out of London for the day.'

They arranged to go to Hampton Court the following Saturday, and Agnes's spirits lifted once more. She made plans and bought something new to wear. In these sudden bursts of sunshine, she found she could bear to look at things.

'Have you gone to the dogs?' Greta inquired.

'What do you mean?' said Agnes. The question seemed suspiciously perspicacious.

'Oh, isn't that what you say?' Greta furrowed her brow like a perplexed student. 'You know, where those skinny dogs run around after fake rabbits and stuff?'

'Oh, I see what you mean. No, I haven't. I don't think it's very nice, though.'

'I'm going Saturday,' said Greta firmly, as if decided by Agnes's disapproval. She grinned mysteriously. 'With London Transport.'

Agnes shrugged, a gesture intended to divest Greta's travel arrangements of the unwarranted importance with which she had seen fit to report them.

'It is cheaper, I suppose,' she said.

She found it hard to talk to Greta sometimes. It made her feel as if she had not mastered even the basic verbal skills required to go comfortably through life.

'Not *London Transport*,' Greta groaned. 'My friend – you

know, the one I met on the tube. That's what I call him. London Transport.' She screeched with laughter. '*It is cheaper, I suppose,*' she mimicked languorously. 'You're such a card, Agnes.'

'I didn't know you'd seen him again,' remarked Agnes stiffly.

'Oh, sure, I see him all the time. He works my station. We have a good time together,' she mused. 'He's kind of weird, though. I went to his house with him one night and he showed me all this stuff.'

'What stuff?'

'Oh, I don't know. Porno mags and stuff, I guess,' she said vaguely. 'Hey, guess where he lives? Somewhere called Tooting – can you believe that? What a place for a train-driver to live, huh?' She made tooting noises like a train and laughed. 'It is, however,' she added with mock sobriety, 'a real dive.'

Agnes felt rather disturbed. She saw how easy it would be to sink without trace into a realm of strange men and nasty magazines and squalid flats in Tooting. One just absorbed what came along, she supposed, as if by osmosis. She had often wondered what would happen if she took up the offers of the men who commented upon her in the street. There was another world beneath the surface of the one she chose each day, a dark labyrinth of untrodden paths. Its proximity frightened her. She wondered if she would ever lose her way and wander into it. She thought of her lover, of her strange job, of her crumbling house, and wondered if she was already there.

Agnes and Nina and Merlin went for a walk; or at least, that's what Agnes said. Merlin said they were going for a moonlit celebration, and he took with him a bottle of wine. Nina said she didn't know what they were doing, but could they please make it quick because she had to meet Jack later. Merlin's aspect of festivity was in honour of the first three months of their communal living at Elwood Street; and despite the new-born whiteness of the first October moon, each privately suspected it had been much longer.

'I don't see why it's such a big deal,' panted Nina as they toiled in the darkness up the Blackstock Road. 'It's not like we've been there a year or anything. Three months isn't an anniversary – it's a trial period.'

Agnes, terrified by the threat of a verdict, remained silent. Merlin gave Nina a friendly shove.

'Get along with you,' he said briskly. 'You and your Roman calendar. This is a pagan ritual, woman. We're going to toast the new moon.'

Agnes was glad they had not stayed in the house with its gloomy crack, which seemed to her to be growing at an alarming rate. Such disintegration was unkind. It seemed to foist upon her the responsibility of propping and bearing. Sometimes the crack appeared larger than life. At others, it was a tiny manifestation of a larger slippage, almost like a gravitational force; a mud-slide, perhaps, tossing her away with its momentum like a cork on a violent wave.

As they reached the park, Merlin suddenly darted away from them and ran off into the darkness howling.

'Oh, God,' muttered Nina as they trailed after him. 'Merlin's rediscovering his pagan virility.'

There was a conspiratorial tone in her voice. They had banded together. Agnes slipped her arm through Nina's as they walked into Highbury Fields. There were no streetlamps in the park. The darkness seemed suddenly private, up against her eyes like blindness. She gripped Nina's arm, wanting to tell her everything; to confess the mortal sin of herself and let the black air absolve her words while her body hid in the shadows. They heard Merlin howl again, and then Nina was gone, darting off into the darkness to find him.

'Come on!' she shouted behind her.

Agnes trotted disconsolately after her. The trees loomed, vague and monstrous. She couldn't see anything. Merlin and Nina's laughter faded into the distance. As she jogged unseeing over the dark grass she felt a wave of panic wash over her and she picked up speed. The road near the park had gone quiet. Everything seemed to be concentrated into the darkness, the silence, the pounding of her blood, the beating of her heart as she ran. It was as if she was without senses, living inside herself. It was as if she wasn't there at all. Her fear turned itself inside out. She kept running. It seemed to her then that she could go on like that for ever.

'Agnes? Can we come in?'

Nina and Merlin put their heads round the bedroom door. Agnes sat up in bed and tried not to look ashamed. She had not disappeared for long, really: she had just run round the park until she had happened by chance on the roadside, where her ardour had been cooled by the sight of houses and cars and she had come home. On her way she had heard them calling for her, and had had a strange sense then of being someone else: a lone jogger returning to a different life, who had heard two friends calling to a girl lost in the woods. She had pitied that poor girl and wondered if she would read about it in the papers tomorrow. Then she had walked slowly back to Elwood Street.

She had hoped to feel a certain snarling, callous independence in doing so, but instead had been able only to think of a time when, aged about twelve, she had taken her bicycle and pretended to run away. She had pedalled until she reached a grassy bank about a mile from the house, and then had dismounted from her steed, mounted the bank, and lain leisurely down to look at the sky. When it began to grow dark and she had judged enough time to have passed, she had climbed back on to her bicycle and had pedalled home, to find that her parents had worked themselves up not into the hoped-for lather of loving anxiety, but into a state of uncontainable anger. She had been shouted at, smacked, and sent to bed, where she was left to ruminate upon the now-proven fact that nobody loved her.

'Are you okay?' said Nina, looking at her strangely.

'What happened?' said Merlin, hovering uncertainly by the door.

'I'm fine. Sorry,' Agnes said, as if they might have preferred to find her lying mauled by a mugger's knife beneath some tree. 'I don't know what happened. I was running after you and I couldn't find you. So I came home. I was frightened.'

Merlin nodded vaguely. Nina looked pensive. They didn't believe her. They thought her strange, she knew. They would not blame the difficult world. Everyone else dealt with it. Why couldn't she?

'What's wrong?' demanded John, slamming the door to his bedroom. He lunged towards her pugnaciously and then brought himself up short.

'Nothing,' said Agnes, attempting flippancy. 'Your bedside manner could stand some improvement, though.'

'Oh, come on,' he said more softly. He sat down beside her and put his head in his hands. 'What have I done to deserve this? I thought I was being reasonable. I mean, what is this?' He indicated the half-shut drawer of his desk, out of which letters and papers, hastily replaced, erupted incriminatingly. 'What are you looking for?'

'I just want to know if you're seeing someone else.'

He wasn't, of course, she knew that. He would never have denied himself the pleasure of telling her. She would have found that simple, in any case, a jealous ague, mild in comparison to the mad fever which currently gripped her. She phoned him in the middle of the night, too, not saying anything, just wanting to hear what he sounded like when he was alone. He made a fist and swung it in the air, then walked to the other side of the small room. Maybe small rooms were the problem. They could never see each other properly.

'You won't find what you need there,' he said, looking at the burgled drawer. 'In fact, I don't even know what you need.'

'You should do,' she replied. He had made her need it, after all.

'But I've given you everything,' he said. His tone was quizzical, interested, as if she were an experiment that had got out of control, a monster he had inadvertently created. 'What do you want to do?' he said then, jokingly. 'Eat me?'

She felt his cruelty slide insidiously into her like a knife. How could she explain, when he made a mockery of the truth, that the smoke in his eyes was but a whiff of the raging inferno below? That what she showed him were but tiny lesions atop a deep and raging cancer? She wanted him to be mother and father to her, to rewrite her history in his hand, to exhume all her years and bury him in their place; kill all of her that never knew him and forget the rest. She wanted him dead or alive, and her feelings were terminal.

'I want – I want to *believe* in you,' she said finally.

'Like fucking God!' he exclaimed almost gleefully. 'That figures.'

He exalted for a moment at this pinnacle, as if it were what he had always wanted, as if he had wanted all along to see how far he could make her go. Then he got up and strolled impatiently around the room, losing interest. She felt then as if she would surely die of him. Outside the summer evening faded quietly to darkness. She sat perfectly still and waited for him to turn around. She needed to see his face. When he finally faced her, he appeared surprised that she was still there. He looked at her doubtfully, appraisingly; as if, she thought, he'd never seen her before. As if she were something in a shop he was deciding whether to buy. He looked at her with a kind of weary langour: he wanted to be home, unencumbered by packages, away from this madness; he wanted to be alone.

'You're like – you're like some kind of black hole,' he said curiously. He sat down in an armchair and for the first time looked at her as if she frightened him. 'You consume me.'

Chapter Sixteen

LOVE was uncourtly at Hampton Court: it divorced, be-headed and died; divorced again, was beheaded an improbable twice, but still, ultimately, survived. Love conquered all but the loveless, and even then sometimes other things got you first.

Like disease, Agnes thought, or maybe childbirth. The dimly ornate bedchamber, which they were surveying from behind its restraining rope like visitors to an asylum, seemed suddenly racked with screams as an heir clawed his way out from a cloying, unanaesthetised womb; his mother two-headed then, like a mythic beast. The rules were different in those days, she thought, but the game was the same.

The house and gardens lay posing like two beauty queens, competing for the beholder in whose eye they might see their rival beauties briefly borrowed. He was beguiled by the gardens, she transfixed by the house; each sensing something of their own shadow in the other's choice which made them defend their favourite hotly. A strange discomfort arose between them, a kind of twinnish mistrust, as they remembered that while each possessed the properties of beauty, together they formed something that made people stare.

It had occurred to her to wonder if he might simply be tired of her; had crossed her mind like a delayed commuter over a busy station, too frenzied and obvious to be interesting. As an insomniac of the heart, Agnes found such admissions unwise; they could keep her awake at night, tucking the darkness round her like an eiderdown of oblivion. The worst of it was that she sympathised with him.

As they crossed the moat into the cool belly of the palace she felt them both to be absurd. Like fish, their confluence depended on a common environment without which they flopped and gasped separately. It was easy to love in dim bars and dark bedrooms, but their bond could not withstand historic transposition. The fact that he was tired of her actually came as no surprise; that she was tired of herself even less so. What disturbed her was the alertness of her need for him amidst all this somnambulance. It beat in her like a heart, unfathomable. Something had been exchanged in those early hours when he had still been free to choose her, and he had been paying for it ever since. She would appear on his doorstep in years to come while he hid behind curtains with a frightened wife and bewildered children, reminding him that once he had singled her out. It was not about affection or delight. It was a game she had to win.

As they walked into the courtyard, straining and chaffing like strangers, it all became sadly plain: this addiction, this great mistake, this misdiagnosis that was love.

Henry VIII, many-headed and self-perpetuating, regenerated lives and wives like an earthworm. Agnes felt they would have understood each other well, she and this builder of mazes; his house a virtual reality of simulated tricks, with its secret gardens and hidden doors, corridors of lust and back passages of intent. It spoke of a mistrust she shared. They would indeed have got on well; both lovers, neither beloved.

She perused their portraits: six wives, love's carrion. She and Henry could have compared notes. Henry VIII, in love with love, fat with the flesh of women. There was, she knew, no satisfaction for that kind of hunger. Like her, what he sought was but his own reflection. What he fought for was but the survival of his own fittest self. He looked for love and he found a beast; and the beast was no one but himself. The nature of the beast, then and now, was that it destroyed what it craved the most.

The courtyards boring through the centre of the house gave the surrounding buildings a prisonish look, their windows bound with steel bodices through which wan, womanly faces might be supposed to peer. These orifices, together with the several low doors which studded the walls at regular intervals, seemed almost elided by the lacy skirts of mosaic and brick, through which the leering tongues of gargoyles erupted beside stony cameo faces trapped like sailors behind portholes. Above, pairs of narrow chimney stacks soared to the sky like outflung legs, cross-bound and gartered. Straggling groups of late tourists hovered uncertainly in the October sunlight.

Agnes saw her lover disappearing beneath a cool arch at one end of the courtyard and followed behind at a safe distance. Once inside, she discovered a great stone staircase which appeared to lead to the body of the house, and the sound of receding footsteps furthermore informed her that he was but a short distance ahead. She climbed the stairs quietly. He had seemed distant and inclined to solitude, and she did not want to jettison what she knew was her last chance by yapping at his heels like a vexing dog. Reaching the landing, she caught him drifting into one of the vast drawing-rooms, and she watched him from the doorway as he paused in front of a large canvas. On it, a naked woman reclined against a grassy bank, the geography of her copious flesh bruised and mountainous compared to the manicured green of her setting. Agnes felt rather offended that he should so mysteriously choose to contemplate such an object – and she in all her lissome superiority so close at hand!

She crossed the room quietly and stood by him, the breath of acknowledgement between them as faint as that of two strangers at an art gallery, each cowed into dalliance by the erudition of the other.

'She's beautiful,' Agnes ventured, hoping with the lie to provoke a denial which would affirm both her charity and her own charms. Moments later, casting a glance beside her to check upon the progress of her missile, she saw it had been vainly fired. He had sauntered off, leaving but a mirage of scent and an airy bodily impression behind him.

When she was younger, she had used to indulge in romantic daydreams concerning the as yet unspecified character of her future partner. She had wondered where he was and what he was doing, and had vaguely hoped by such contemplation to establish psychic links between them which might one day render him more securely hers. She wondered now if she had ever been visualised thus in a stranger's mind. Beams of sunlight slanted across the empty room, whirled with motes of dust. It seemed important, just then, that she should be tethered here by something stronger; that being here was part of something larger, someone else's plan.

She no longer observed the future as if from the passenger seat of an aeroplane: a pleasant trip, with but the slightest frisson of fear, to a certain and even more pleasant destination; the high peaks of mountains in view, with fluffy clouds obfuscating the terrible plunge to their craggy feet. Now she was earth-bound and afraid, grinning stupidly at the sky and wondering how things stayed up there. She fingered her future like a set of flimsy negatives: a world of dark skies, glaring shadows, black smiles and certain death.

Agnes Day was lost, but only in so much as her lover was not to be found. She wandered down a long corridor and read from a sign that Anne Boleyn had fled over those very boards after receiving news of her imminent execution. For reasons which did not require elucidation, the passage had been named the Screaming Gallery.

Anne Boleyn had six fingers, Agnes recalled. Despite her

deformity, Henry had loved her passionately. She wondered how he felt as her head thudded to the ground. It was an act of power, but also perhaps one of love. She thought of the desecrated Anne. To be so loved – what must it feel like?

She perused the tapestried dining-hall and imagined it full of bearded men spearing unspecified cuts of meat with knives. She examined faded tapestries depicting one-dimensional horses and women with shrunken bodies and enormous heads like embryos. She had hoped he would see her thus absorbed and be impressed by her self-sufficiency. After a while, however, she grew tired of her attentive posture and set out towards the kitchens, as if there might be some titbit there to comfort her.

Some time later, lodged in a circuitous passage like something indigestible, she knew she was lost. She retraced her steps and recognised nothing surrounding her. She hadn't been paying attention. The corridor was deathly quiet and she supposed she must have wandered into a tourist backwater at the back of the house. She sat down on a step and remembered a time when her parents had taken her to a market in Mexico, where they had gone for a family holiday. It was dark, and they were cruising the chattering streets in a leisurely manner before dinner, fingering the stalls in a desultory way but really there to absorb the music and cheerful banter, the foreign faces and smells of cooking. They had all been rather uplifted by the scene, she remembered, until they had come upon a stall selling silver jewellery where Agnes, aged six and voraciously acquisitive, had become fixated by a small ring with a blue stone.

She had asked at first politely for a deal to be struck in her favour, and once refused had offered bravely to sacrifice several weeks of future pocket money in its preferment. Her father, who knew perhaps from experience better than to broker in futures, had cruelly cited the several smaller and inferior purchases with which her pockets were already filled. Had she known then, she calmly explained, what awaited her now, she would never have squandered her means so thoughtlessly. Her father had seemed to find this an amusing reply, and had claimed it was an apposite enough description of life. Far from rewarding her for her philosophy, however, the adult party had shortly after wandered off to sample other diversions. The assumption that she would merely follow behind them inflamed her with rebellion. She stayed exactly where she was, despite the grinning stallholder's increasingly frantic and incomprehensible gesticulations in the direction of her retreating parents' backs. Some time later, when they did not return, her sensations of power began quickly to evaporate; and compounded by the double blow of the failed purchase, which had created in its wake an aversion to what was already hers, she became engulfed by misery.

Finally she had run after them, but the scene which only minutes ago had seemed so bright soon became dark and menacing. Her family was nowhere to be seen amongst the leering faces, their putative cries drowned by jangling music and harsh foreign voices. She darted down alleyways and through unfamiliar squares until finally she had sat down on a step and cried at her punishment; for that, surely, was what it was? She had ceased to please them and they had dropped her in the street like an empty sweet-wrapper, never to return.

She had never been able to remember the conclusion to that story. She had no memory of tearful reunions. Sometimes, she used to think that perhaps another family had found her crying there on that doorstep, and had taken her in and brought her up as one of their own, without telling her.

Things between them had, she supposed, come to a stage where the phrase suggested mutual obstruction; and yet there was a lack of verbiage, of event and gesture, which, though she knew herself to possess flaws, hinted at the additional presence of a mystery which might redeem them. He was holding something back; or rather, he was letting it out, for had she not noticed it? Normally the best kept of secrets, now he was dropping clues. His evasions and silences were becoming pointed and obvious. He longed to be away from her, that much was plain. Pleased with her detective work, Agnes did not trouble to peer too closely at its implications for fear their content, like something artificial, might harm her.

She had never thought their relationship would be ended, for the simple reason that it had never really seemed to begin. They had merely drifted together, she supposed, like a commonplace; the soggy detritus of two gappy lives which would drift apart again at the next convenient tide. She had heard of such a thing as a casual encounter, and yet she had applied her old formulas to the stark patina of its reality as if she knew nothing. She had dragged out her suitcase of emotions and strewn its contents over a chair like a travelling saleswoman.

Once, in the darkness of her north London room, she had gazed upon his tender neck and told him that she loved him. He had said nothing, of course, fixing her with eyes which could have been empty or full depending on the light, and had left her to draw whatever conclusions she wished. She had said it again, and again, as if trying to shock him, but the threat of madness had stopped her before he did. She expected at least a dénouement in exchange for all this mystery.

She got up from the step and looked out of the window. It gave out on to the garden, and she realised she must be directly below the large drawing-room in which she had last seen him. A low filter of mist hung beneath the pale afternoon sky. The sand-coloured paths carved into the smooth lawn fanned symmetrically out from her vantage point like sunless rays. This, after all, was the very centre of things. Perhaps it would not be so bad, being without him. She would have the time to do other things: she could take up sport, clean her room, get things done. It would be like recovering from a long illness.

She saw him then, strolling past a tree and over a lawn as if he owned it. His separateness pained her. The house ticked quietly around her. He was, perhaps, readying the executioner's axe before her very eyes. She pressed her face against the cool glass and felt it joined by other ghostly faces. He had left her here in this feminine mausoleum, this connubial death-row, as if to do so conformed with his sense of etiquette. She was not like Henry, the master of ceremonies, the magician with his disappearing wives. She was a Christian, not a lion. She was a wife, six-fingered.

The tree, which was in fact two trees grown from a single root, was beneath its glamorous foliage a sharp-clawed and vicious thing. With its dragon hide and single chicken foot, it crouched like an old woman in the cave of its skirts where Agnes, hiding from the truth, took shelter. Once there she felt a momentary shame, as if in spying its arthritic limbs and ugly knotted joints she had violated its privacy, like a voyeur at a drowning gorging on the veined blubber of a dead woman. It had always troubled her that she might suffer humiliation at the hands of death as well as those of life; might be found with her nightdress hitched ignominiously over her head, her body white and flaccid as a fallen moon on some dark river bank. Or perhaps smashed open like a watermelon on tarmac, her juices messy, the stench of her making policemen gag. Then again, something less dramatic: old age and desertion could find her three days' dead in a council flat, tumescent and blue in a bath-chair. What could one do? Except surrender to it, long for it, as now with the secrets of her body on her lips like a tactless remark. She crouched by the crippled trunk in the dirt, uncaring. The gardens were quite still beneath the pale bowl of the sky, flat on their back in the late afternoon sunlight. Agnes sensed an air of virginal subjugation in their exquisitely trimmed and flowered beds; the lawns too smooth, the trees honed and shaped like ice-cream cones. There were no wild and clumpy patches, no grinning daisies or feisty nettles or other imperfection to proclaim life.

There would – and nothing was more certain than this – come a time when she was no longer expected to behave so properly. The thought almost cheered her up. She would be sundered from herself as surely as Anne Boleyn's head from her shoulders, watching it all from a great height and laughing, perhaps, at those who were cleaning up the mess and thinking as she had a moment ago that they would not want to be seen dead anywhere. She wondered that the mere thought of it did not drive people to greater extremities: hiding madly beneath trees, peering out between the branches, a lover nowhere to be seen.

When Agnes spent her first night with John, they had known each other for several weeks, she recalled, and in that time had seen many films, some of which had laid out unsparing as a map the details of nights as yet unspent, words unspoken, injuries unfelt and partings unimaginable. When, after several lifetimes of experience in dark cinemas, the subject of sex seemed to Agnes to be accompanying them like a grumbling chaperone on their outings, she had begun to worry at his failure to acknowledge it. She had brought it up one evening herself as he walked her home, and though she knew she had not managed to pronounce the word with the comfortable familiarity she had aimed for, she was still astonished to be met by shrieks of mysterious laughter.

'Why are you laughing?' she had cried, stopping in the street and facing him furiously.

'I'm sorry,' he had said wiping his eyes. 'It was just the way you said it. "Shall we have 'sex'?" ' He mimicked her cruelly, with a school-marmish emphasis on the last word. 'Look, I don't want to rush you, okay? The ball's in your court.'

Left to content herself with that rather lewd-sounding epithet, Agnes went to the doctor and got a prescription for the Pill. Following the instructions on the packet carefully, she had taken them for a full month and during that time had developed a knowing air which suggested she was a woman of the world. As her time of readiness approached, she had informed John of the imminent arrival of his visa to her unexplored territories, and he had marked the date as if arranging a business meeting. Spontaneity, then, had not been a noticeable feature of her blooding; and it was for this reason, perhaps, that when they met on the day in question, and spent it assiduously together as if preparing for an exam, their conversation had been somewhat laden with uncomfortable silences and tense asides. As evening drew near, Agnes had become stricken by terror at his oddness. Surely he wanted to do this? Surely everyone wanted to? She had thought at the time there must be something wrong with her, but it was not until their innocuous fumblings had somehow come to a fruition she had observed rather than shared that she knew for sure.

'Are you all right?' he had said, rolling off her and staring at the wall.

She allowed herself to move her limbs, which ached from the rigid concentration with which she had maintained the position he had indicated for her to adopt some time ago. She turned on to her side and extended an awkward arm towards him, draping it over his ribcage like something tranquillised. Her lack of affliction worried her. Why shouldn't she be all right? What was supposed to have happened?

'I didn't feel a thing,' she said, aiming for cheerfulness.

At that he turned away from her completely, shrugging her arm from his side. Agnes realised that politeness was perhaps not the order of the day.

'I'm sorry,' she said.

'It's okay,' he replied, misunderstanding her. 'A lot of people aren't that good at sex. Don't worry about it.'

Had he circumcised her like an Asian bride, he could not have rendered her more effectively his. That night she lay awake confused and cried for fear of him; although later she was to cry at the thought of how easily they could never have met; and later still, at the fact that they ever did.

Though it was growing late, he suggested they go and look at the maze.

'Get lost?' she said, wishing she'd had the courage to abandon the interrogative inflection. 'At this time of night? We'll never find our way out in time.'

He had found her drinking tea in the small garden cafeteria, where she had gone giving up all hope of him. The manner of his discovery had annoyed her, for she had spent at least half an hour in the garden striking winsome poses of contemplation against various horticultural backdrops in the hope that he would happen upon her and be struck afresh by love. Eventually, however, she had grown cold and miserable and had stomped off in search of more reliable sustenance. His neglect stabbed at her heart, but shame at her presence in the tawdry tea-room left her no choice but to forgive him. Perhaps all was not yet lost. She could, after all, entrap him in the maze. She got up from the grubby table, her brown tray abandoned like a past life.

In the maze, Agnes suspected cheating, for it was surely not a superior sense of intuition which had sent him darting away from her down one alley and then another until she had lost him. Perhaps he had studied a map of it before they came or – worse still! – had spent those hours in which she had vainly searched for him in here, working out the best route. She had known men to do such things in the spirit of competition. They liked to trick and confuse her, setting up traps and then bursting in to save her with a victorious Ha! She chose an avenue at random and tried to memorise various leaves and twigs as she went, lest she should pass that way again.

A large bee cruised lazily around her head and then dived suddenly close to her face. She sprang back wildly as it boomed past her ear. Unobserved in the quiet green tunnel, Agnes twitched and laughed nervously. The sky overhead was leaking a dusky blue light and she wondered what would happen when it grew dark. Would they send in an efficient patrol to round up stragglers, or would they perhaps shout directions over a loudspeaker, the whole thing becoming suddenly like a sea or mountain rescue as their charges emerged forlornly, shaken and grateful? The sound of a child laughing caused her to jump. She looked around but it had evidently come from one of the adjacent corridors, for her own was empty. She had not realised how close they all were. Far from being comforted by the sound she felt menaced by it, like a blind person. The tall hedges chirped quietly around her. She wondered how her life had arrived at this moment: a path, a darkening sky, a child laughing, herself alone.

Some time later she gave up all hope of trying to maintain a sense of direction. She had heard that a monkey, given a typewriter, would in time produce the works of Shakespeare, and with new confidence in the genius of randomness she began turning and weaving aimlessly.

He would, by now, doubtlessly have found the centre and would at this very moment be lounging in it, triumphantly smoking a cigarette to mark his arrival. He would perhaps leave the glowing butt for her as testimony to his superiority, before sauntering out into the park where the warm street-lamps and night-time traffic on the road nearby invited him back into the city; she left trapped in the riddle of his rejection, the past he was putting behind him.

She turned into a particularly promising avenue and found it to terminate in a dead end. She wondered if she would always have to work so hard to find the point of things. She wanted to be sought rather than to seek. She wanted to be the point herself. In her mind they lined up, the people who had known her: a series of haphazard collisions, a motorway pile-up of twisted steel, their ruined fenders caught in a kiss, their bodies locked in a massive, involuntary, destructive embrace. She wondered if she had caused this noisy mess of tangled limbs and broken hearts; had gone the wrong way, steering crazy joyless arcs in the darkness, shooting the lights in the hope of encounter. John had once told her that if she gave people the freedom to leave, they would in all probability choose to stay. Agnes, in a state of emergency, could not contemplate the perversities of a free market.

She heard the sound of footsteps approaching down one of the dim tunnels. She looked up and made out the shape of a man. For a moment her heart leapt in a joyful arabesque at the thought that her lover had come to find her. As he grew closer, however, she saw that it wasn't him. She tried to tug the smile from her face, but he saw it and looked at her curiously, perhaps wondering if he knew her.

'That one doesn't go anywhere,' he said, indicating the path from which he had just come. He dug his hands in his pockets and trod heavily past her.

Agnes sat on a bench in the centre of the maze. It was nearly dark now. Only a few minutes earlier, a bell had rung into the silence to signal the imminent closure of the area. Really it was a sordid affair. She gazed round the grim enclosure with its overflowing bins and cigarette-strewn floor, its single tree graven with the names of lovers. She wondered who they were, these people who saw fit to advertise their union in a place they would not see again; or perhaps would see later, alone, knowing now what they had so desperately wanted to know then, blushing perhaps at their faulty arithmetic which, in calculating that one and one made one, implied that now they were half the people they once had been. Perhaps they would add dates, like tombstones.

Two people came into the small clearing. Agnes watched them as they congratulated themselves. They paced its small distance like a prison cell and waited for something to happen. When it didn't they looked at her suspiciously and then ambled back into the maze. She smiled to herself knowingly. There was nothing here. It was a hoax, an illusion of significance. She had lingered here merely to explore its pointlessness.

'What was the point?' she had said when he told her. 'What did you want from me?' And then, angry at his silence: 'Why did you bother?'

The fact that there was someone else, that there had always been someone else, would cease to hurt in time. She had found him here, leaning against the tree with prophecy in his bearing, and in her foolishness had thought this augured well. He had surprised her, in any case. She wondered that he had told her at all. She would suffer for that later. For now, scavenging for clues in the empty room of his motive, she was content to be a fool. The bell rang out again as a low moon crested the sky like a lone, slow-motion surfer skating a vast blue wave. She couldn't stay here. Here was the moment that could not be hung on to. That things couldn't just stop was one of her main complaints against the world. She would take the train home, he having taken the car.

Chapter Seventeen

'TRY four,' said Nina, popping open a can of beer.

A small volcano of foam erupted through the aperture and she swiftly applied her mouth to it to catch the spillage. It was Sunday, and they were gathered indifferently together in the sitting-room like the wreckage of a rough weekend.

Merlin groaned and picked up the remote control, which he aimed at the television set. A picture of a large monkey nonchalantly scratching itself appeared on the screen.

'Wildlife,' he said. 'We were watching this before, Nina. You told me to turn over, remember?'

'Oh, yeah. How about three?'

'Game show. Large spinning wheel, ugly spectacle of human greed and suffering.'

'Two?'

'Documentary on rise of capitalist economies. Same thing.'

'One. Put it in one, Merlin. We have no choice.'

'Walls have fallen over such things.' They had spent most of the afternoon watching the liberation of Eastern Europe on television. Merlin flicked the remote control again. 'Look, one's a Western. Everyone happy with this? Agnes?'

'Fine,' said Agnes. She had been strangely disturbed by the scenes on the streets of Berlin and Budapest. Through the jiggling of a hand-held camera, they had witnessed the rough, unscripted love of humanity for itself; a far cry from the world of svelte, film-star embraces and edited dialogue in which she lost herself nightly. She had felt almost embarrassed by the reality of it.

'I love these movies,' said Nina contentedly. 'The women always look so amazing. Orange hair and beauty spots. Really fake.'

'They look like inflatable dolls,' Merlin agreed. 'Maybe we'll start getting *Easterns* now. Frontier dramas with consumer durables.'

'They're propaganda films really, aren't they?' said Nina, still watching the screen. 'Like those ones they made about British factories during the war.'

'No, those were morale boosters. Westerns are just fiction, really. No one believes it was like that any more.'

'Well, that's what I said!' replied Nina petulantly. 'Propaganda. It's just outlived its significance, that's all. The only difference between these and the war films is that we still believe we run the world.'

'I don't think you can compare them like that.' Merlin put his hands behind his head and looked at Nina expectantly.

'Why not?'

'Well, for a start it sounds like a conspiracy theory, which suggests a lack of moral vision.'

'Oh, really?' said Nina sarcastically. 'So, when we butcher and proselytise it's enlightenment, right? But when anyone else does it, it's persecution. That sounds like a moral hallucination to me.'

'We needed to win the war,' Merlin replied calmly. 'And I would go so far as to say it was one of those rare historical situations when there was a clear case of right and wrong. And we were right.'

'Oh, come on!' said Nina. 'Do you really believe we charged in there for charity?'

'Charity?' exclaimed Merlin. 'That's an outrageous thing to say! Tell that to six million Jews.'

'We didn't care about them, did we? They were politically secondary! We were more worried about munitions factories than camps.'

Agnes stood up, white-faced.

'Can't we just enjoy the film?' she said. Her voice warbled nervously. 'I mean, can't we just watch a film without – without holding a full-scale political debate? Why does everything have to be taken so seriously?' The other two were looking at her in astonishment. She headed for the stairs. 'Why do you have to take everything so seriously?'

'Look who's talking,' said Nina audibly as Agnes retreated.

'Oh dear,' said Merlin.

'I got a letter from London Transport this morning,' said Greta dolefully on Monday.

She had, it seemed, tired of her underground admirer, but his affections were not to be so easily derailed.

'What did it say?'

'Say is putting it a bit strongly. Grunt would be more accurate.'

Greta's hand dived into the packet of biscuits in front of her and emerged triumphant.

'The guy's a fruitcake,' she continued between bites. 'I'm amazed he can write. Cookie?'

'Oh, thanks.' Agnes took one and began to chew it. The soft, sugary mass on her tongue comforted her momentarily and was gone. She took another. 'At least you're getting some attention,' she said.

It had been meant as a joke, but instead had the effect of sounding out the depths of her own desperation. Greta laughed loudly, her lipsticked mouth studded with crumbs which Agnes wondered uncomfortably if she should tell her about.

'Yeah, it makes you feel kind of special getting fixed on by people who are funny in the head. Did I tell you he's been hanging around outside my house?' She inspected her nails. 'I mean, we went out on a few dates and now he's behaving like a pervert. I hate dates. Dates are things you eat.'

'You've got some crumbs on your lip,' said Agnes, who was beginning to feel upset.

Greta grinned and put her hand into the now empty biscuit pack, her fingers upon withdrawal laden with the offending matter.

'Gee,' she said hilariously, implanting a thick layer of crumbs over the meagre few already there. 'Have I?'

The bus home was so crowded on Tuesday that Agnes could not get a seat. She stood by one of the doors instead, whose dark glass panel steamy with the oppressive breath of human-kind informed her that she looked wan and hollow-eyed. She gazed at her reflection, sucking in her cheeks a little to deepen its shadowy aspect of suffering. The bus shuddered to a halt and the doors sprang open with a compressed sigh. A wave of sharp night air broke unpleasantly over the damp warmth of the interior. Agnes, moving to one side so as to allow others to disembark, now caught her fugitive reflection in one of the large fish-eye mirrors angled for the driver's benefit from the ceiling. In it, her face appeared alarmingly large and pasty, with pores which gaped through an oily sheen of make-up. She looked away quickly, her heart plummeting.

'Oh my God!' said a man's voice just then. 'Oh my God!'

Agnes looked up. The man appeared to be looking at her. The other people in the bus were looking at her also, their faces blank as a row of sunflowers.

'It's you!' he said, peering and smiling uncertainly. 'It *is* you, isn't it? Oh my God!'

'Excuse me?' said Agnes, as quietly as she could. She hoped he would take the hint and lower his tone.

He was middle-aged, with a face which seemed intelligent but trampish clothes and a lingering odour which proclaimed that even if he was, it certainly hadn't got him anywhere. Her heart pounded with embarrassment as she saw that he was mad, and had singled her out as the subject of his rantings.

'You're the lady in the pub,' he said, smiling again in a manner which seemed contradictorily urbane. 'Aren't you? God, how embarrassing.'

'Why is it embarrassing?' said Agnes, and was surprised to find that their audience found her curiosity amusing.

'Well—' He was still smiling. 'I was in the pub and I'd had a bit to drink – is it you, actually? Is it? The lady whose handbag I was sick into.'

A few titters of revulsion emanated from the back of the bus. Agnes felt unusually calm. She smiled back at him and addressed him in her most authoritative voice.

'In that case, I'm relieved *not* to be her,' she said, casting a conspiratorial glance at the other passengers. They responded with a hearty gust of laughter.

The man looked nervously at them and then back at her. He appeared confused. The bus was alive with comment and several people looked at her approvingly. They liked her style. The man shook his head and walked lurchingly to an empty seat at the far end of the bus. He appeared crestfallen. Agnes got off two stops early and walked home in an agony of guilt.

On Wednesday she came home to find two men in boiler suits tapping expertly at the sitting-room wall.

'Council,' said Merlin as she bypassed the group on her way upstairs. As if urging her to join in, he added: 'They've come to pass the death sentence.'

Agnes lingered reluctantly. She wanted to be alone.

'How long have we got?' she said.

Neither of the men appeared to hear her, so Merlin repeated the question.

'Hard to say,' said one of them. 'Could be ten months, a year tops. What d'you say, Gavin?'

'I'd give 'em three months, mate,' said Gavin cheerfully. 'First you got your subsidence, right? That won't really bother you for a good while yet but then, this time of year, you've got your damp and cold to think about. It's exposed all down that side, see? 'Less someone cares to pay a few grand to get that crack seen to and the wall supported on the other side, well, as I say, I'd give you three months.'

'So what you're saying, Gavin, is it's their choice.'

'Quality of life,' said Merlin as an aside to Agnes.

'As I say, unless someone wants to have it fixed up, that's about the size of it,' said Gavin.

'But what if we can stand it?' interjected Agnes. 'What if we don't mind the cold and damp? We could stay here for another year?'

Both men looked at her and grinned.

'You've got a right one here,' one of them said to Merlin. 'A right masochist.'

On Thursday Agnes pleaded a headache at work and went home early. She got in the bath and lay there until the water grew lukewarm and her body appeared to be marbled with a bluish tinge. She remembered at school the nuns used to have giant bath sheets which fitted over their heads and draped over the sides of the bath so that they wouldn't be able to see their own naked body lying there in the water. At least that's what some of the girls had said, claiming to have seen these strange plastic contraptions hung out to dry in the kitchen garden. Agnes would have liked to have had one now. She could lie still beneath it like a subterranean canal, cavernous and secret. She wanted to be hidden from herself. She would feel safe then, protected, like the time her father and brother had buried her up to her neck in sand on the beach and she hadn't been able to move; but she had felt warm, and light with the irresponsibility of it. Just her head grinning bizarrely out of the sand. She would be a limpet clinging to a rock, she thought now, if she could. She thought of a room full of bathing nuns, their shaven heads sprouting from the plastic in rows like tomato plants, and she began to laugh. Her laughter sounded all through the empty house. She thought of her father and brother running away down the beach, shrieking with delight at her predicament. She had laughed then, too, until it had begun to dawn on her that they might leave her like that and never come back.

On Friday, Agnes was called into Jean's office. They each sat down on the appropriate side of the desk.

'Now,' said Jean, arranging her small hands neatly in her lap. 'You probably know that this is the time of year when we try and give people a little extra money if we think their work is up to standard.'

'No,' replied Agnes. 'No, I didn't.'

She saw her lover as if from the prow of a boat. She was being borne off to sea while he lounged nonchalantly on the quayside, looking at her like a stranger as she passed. She waved her hand and he peered back, as if into strong sunlight.

'Well, we do,' said Jean. 'Anyway, dear, I'm afraid we've decided to withhold your bonus for a while.'

'Oh.'

He had never had any intention of coming with her, after all. She had just happened to pass randomly through his life, like a tourist.

'I discussed it with the Managing Director, and it seemed to us that you haven't really settled down yet. We decided to give it a bit longer and then make a decision.' She paused, and then continued in a sharper tone: 'You do understand what I'm saying, dear, don't you? You haven't settled down!'

Jean spoke loudly, as if to a deaf person. Agnes looked at her. She had no eyebrows, merely pencilled lines which, perhaps applied in haste, gave her the look of one apprehending a surprise attack. The delayed import of what her employer had been saying became clear to her. Agnes understood she was about to lose her job. Jean was right. She suddenly felt decidedly unsettled.

'You're right,' she said.

'You haven't settled down,' replied Jean, repeating herself with surprise. 'You haven't really come to terms with the system. We just don't think you're putting your all into it.'

Agnes felt strangely comforted by these words. Having never really cared about the office or the people contained within it, she had assumed that she, likewise, had eluded their notice. The attention such criticism implied was almost warming. She began to cry.

'I'm sorry!' she sobbed. 'You're right. I'm sorry.'

'Oh dear,' said Jean, fumbling nervously on her desk-top for a tissue. 'There, there.'

'It's just all been so awful. So awful!'

'There are other jobs, you know, dear,' replied Jean briskly. 'You don't have to work here if you find it so awful. Perhaps it's for the best.'

'No!' Agnes reached over the desk and clutched her hand dramatically. 'It's not the job, I promise! I like it here, I – please don't make me go!' she pleaded. 'I've just had a bit of a hard time recently. Personal reasons.'

While there was little in her life that wasn't personal, nevertheless the term shamed her. She disliked underselling the drama of her turbulent heart. Jean creased her pencilled eyebrows with puzzlement.

'I promise I'll make it up to you,' swore Agnes impetuously. She released Jean's hand, which had been lying limply in her own for some time. 'I'll settle down, I promise! Just give me a month and I'll show you. Please!' She fixed her with martyred eyes. 'Please.'

Having always nurtured a secret belief that she had been born in the wrong century, and would have been far better employed in one where she could have spent her days on a chaise-longue scheming how to ensnare a wealthy husband, Agnes had disdained the modern world of work in the hope of better things. Such a perspective, subverted though it was, sat uncomfortably alongside the egalitarian flavour of her political beliefs. In private moments she reasoned that her idiosyncratic personality would not conform to iron-cast office hierarchies; and while she was haunted by the idea that she might not be normal, she religiously avoided any activity which might serve to make her more so.

Working late on Friday brought upon her a plethora of new sensations, not all of them pleasant. On the evening in question she expended as much effort on quelling her emotional uprisings as on any extraneous proof-reading. Her whole being seemed to revolt against the engagement of her mind with anything which did not directly concern it; but as she took the bus home through the night-time city, she caught a glimpse of a small but comforting interface. The truth was that she felt rather better. Indeed, she felt almost virtuous. She settled back wearily into her seat, meditating upon the integrity of labour.

The days in which he had not called had accumulated like dust on a mantelpiece. She had raked through the ashes in the hope of uncovering something the flame of his rejection had spared. The truth, in the end, was that with no one around any longer to take responsibility for wasting her time, even she could not bear the thought of doing it for herself.

Chapter Eighteen

AGNES started walking home from work at night. It was a long way from Finchley Central, and the money saved did not justify the expenditure of effort involved. This new practice was, however, not part of a plan for economic stringency. It was more of an extension of the secret life of solitude Agnes had lately felt herself to be living.

The first time she had attempted the strenuous hike through the congested hills and vales of north London, it had not been through choice. She had arrived at the bus stop to find her purse empty of change, and with the uncertain logic of such trying moments had decided she could as easily walk the three or four arduous miles homes as the two hundred yards up the high street to the nearest bank. It had taken her over an hour, and she had arrived weary but exhilarated, to find the house dark and silent. The others had apparently gone to bed, and as she made a solitary cup of tea in the kitchen and carried it upstairs she realised this state of affairs was rather pleasant. The part of the day in which one had to field questions and explain oneself now seemed to her the most arduous. She drifted around her darkened room for a while like an intruder, touching things. The next morning she got up early and left for work before the others were awake.

Agnes had never been one for being alone. She had always felt herself becoming blurred around the edges after an hour or two and had gone to seek more stimulating company.

Now she began rather to enjoy the sensation of encroaching invisibility. It became something of a challenge. How long could she go without calling on her friends for support? Would they worry, wondering what had happened to her? Would she become mysterious and desirable with absence, returning to find herself somehow nicer, her life enhanced? In the old days the house had been her nerve-centre, for as well as providing the solaces of friendship it had been a hub of news: phone calls, letters, unexpected callers, all of the things which pumped her heart like a life-support machine emanated from home. The fact that now she dreaded its quiet telephone and reminders of bills unpaid did to some extent facilitate her protracted absences.

She walked down into East Finchley, under the railway bridge, and on towards Highgate. The winter darkness was sharp and clear, but the streetlamp turned the sky a muddy brown. Her feet pounded on the pavement. Her breath came out in misty dragonish puffs. The rhythm was almost mechanical. She liked the way her mind emptied of nebulous worrying thoughts when she was walking, and housed instead a set of honed perceptions. She had little experience of such intentness.

As she approached Highgate she stopped at one of the garish late-night garages, which hummed and glowed incongruously by the roadside like spaceships, to buy some chocolate. Normally Agnes would never have eaten such a thing, let alone in the street, but her midnight perambulations had begun to lend her a certain immunity to the common gaze. Initially she had been troubled by the stares of occasional passers-by on the lonely pavements, especially the men, who looked at her first as if wondering what she was doing out alone so late at night, and then away, perhaps frightened of the implications, already seeing themselves accused. She wondered if they sensed her fear of them and were ashamed. Later, when habit had dissolved her fear of strangers, she thought it was they who were afraid. She knew how she must look: peripatetic, unwanted, a mad glint in her eye. It was almost enjoyable.

She passed through Highgate village and began to walk down the long hill to Archway. Buses lit up like moving blocks of flats whooshed past her. A car sped by, its horn blaring, arms waving from the windows like streamers. Her heart pounded with surprise. A film of sweat sprang up beneath her clothes. She took out her bar of chocolate and began to unwrap it with shaking hands. Only a moment before she had felt immune, her identity a faint question mark over her head. Now she wondered what on earth she was doing at this sordid roundabout, when it was so late and cold that any normal person would have longed to be home. Suddenly she too longed to be home. A delayed flame of pain shot through her, illuminating her in the darkness. She tried to cross the road and was met with a barrage of horns.

Finally she reached the Holloway Road. She took a piece of chocolate and put it in her mouth just as a man walked past her on the pavement.

'You'll get fat,' he said. His face was concerned.

'Just – just piss off!' Agnes shrieked as she hurried away.

By the time she reached Drayton Park she was almost running. She crammed more chocolate in her mouth, but her breath seemed unfortunately to collide with it on its way out and she began to choke.

'Hey!' someone shouted from across the road. 'Hey, you!'

She quickened her pace with terror. She could hear footsteps behind her.

'Good God, Agnes,' said Merlin, overtaking her and then stopping in her path. 'What on earth are you doing?'

'I – I don't know,' replied she between coughs and gasps. 'Someone was shouting. I was scared.'

'Oh, that was me. I was only joking. Hey, you've got chocolate all over your mouth.'

They walked back to Elwood Street. Agnes wiped her mouth surreptitiously on her sleeve.

'Do you fancy a drink?' said Merlin when they got in. 'We could go to that pub on the Blackstock Road. We could have a chat.'

It was a long time, Agnes realised, since she had been out.

She went upstairs to change into other clothes. She wondered what Merlin wanted to talk to her about.

She and John had always used to argue when they went out. It was something to do with the ritual of spending money on formalised pleasure – it begged to be despoiled. Once, in a restaurant, he had spied a female friend on the other side of the room and had gone to stand at her table like a suitor, talking and waving his arms animatedly. Their food had come and still he did not return. Agnes had tried vainly to catch his eye but he hadn't looked at her. She didn't dare to go over there herself and drag him back to the table. She had waited for over half an hour in a sweat of embarrassment and jealousy, ridiculous and alone at a table laden with food, like a mad old divorcée. Eventually she had begun to cry. When he returned to find her like that he had been disgusted and had left the restaurant, flinging a ten-pound note down on the table.

She took off her clothes and chose different ones, but was distressed to find that they would not fit her. She had put on weight. She climbed back into the first outfit. Merlin called up the stairs to her. She fumbled with a lipstick, sweating with panic.

'I feel like I haven't seen you for ages,' said Merlin when they were ensconced in a velveteen booth. The table before them was scattered with unused beer mats, beside which crisps floated soggily in dark liquid circles. 'You've got a secret life. You never come home any more.'

'Overtime,' said Agnes. It sounded more like a comforting hot drink than a spiritual struggle.

'Really?'

Merlin regarded her with grinning amazement. She stared back at him, and was disconcerted at her sense of having never really looked at him before. He had new glasses.

'You've got new glasses,' she said.

'What?' He looked bemused. 'Oh, these. No, I've had them for ages. Come on, Ag, don't change the subject. Tell me about your secret life.' He peered at her suspiciously. 'What are you up to?'

'Nothing.'

'Oh.' He seemed disappointed. 'So why don't you ever come home?'

'I told you. Overtime.'

'Oh. I thought you were joking.'

'Well, what did you expect me to say? I'm having some affair that I can't tell you about?'

'I'll admit I was thinking along those lines.'

'God, well, I'm sorry I can't give you anything as exciting as a man to talk about. It's just my boring old job.' A gorge of anger rose up into her throat. 'Maybe you'd like to find someone more desirable to have a drink with, Merlin. I mean, God forbid that I should dare to talk about my boring old life. I probably shouldn't be out, should I? I should be in purdah. I should ring a bell and shout "single"!'

Merlin, to her surprise, began to smile. His reaction would have driven Agnes to further excesses of outrage had she not soon perceived that he seemed to be looking at someone else. He smiled again and waved his hand.

'Friend of mine,' he said. 'Hang on a second. I'll be back.'

He got up and went to a table where a blond girl was sitting. They greeted each other effusively. Agnes fiddled uncomfortably with a beer mat. A man came into the pub and sat down at the bar. He was looking at her. She looked back defiantly. She felt rather audacious after her outburst. He was bearded and wore a respectable suit. Presently, he got off his bar stool and came over to her table.

'I suck girls' cunts,' he said calmly, standing before her.

Agnes looked at him dumbfounded. His choice of vocabulary left her own impoverished. She managed to shake her head. He shrugged, smiled at her briefly, and then turned and went back to the bar.

'Who was that?' said Merlin, sitting down.

'I don't know.'

She was still in a state of shock. She had never heard anything so disgusting in her life. One never knew. Really, one knew nothing at all.

'I want to go home,' she said.

'Oh. Whatever you say.' Merlin drained his glass, his Adam's apple moving up and down like something alive trapped in his throat. 'Okay, let's go.'

They got up to leave. The man turned around and stared at her; like someone normal, someone in a crowd, his face boarded up like a derelict place.

'It's happening to me,' Agnes told Greta. 'What happens to you – you know, when people come up and say strange things? Well, it's happening to me.'

'Maybe the world's just getting meaner.' Greta shrugged.

'But there must be more to it than that!' Agnes cried impatiently. 'Haven't you ever wondered why it happens? What makes people think they can just come up and – and say anything they like?'

'Yup, it's a mean old world,' sighed Greta. 'All you can do is be mean back.'

Agnes gave up. She sat down at her desk and found herself too distracted to work. Finally, she got up and decided to get some fresh air, albeit at the risk of further accosting.

'You can't show people you're sad,' Greta announced as Agnes reached the door. 'What goes around comes around. They sniff it out. Like goddamned dogs. Then they give it right back to you, only worse.'

The crack in the wall now stretched from floor to ceiling. Agnes had tried to camouflage it with posters but they peeled off with the damp, resulting in a worse defect on display than the concealed original. It was November now, a month of iron skies and stormy nights. As the cold seeping into the house turned from an invigorating freshness to a disturbing presence, Agnes felt the sensibility of change being forced upon her; for she saw in the long, cavernous fault intimations of the irretrievable sundering of future from past.

'Why do you worry so much about where you're going to

be after you die?' John had once said to her. 'You never give a second thought to where you were before you were born.'

Nina was usually at Jack's house in the evenings, but when he went away for a few days she came back. When Agnes came home she found Nina in the kitchen cooking supper.

'Do you want some?' Nina asked, indicating a pile of as yet unassembled ingredients.

'Oh, thanks,' said Agnes, taking off her coat. She hadn't spent time alone with Nina for weeks. She wondered what they would talk about.

'Jack tells me you had a contretemps with his friend in Hampton Court,' Nina announced presently, resolving Agnes's dilemma.

'That's right.'

'So have you heard from him since then?'

Nina removed a cucumber from its cellophane packaging and began to slice it.

'Who says I was expecting to?'

'I dunno. I just supposed you were. You do have a history of post-coital obsession, you know.'

Nina began cracking eggs to make an omelette. Agnes looked at the empty egg carton which read LAID AND PACKED THE SAME DAY, and thought of how many times she had been.

'I don't want to hear from him,' she said.

'Fine. I think you're well out of it.'

'Well, fine.'

Agnes tried to remember the last time she'd had a warming conversation with Nina. There was something gritty and abrasive between them which rubbed every time they spoke.

'So what was he like in bed?' said Nina presently, obviously mistaking the moment for one of intimacy.

'Fine!' Agnes gushed.

It irritated her that after everything she still felt a residual loyalty to him. It was almost atavistic, like an instinct that should have been phased out by years of evolution and feminism. Nina was facing her expectantly, apparently awaiting further revelations.

'Actually, it was strange,' she confessed.

'What do you mean?'

Agnes contemplated her position. What if Nina should take the side she herself had just deserted, and conclude that his dysfunction was no one's fault but her own? She seemed strangely alerted to the presence of a mystery, in any case, standing there with arms crossed, waiting.

'Well, you know what he's like,' Agnes offered. 'He always seems half-asleep or something. He makes you want to check his pulse.'

'What do you mean, "strange"?' Nina persisted.

'Well—' She felt herself writhing. 'He didn't – he couldn't – I tried, I really did, but it never made any difference because he still didn't—'

'Come?' interjected Nina smoothly.

'Yes,' breathed Agnes. 'I thought it was my fault.'

'No,.it's pretty normal.'

'Is it?' She felt almost smug. 'It's never happened to anyone else I've been with.'

'No.' Nina looked at her oddly. 'I meant it's normal for people like him.'

'What on earth do you mean?'

There was a long and awful moment of silence. Nina turned away and began absorbedly chopping vegetables.

'I shouldn't have said anything. Forget it.'

'No!' Agnes cried. 'No, I won't forget it!' She banged her hand dramatically on a counter-top for effect. 'So – so just tell me, okay?'

Nina looked up at her coolly and then returned to her vegetables.

'You asked for it,' she said above the ominous thud of blade against board. 'If you really want to know, he's a smackhead.'

'A what?'

'Smackhead. Heroin addict, for God's sake. I thought you

knew. They often have problems like that – sexual problems. I thought you knew,' she repeated.

Agnes wondered if she understood what had been said. The words appeared to be floating around her in big inflated balloons, like a comic strip. She thought of the gaunt cipher of him, the quiet greedy suck of his presence; his long silences behind the bathroom's bolted door when she had thought he must surely be dead or sleeping; the heat of him, his black bullet eyes saying nothing.

'How could I know?' she said then.

'How could you not know? What, are you blind? How could you spend all that time with a person and not know a thing like that?'

'He didn't tell me.'

'Well, that explains everything,' Nina said sarcastically.

'Well, how did you know, then?' said Agnes as the strange fact of it occurred to her. She was beginning to feel sick. 'How did you know? Did he tell you? Did he?'

'No. Don't be stupid.'

'So who did?'

'Jack.'

A sudden surge of adrenalin made her feel almost buoyant. She put her hand on Nina's shoulder and forced her to face her. Nina's face betrayed a fleeting shadow of fear at the physical contact, as if it suggested things had got out of control.

'Why didn't you tell me?' Agnes demanded.

'There was no reason to.' Nina shrugged away Agnes's hand. 'And anyway, Jack asked me not to.'

So that was it, then. If only she had looked, how much she might have learned! Had she but guessed at the shady deals, the backhand bribes, the double-crossed hearts of others, for how much might she sooner have forgiven herself? It was Agnes's nature to emulate others, not to judge them; how happy they must have been, with her to please them as well as they pleasing themselves!

'*He* obviously didn't want you to know,' Nina conceded.

'Otherwise he'd have told you, wouldn't he? Look, maybe he was embarrassed about it. Maybe he didn't want to hurt your feelings.'

'What?' Agnes laughed wildly and Nina looked startled. 'What was it you said to me that time, about men being animals? So what are we saying now – that he didn't want to hurt my *feelings*? You're obviously a believer these days. I suppose you also knew,' she added, triumphant at having a revelation of her own to hand, albeit one which could inflict injury on no one but herself, 'that he was seeing someone else all along? Maybe you thought I shouldn't know about that as well.'

'I didn't know that, actually. Was he really?'

'Don't bother defending him!' Agnes shrieked. 'I won't listen! I know where your loyalties lie – I won't be making that mistake again!'

'Oh, for God's sake,' Nina snapped. 'Don't get hysterical. You're behaving like he's a serial killer or something. Or maybe – ' she looked at Agnes curiously – 'maybe you really are as innocent as you pretend to be. Maybe you needed to wake up. If you ask me—'

'I don't ask you!' Agnes cried, putting her hands over her ears and turning to leave the room. 'In fact, I don't think I even like you very much.'

Chapter Nineteen

AGNES Day was letting herself go. The phrase did imply a certain freedom from imprisonment, but its effects were far from captivating. Hair sprouted freely over her unmown slopes, where bulges swelled like molehills. Skin sagged here and flaked there, puckering like a contour relief map. A distinct whiff of human flesh could be caught in the groves where exotic flowers used to perfume the air. Surrendering to the final molestation of art by life, Agnes abandoned her brush and palette and barely faced the world.

By becoming that which she had always feared – or perhaps had always feared she already was, underneath – Agnes knew certain things would have to be sacrificed. Men no longer looked at her as she passed, and while initially her heart had plummeted at the realisation, her spirit nestled further into the safe folds of a hermaphrodite sensibility. To think of herself as undesirable was second nature; to read it in the eyes of others was something else altogether and required some defence. She would give vent to her feelings in the privacy of her room at night, when she would cry and claw at her body with rage.

Eventually, however, she came to see that her despoilment carried within it its own defence. Her blank face and new folds of flesh were at once her protection from the world and her submission to it. They made her invisible. In times of despair she was tempted to return to her old ways, but never tried for fear of discovering that she couldn't. Her renunciation of those things seemed to her then to have meant nothing but the death of everything she had once held dear.

Her career at *Diplomat's Week*, meanwhile, began to flourish. She became expert at locating errors and discrepancies, and on more than one occasion saved the day by insistently carrying out last-minute checks even as the pages were being borne off to the typesetter's. She wrote an article for the magazine and was surprised to find it accepted. She suggested new formats and saw them pass into legislature with scarcely a blinking eye.

'We might have to give you that bonus before long,' said Jean beamingly, who of late had been observing rather than participating in this show of labour.

'How about me?' said Greta. 'I have to watch her. It makes me tired.'

Like someone who had come out of hiding, Agnes began to speak openly about her work with her acquaintances. In doing so, she discovered that it was possible, with but a modicum of glamorous embellishment, to make almost anything sound interesting if you described it in the right way. She talked about deadlines and copy dates, hymned galleys and bromides, discussed at length with fellow publishers the problems one encountered in the company of typesetters and printers. One companion was evidently so moved by her narrative that he offered to come and meet her for lunch so that the scene might be evoked in his mind more clearly.

'Where's your house?' he questioned imperiously.

'Highbury,' replied Agnes in bewilderment, before realising to which establishment he was referring.

What irked her was the malevolent coincidence with which the application of her workmates seemed to falter in direct proportion to her own increase in zeal. At first she had thought this was merely the fault of her own altered perspective, but it soon became clear that Jean and Greta had fallen prey to rogue circumstances. Greta seemed detached and morose; Jean, on the other hand, radiated a nervous joy of the type which automatically generated its antithesis in those who encountered it. She had lost weight and begun to wear make-up. She arrived late, appeared distracted for most of the day, and left early. Agnes wondered if she and Jean had somehow exchanged personalities in a midnight astral collision.

'She's like a goddamned mosquito,' complained Greta. 'Zip zip, buzz buzz – THWACK!' She grinned. 'I used to have this really neat electronic insect exterminator back home.'

The strange coincidence of Jean's new-found ecstasy with a sudden recurrence of phone calls from someone called David from the Church of Christ the Evangelist, as he unfailingly announced himself, could not but solve the mystery.

'So what's with this David geezer?' Greta boldly asked. She had lately taken to spicing up her narrative with eclectic touches of native vocabulary. Agnes saw it as a bad sign that she had resumed relations with London Transport. 'Are you two going together or what?'

'In a manner of speaking,' Jean replied. 'If that's how you want to put it.'

'I do,' Greta assured her.

'Well, I suppose we do see each other quite often,' replied Jean, feigning a puzzlement designed to suggest she had never thought of it in quite that way before. 'He's a very nice man – so, so dignified, if you see what I mean.'

'Dignified Dave,' said Greta rolling her eyes. 'Hot damn.'

Further questioning revealed that David was a born-again Christian and that Jean had lately taken to accompanying him to church. It was really very interesting, she said. Quite fascinating, in fact.

'She must love him,' opined Greta as Jean left the office. 'She must love him a lot.'

When Agnes thought of love, she saw her lover, or her ex-lover as he should now be called, thus in visions: the sucking syringe finger, the sweet steel needle, penetrating himself as he had her once upon a time. She knew nothing could compete with the liquid love he channelled into his own veins, careful not to spare a drop, no love, ultimately, lost between them. She decided she should get an AIDS test and asked Nina pointedly one Saturday morning how one could best contrive to have such a thing.

'No need,' said Nina shortly, unruffled by Agnes's accusing eyes and brave tone. 'He wasn't a junkie. He didn't use needles.'

She returned to the perusal of the magazine in her lap, while Agnes experienced a surge of annoyance, unmitigated by relief, that she should have to request details of her lover's intimate habits from her treacherous ex-friend.

Curiosity, however, compounded her plight and she could not refrain from asking: 'So how did he do it, then? I mean, how did he actually take the stuff?'

'Smoked it,' said Nina, not actually adding 'stupid' but severely implying it. 'Needles are sleazy.'

'Thanks a lot,' said Agnes, in a tone which required no subtext.

It was after that that she really felt for the first time she had lost him. It was almost as if she was disappointed by this latest intelligence, dependent as she had been on the depth of his malignity to fuel her own angry responses. When she was younger, she had used to think in moments of severe pique at her family that they would all be sorry if she died; and death had seemed a small price to pay for the satisfaction of remorse. Now, imagining him going about his business with a conscience clear and bright as a lightbulb, she realised that such vengeance was not to be hers. He had done her no wrong, apart from preferring someone else. And whose fault was that?

'You should smile more,' John used to say to her. 'You look better when you smile.'

It had never occurred to her to point out that if she had felt better, she would by implication have smiled more, for rearrangement was an inexorable part of their routine. He would tell her to wear this jacket, change that shirt, do her hair this way instead; and she really saw no reason why the expression on her face should not fall within the territories under his jurisdiction. He wanted to improve her, presumably so that he could love her more.

'When I phone you up,' he said one day, 'you're always in. Why is that?'

Whenever he was due to call, she always waited faithfully by the phone, dispatching other callers hastily lest he should find the line engaged and refusing to leave the house for a minute.

'Well, it would annoy you if I wasn't there,' she reasoned, although bewildered by his question. 'Wouldn't it?'

'Not necessarily. Sometimes it's good to be frustrated. It makes things more exciting – it makes the object of your frustration more desirable. Do you see what I mean?'

'No, I don't. I don't see what you mean. Are you saying you want me to go out specially when you call? Is that what you're saying?'

'Forget it,' he said lightly.

She couldn't forget it. His perversity upset her. She knew it was all in the interests of making him love her more, but it looked to her as if he was running out of ideas. Until now, he had never actually asked her to love him less. Nevertheless, once or twice she did run to the bathroom at the sound of the telephone ringing and had leaned against the locked door, her heart beating senselessly until it stopped. It hadn't seemed to change things much.

Nina spent even more time at Jack's house after her argument with Agnes. Merlin started working late. Sometimes he and Agnes would meet in the kitchen at unsociable hours and they would stay up and drink beer while Nina's room lay dark and empty above them like that of a missing child.

'It's like when someone walks out during an argument,'

said Agnes one night. 'You're left with all this anger and nowhere to put it. It seems really unfair. I mean, she started it, right? It was her fault. She should apologise.'

'You did say, if I remember correctly, that you didn't like her very much.'

'I don't.'

Merlin leaned wearily into the sofa.

'You have to,' he said. 'All our names are on the lease. Besides, she's your best friend. You have to like your best friend.'

Agnes told him about her early experiences of best-friendship at school, where the title was nothing if not transient and could be purchased or lost for the small price of a treasured object – a coloured pencil perhaps – given or withheld, or a favour done. 'Swap me your rubber,' came the cry. 'I'll be your best friend!'

Never one known for her stock of fancy stationery, Agnes had always found best friends to be in short supply. Once or twice she had purloined one with the bargain-basement currency of loyalty and love, but this kind of investment became more risky in view of the inevitable transformation of friend to enemy which had characterised relations amongst her peer-group.

'It was always worse if you'd been their real friend,' she said. 'When they turned against you it meant they knew things about you. I don't know, it was just worse.'

'Well, presumably it was more hurtful,' said Merlin. 'But why did they turn against you in the first place? What did you have to do?'

'Nothing. It just had to be your turn. Someone would suddenly say, "I think so-and-so needs to be taken down a peg or two, don't you?" and that was it.'

'The call to arms.'

'I suppose so. Everyone knew what to do. It was all very matter-of-fact.'

'Did anyone ever refuse to join in?'

'Yes, sometimes. They were like invisible people, though.

143

Outcasts. No one ever talked to them. Thinking about it now, I suppose they were actually quite brave. I would never have dared to do that.'

'So why – why did the bullied become the bullies, if you see what I mean? How did people have so much power one minute and then none at all?'

'I don't know. I've never really thought about it. Once you've had power over people, maybe they hate you more. At the time, it was just what you did to protect yourself.'

'But there must have been a ringleader,' Merlin insisted. 'Someone who never got it in the neck. You must have had a leader on your terror campaigns.'

'You're right, we did. Her name was Christine Poole.'

'You shivered as you said it!' Merlin said gleefully. 'I saw you! Christine Poole. Creepy name. Does she haunt your dreams?'

'I suppose she does.'

'Let's go and find her!' cried Merlin. 'Let's go round and do her over, shall we?'

'I don't know where she lives,' said Agnes, smiling weakly.

This was actually a lie. Agnes knew perfectly well where she lived. It was in an unremarkable terraced house in their local town at home. Once, when she was home from university, she had seen her walking down the street. At first she hadn't recognised her. She seemed so much smaller and drearier. She had permed hair and a haggard face, and she was pushing a pram. They had almost collided on the pavement, as if thrown together by the fugal force of their shared past. A flicker of recognition had passed between them. Agnes had thought of all the times she had dreamt of this meeting. It was to be a form of revenge. She had planned to be beautiful and successful, maybe with a man on her arm. She had even thought of clever vicious comments and cutting remarks. In the event, however, the girl had shunted the pram off the pavement to let her pass and they had gone their separate ways without a word. Agnes had glimpsed her feet as she passed, crammed into cheap stilettos.

At the time she had felt sorry for her, and pity had assuaged her vengefulness. Christine Poole, after all, had got what she deserved. Now Agnes was not so sure about things. Now, if she went to visit her, as Merlin suggested, she didn't know what would happen. Now she was the one with failure written all over her. She was not so certain of defeating Christine Poole. She thought of Nina, and it occurred to her that nothing might have changed.

'Where's Jean?' said Agnes as she arrived in the pub, where they had planned to hold an editorial meeting to discuss the latest issue of *Diplomat's Week*.

'With born-again Dave,' Greta replied. 'The rave from the grave.'

She drained her glass and set it down on the table. Agnes took off her coat and sat down heavily beside her.

'Great,' she said. 'Marvellous. And do you think she's going to find the time between – between hopping in and out of bed or whatever it is she's doing to put in an appearance?'

'Jean dates for Jesus,' said Greta laconically. 'She's got all the time in the world.'

Agnes picked up the copy of the magazine which was lying on the table. It looked much better; in fact, it was quite good. She turned to the article she had written on women in politics and saw that the byline read 'By Agnes Hay'.

'Who cares?' she said, flinging it back on the table. 'No one else seems to. Why should I? I don't want to talk about work anyway.'

'Aw, honey, what's up? Don't tell me your industry pill has worn off.'

'Well, someone has to do it! We can't all just be – be mooning around about men the whole time.'

'You too have mooned,' observed Greta. 'In fact, you were pretty much a full-time mooner until a few weeks ago. Let the old hag have her fun, sweetie.'

'It just annoys me that women have to fall to pieces every

time a man shows any interest in them.' She lowered her voice. 'I mean, I know because it happened to me.'

'My name is Agnes Hay,' Greta cackled. 'I am a Woman Who Loves Too Much.'

Agnes went to the bar and bought two vodkas with tonic.

'Why does everyone have to criticise me the whole time?' she said when she got back. 'It seems to have become obligatory. It seems to have become a bloody national pastime.'

'What do you mean?' said Greta, pronouncing the phrase as one word. 'Gee, I didn't mean to make you feel bad. I was just playing around.' She raised a concerned hand to her own forehead, as if suspecting a tropical fever might have gripped her unawares. 'Gosh, I'm really sorry. You're the best, really you are. God, that was so mean.'

Agnes could not argue with so comprehensive a display of remorse.

'Don't worry about it,' she said. 'You're probably off-loading anger about something else.' It sounded stupid, so she added: 'I mean, we all do that sometimes, don't we?'

'Do we? That's really smart.'

Agnes didn't think it was that smart. She would have preferred people to keep their emotional goods on board.

'Why can't I say things like that?' Greta continued. 'I can't explain things to save my life. You have a way with words.'

'Do I?' said Agnes, feeling at a loss for them.

'Sure. Hey, I had a dream about you last night. It was really weird, you were standing on the edge of the ocean chucking these things into the water.'

She paused as if to signal the completion of her narrative, and Agnes experienced a moment of frustration at this early proof of her friend's recently proclaimed defect. In general Agnes disliked the incessant fascination of others with their own dreams, analysing them like works of genius thrown up by their dormant imaginations. For her own part she rarely dreamed; such bizarre and wishful fantasies as her mind manufactured were indistinguishably fused with the reality of waking life, broadcast in daylight like an unwatched television set in a corner. The images which visited her in the night were but the residue of her conscious censors, from which she woke sweating and tortured.

'What do you mean?' she said. 'What things?'

'Well, they were these really beautiful things, kind of like glass but lots of different colours. Each one was different, they were all different but part of the same thing if you see what I mean. I couldn't believe it when I saw you just throwing them into the water because they were getting all ruined and I was shouting for you not to do it, but you kept chucking them in. It was like you didn't care, you know? So anyway, I promised myself then that I'd tell you when I saw you. Not to do it, that is.'

'Not to do what?'

'How should I know?' Greta grinned. 'Not to ruin the damn pieces of glass, I guess.'

'Do you often dream things like that about other people?'

It seemed strange that she should have been discovered standing alone by some desolate ocean in someone else's mind. It was almost as if she remembered it herself.

'Oh, sure. Once I dreamed this friend of mine's father was going to die in this horrible car crash, and then next day he did.'

'And had you told him?' said Agnes, aghast.

'Of course not! Would you want to know a thing like that?'

'I suppose not,' said she, feeling rather chilled. 'I wouldn't want the responsibility of having to decide, though. Didn't you feel guilty?'

'Why should I?'

'Well, perhaps you could have prevented it.'

As soon as the words were out of her mouth, Agnes felt horrified that she should have said such a thing. What if Greta took it to heart? What if, filled with remorse, she should go off and inflict some terrible damage upon herself?

'Well, I thought of that,' said Greta, apparently unperturbed. 'But then I decided, well, if that's his destiny, what difference would it make? My telling him would be included in it, if you see what I mean. I guess I was just unlucky to tune in to his future. Most people ignore things like that anyway, like in that play – you know, the one where that fortune-teller says to the Roman guy that he's going to get knifed if he goes to the meeting but he goes anyway?'

'*Julius Caesar*.'

'Right. Like that, anyway. I just kind of carried it around with me. Other things too.'

'Like what?'

'Well, mostly about myself. Feelings I have, kind of like premonitions. At the moment, say, I've got a feeling about that guy.'

'Which one?'

'London Transport, you know. About him. Weird.'

'Why on earth don't you do something about it?' cried Agnes.

'What could I do? That's not how it works. I'm just spooked. It doesn't change the way things are. My grandma was the same.'

'What happened to her?'

'She went crazy.' Greta rolled her eyes and laughed. 'Well, she was always kind of crazy.'

'But what you said to me the other day, about not letting your sadness show, remember?'

'Sure.'

'Well, couldn't it just be that? I mean, it isn't as if you're jinxed or anything.' Agnes was growing uncomfortable. She felt herself edging away.

'Don't worry,' said Greta. 'It's not infectious. What I said to you, well, that may be true. People are pretty much self-fulfilling prophecies. The premonitions are different, though. That's more like remembering things that haven't happened yet. It stinks.'

Agnes thought about this for a while.

'But where does it come from?' she said finally. 'It's not as if you make the things happen just by seeing them. And why is it always bad things?'

'Don't ask me.' Greta shrugged. 'This mystic lady once told me I had the evil eye. She was a bitch. I said to her, lady, if I had the evil eye, I'd be watching you squirm.'

'Gosh,' said Agnes faintly.

'The best one was this old witch from Regina who told me I was experiencing karmic grief from another life.' She snorted with laughter. 'Maybe I need to be born again. Maybe I should hook up with Dave.'

A mad person accosted Agnes on her way home, accusing her of being a spy for the social services. She got off the train and walked back to Highbury.

Chapter Twenty

AGNES was in a bar in Islington, a place where people sipped Italian coffee served by French waiters as if they had never lived any other kind of life. Agnes drank beer from a bottle and waited for Merlin, who was coming there straight from work. They were going to see a film together; perhaps something with subtitles, Agnes thought, to fit in with her mood. She contemplated the grey marble moon of the table-top, with its folded newspaper and elegant foreign bottle. It was almost convincing. She could live another kind of life; could go to a place where such things were details of a more extensive canvas, rather than lonely still-lives against a background of dirty streets and cold cloudy skies. Perhaps she would accrue depth there, like a foreign film, with the mere fact of difference lending her a certain mystery.

'Sorry I'm late,' said Merlin as he arrived. 'I've been terrorised. Bomb scare.'

He took off his coat and put it on a vacant chair. The smell of damp wool pervaded the air. It reminded Agnes of congested buses and discomfort. He didn't look very well, she noticed; not exactly ill, but with that pinched, worried look she had begun recently to notice in her own features. She wondered what was wrong with him.

'Shall I have something with a lime?' he was mumbling, scanning the menu. 'Or maybe something with caffeine. Coffee with a lime. What are you drinking?'

Agnes turned her bottle around so that the label showed.

She had begun to feel less ingratiating of late, especially towards men. It had occurred to her that emanation generated a certain type of vulnerability. It made one a known quantity, and thus easier to injure. She wanted to be more reserved and hence tougher, like Nina.

'Does that come with a lime?' Merlin inquired.

She nodded and then shrugged to suggest that the citrus feature was optional.

'Will it talk to me?'

'Don't be stupid,' Agnes allowed.

'Well, don't shrug, then. I've had a horrible day. I can't cope with shrugging.'

Agnes realised she had perhaps chosen the wrong moment to experiment with her new style of gender relations. Merlin was staring fixedly at the menu.

'What time does the film start?' he said, looking up. 'Try and answer that with a shrug, baby.'

'*Baby?*' Agnes precipitantly replied, all concessions for the moment abandoned in the light of this new outrage. 'What's that supposed to mean?'

'Generic term, ironically employed. No offence intended.'

'None taken,' she conceded gallantly. 'Besides, you under-estimate me. Eight and a half shrugs, in answer to your question.'

'Right.' He tried to flag down a waiter and failed. The sleek-haired, black-clothed minions cut sneeringly through the crowded tables like sharks, unapproachable. 'These people are the end,' he sighed. 'Talk about power-broking. We should have them all deported.'

Agnes was moved by his views on immigration to stare at him.

'Are you okay?' she inquired.

'Apart from being temporarily invisible, yes. How about you? You seem a little – on edge.' He contemplated her wearily. 'Hey, what's happened to your face?'

'What do you mean?' Agnes put her hands to her face, searching for hitherto unnoticed deformities.

'Your mouth is missing,' he baldly replied.

Agnes glared at him, speechless.

'Thanks a lot!' she burst out finally. 'Thanks a bloody lot, Merlin. I'm just not wearing any make-up, okay? Is that a problem? Look—' She glanced an old plastic bag fortuitously discarded at her feet and held it aloft. 'Look, I can wear this over my head if it offends you!'

'Agnes, hang on a minute, will you?' he interjected. 'I was only joking, honestly. I like it. It suits you.'

'Well, that's okay, then. As long as the men are happy.'

'Oh, Agnes, you know I didn't mean—'

'Shall we talk about something other than my cosmetic arrangements?'

'Fine.' Merlin's face betrayed an emotion which resembled suppressed laughter. 'Um – work. How's work?'

'It's fine. Everyone's in a funny mood, though, especially Jean. She's got a new boyfriend.'

'Jean has a boyfriend!' laughed Merlin with relish. 'The crone of Finchley Central! The scourge of leisured people everywhere! That's really funny.'

'Why?' said Agnes coldly. 'Does she have to be young and pretty and submissive to deserve a man?'

'That's not—'

'Let's just hope she knows how lucky she is, Merlin. Heaven forbid that she should take it for granted that a member of the hallowed sex finds her attractive.'

'Agnes, you know I didn't mean it like that. I thought Jean was official material. I was only trying to make you laugh. Come on, tell me about it. Tell me how she met him.'

Unfortunately for Merlin, his wheedling tone reminded Agnes of John, who had used to treat her enraged outbursts with precisely that same indulgent manner, which, in her view, should be reserved for fractious children and pets.

'Don't condescend,' she said.

'What? I wasn't! What's wrong with you?'

'Does there need to be something "wrong"? Would it make you feel better if I said I was suffering from pre-menstrual tension?'

Merlin looked at her. Other people in the café appeared to

be looking at her. If there had been a mirror handy Agnes would have looked at herself, but there wasn't. The phrase 'pre-menstrual tension' appeared to be echoing around the tables.

As the first heroic flush of her blitzkrieg passed, she began to grow rather uncomfortable. Merlin continued to stare at her in amazement. Suddenly he started to laugh. His shoulders shook and tears began pouring from his eyes. After a while, it became clear to Agnes that he was actually crying.

'I think we'd better leave,' he gasped.

They waded through the suddenly heavy silence in the café and stumbled out into the rain on Upper Street. Tall buses sped by in ebullient sprays of water. Agnes walked as close to Merlin as she dared without actually touching him. He had stopped crying and in fact seemed quite cheerful.

'Never in my life,' she announced as they approached High-bury Corner. 'Never in my life have I made someone cry.'

This was almost a lie. John had once cried like a crocodile for her – over something she'd conveniently done when he'd already decided to leave her, which action his tears consequently justified – but that didn't count.

'Look!' he had said, pointing to a single drop which crawled down his cheek like a snail, leaving a silvery mark. 'Look what you've done – you've made me cry!'

He had seemed rather proud of it, and Agnes had not had the heart to suggest that this effusion might be owing to that summer's exceptional pollen-count, rather than her own cruelty.

'Well, I was laughing, really,' Merlin confessed. 'But it sort of metamorphosed.'

Agnes decided this was probably not the time to take issue with the laughter, certain as she was that in this case she really had precipitated it, and furthermore that she had done so for reasons which were looking less favourable from her own point of view with every passing moment.

'Anyway, I'm sorry,' she said. 'I suppose I was rather excessive.'

Merlin laughed.

'Yes, I had noticed a certain – what shall we say? – a certain defensiveness in your manner these days. Do I take it that the aforementioned hallowed sex are not your favourite gender at the moment?'

'No,' she said crossly. 'And can you blame me?'

'I suppose not. I'm just being selfish. I like you the way you are – I don't want you to go changing on me. You were going to be my comfort in old age.' He took out a tissue and blew his nose. 'But apart from that minor consideration, you're free to wield your spear anywhere you want. You didn't really make me cry, anyway. I've got other things on my mind.'

'Oh,' said Agnes, trying not to feel offended. 'So what's wrong, then?'

'Woman trouble, I suppose.'

They crossed the road and turned into Highbury Fields. Dark trees dripped heavily around them and the rain grew misty over the grass. Agnes didn't like the thought of Merlin having woman trouble. It wasn't the sort of trouble he was supposed to have.

'So who's the woman?'

'What? Oh, my boss, actually.'

'Your boss? I didn't know your boss was a woman. That's really interesting.'

'Agnes, this is hardly the time for a feminist corporate headcount. I'm trying to bare my soul here.'

'Sorry. God, Merlin, you're in love with your boss. How did it happen? Did it just sort of creep up on you?'

'She did sort of creep up on me, yes. You could say that.' He pursed his lips into a grim smile and dug his hands in his pockets. 'But just for the record, I'm not in love with her. She's in love with me.'

'What?'

He laughed.

'Do I have to be pretty and submissive, et cetera, et cetera—'

'Are you serious?'

'Well, surely it's not that hard to believe, is it?'

'No, of course not,' said Agnes, wondering if he might just be imagining it. 'But what form exactly does this – ah – love take?'

'A good question,' said Merlin. 'She's using it as a power thing, actually. That's why I've been working so late recently. She invents all this work for me, really stupid stuff. She makes me run errands for her just as I'm about to go home. It's not my job, but it's all legitimate work, so there's nothing I can do about it.'

'But mightn't she just be a slave driver?'

'You mean, am I just flattering myself? Give me some credit, Agnes. You'll be asking me if I dress provocatively to go to work next.'

'I was only trying to help! I just thought it might not be as serious as you think.'

'It's bloody sexual harassment is what it is. She puts her hand on my leg every time I go near her desk, for God's sake.'

'Well, in that case you can take her to court.'

'Who'd believe me? You hardly do. Anyway, I'd lose my job, and I can't afford to right now. God, it's such bloody poetic justice that this should happen to me!' He looked up at the darkening sky, blinking and gasping like a fish. 'Why me? I'm a feminist!'

'Maybe it's a sign,' said Agnes, attempting levity. 'Maybe your tribe are calling you back.'

'Maybe.' He laughed. 'I shall cultivate the wild man within. Do you know, I could buy an Oriental wife if I wanted one? The perfect wild man accessory.'

'Where from?'

'An agency. I saw it in the personals, it's called "Thai the Knot". Isn't that sick?'

'That's disgusting. You're disgusting, in fact, for looking in the personals.'

'Boys are meant to be disgusting. Girls, on the other hand, must be innocent and pure. I do it all the time, actually. I saw one today which said "Emma Woodhouse desperately seeks Mr Knightley".'

'And were you tempted?'

'No. In fact, it really annoyed me. People are so illiterately romantic these days. Mr Knightley wouldn't look in the personal columns, for heaven's sake. The whole point of him is that he's already there. Women have got some very peculiar ideas. They want to get laid, but they want it to look like Jane Austen.'

Agnes stared at him. They continued walking and she shook her head. Merlin certainly was behaving rather oddly, although this often happened to people, in her experience. One brush with the rudiments of love and they became card-carrying experts on the opposite sex.

'Where are the proofs for the restaurant section?' asked Agnes.

'Sorry, dear,' said Jean after a lengthy hiatus. 'I didn't quite catch that. What did you say?'

Greta came into the office and sat down leadenly at her desk. Her eyes were wide and filmy, like a sleepwalker's.

'Proofs,' repeated Agnes. 'Restaurant section. This week's issue. Remember?'

'Someone called,' interjected Greta, appearing to wake up. 'There was a call for you earlier, Jean. Some guy.'

'Who?' Jean suddenly became mysteriously alert. 'Who was it? A man, you say?'

'Yup.' Greta grinned slyly. 'He did mention his name, but I forget what it was.'

'Well, how did he sound?'

'He sounded kind of – dignified.'

'Was it a deep voice?' persisted Jean. 'Deep and well-spoken, with a slight lisp? A very charming lisp, actually. You'd hardly notice it.'

'Yup.' Greta nodded. 'Sounds like ole Dignified.'

'I'll be back shortly,' said Jean, dashing for the door. 'I'm just going to my office.'

'That woman kills me,' said Greta, yawning. 'She's such a card.'

★

Agnes slammed into the house in a state of considerable distemper. She had been forced by the nonchalance with which the editorial department was approaching its deadline to stay late in the office, working alone while the cleaners emptied bins and vacuumed floors around her. Watching them sanitise the unsavoury detritus of her day she had been besieged by feelings of shame and guilt, and had attempted to engage them in pleasantries. Not beguiled by her condescension, however, they had roundly rebuffed her overtures and left her feeling that a mysterious exchange of power had taken place, the precise manoeuvres of which she was not able to fathom.

She went into the sitting-room and found Nina and Merlin huddled on the sofa like two conspirators.

'We have great news!' Merlin exclaimed, seeing her. He nudged Nina. 'Go on, tell her.'

Agnes sat down on the edge of an armchair. She didn't like news these days.

'What?' she said suspiciously.

'We're not telling you until you look more excited,' said Merlin obstinately.

Agnes felt her backbone sag with frustration. She restrained herself from informing them that, had she been able to manufacture such pleasant emotions at will, her life would undoubtedly today be very different.

'I got the job,' said Nina abruptly. 'I'm quite pleased, actually.'

Agnes had not known she was applying for one. She looked from one to the other of them in bewilderment.

'Just think,' said Merlin, coming to her rescue. 'Our girl on the pages of a national newspaper! Elwood Street at the whirling vortex of the mass media!'

'That's great,' said Agnes, more confused than enlightened by Merlin's rather baroque explanation. 'Great.'

Nina looked at her closely and then shrugged.

'Don't overdo it,' she retorted. 'You might actually sound as if you meant it.'

She got up and left the room. Merlin watched her go and drummed his fingers anxiously on the arm of the sofa.

'It wasn't my fault!' Agnes protested. 'I didn't know about her job.'

'I know,' sighed Merlin. 'But couldn't you – well, couldn't you at least have *pretended* to be pleased?'

Agnes had many memories of doing things against her will, but one occasion had always stuck particularly prominently in her mind.

It had happened when she and John had gone back to his house one night after a party. Sometimes they went back to her house, but more often these days they each went home alone. On this particular night, however, although comforted by the acceptance his invitation implied, Agnes had not felt much in the mood for the rites which were its usual conclusion. She was tired and had drunk too much, and had broadcast these symptoms several times on the way home in the hope that he would not press her into further denials once ensconced there.

'Let's go to bed,' he had said as soon as they arrived; and Agnes did, snuggling up against the far wall so that their bodies would not touch, with as much of the aspect of an ailing child as she could muster.

He switched off the lights and got in beside her at a respectable distance, but scarcely five minutes had passed before his hand reached over and began caressing her. She sighed and attempted to feign sleep. His hand continued its wanderings undeterred. Suddenly, with one jerk of his body, he was pressed up behind her.

'I – I don't really feel like it,' she said, troubled more by her own aversion than his persistence.

He hadn't replied, appearing for a moment to desist, but seconds later she felt his hands on her again. He sat up in the darkness and turned her reluctant body on to its back.

'I don't want to!' she had daringly cried.

His face was cloaked in shadow, but all the same she could have sworn she saw him smile. While it was going on, a curious form of revenge had occurred to her. She would do nothing. She would play dead and see how he felt about that. Her body lay inert, as if on a marble slab. Her arms lay still be her sides. Unperturbed, he had merely arranged her limbs for her. She waited for what seemed like hours while he gasped and sighed above her, but he did not seem troubled by her lack of participation. She imagined then that he was raping her. On to the oval blur of his face she imposed that of a stranger. So this is what it feels like, she thought. As he pumped and shuddered, her mind seemed to be growing further and further away until she appeared to be observing events from the ceiling. A lump of anger sat heavily on her chest. She tasted resentment, oppression and rage on her tongue like foreign foods. She had always known those things were there – she had read about them, after all, in books – but it seemed then as if she had simply never chosen to experience them for herself.

'Thank you,' he said finally, flopping down beside her while she lay still and opaque as a moonlit sea. 'Thank you.'

He hugged and kissed her passionately. At one and the same time she suddenly felt deeply, achingly guilty, and terribly afraid. He got out of bed and paused to look down on her benignly and touch her cheek.

'Agnes, will you marry me?' he said.

'What?' She sat up. 'What did you say?'

She felt she had finally discovered how to make him love her. She felt punished, grateful, devious and rather sick. It was so easy!

'I *said*,' he repeated, a smile which in the shadowy room appeared oddly contemptuous spreading slowly over his face. 'I *said*, would you like a cup of tea?'

St Joan's in Highbury Barn was an arkish construct. Agnes would eye it nervously as she passed, disapproving of its squat modern form and wide wooden belly. Such aesthetic disdain was a natural by-road off her main omission. Had the church been more attractive, the implication ran, she would surely have entered it by now. As it was she slunk guiltily past it like an old people's home in which a decrepit, lonely great-uncle sat forlornly awaiting her visit.

Of late, however, things had changed. Agnes had begun to nurture a dawning awareness of a lack, a growing vacancy at her core. She was ripe for conversion, but while in others such a need brought with it the danger of being brainwashed by a religious sect or enrolling in night classes, Agnes's mettle had since birth been cast in a mould which dictated its own *modus operandi*. Feeling the call, then, she had taken her sorrows up the hill to St Joan's in the hope that by now some wonder of modern theology might have invented a panacea for them.

Once inside she felt slightly disappointed. She had missed the service and the church was empty save for a few worthies busying themselves with the tidying up of hymn-books and parish newsletters. She sat down in one of the wooden pews and waited for her spirit to be claimed. The pedestrian setting, however, did not facilitate access to the Presence. Perhaps she needed incense and a pre-pubescent choir. She found herself thinking about the new issue of *Diplomat's Week*. It was to carry another of her articles, which she hadn't quite finished yet. Merlin crossed her mind and she considered his predicament briefly. She thought about Tom. She ought to phone him.

While it was at least pleasant to have time to think, her ruminations had the effect of making her want to leave the church so that she could attend to them. Her eye wandered impatiently over the altar, behind which hung a crucifix bearing the usual gorged and bloodied simulation of agony. She regarded it indifferently. There had been a time when such representations had transfixed her with their animate, piercing gaze, causing her heart to sing with hope and grief. She had changed, she knew, but she didn't quite know how or when. Like an old car, the addition of new parts over the years had left little of her original material, but her form remained unaltered. Could she, she wondered, still be said to be the same person?

Indeed, it seemed to her now that there had been a time when *all* her emotions had been as spectacular and colourful as a firework display. She had always known she was meant to feel things. She had believed she was special, so open was she to pain and love. Or was it only that she had indulged such emotions to protect herself from any lengthy contemplation of duller things: boredom, loneliness, failure, all of the things which hovered outside the door like tax inspectors, vigilant and malign?

Sitting there, it all became horribly clear. This dullness that seemed to inhabit every corner of her spirit was nothing but the unpainted, unadorned face of reality. She had no resources herself to enliven it. She had always captured emotions and then visited them like animals at a zoo, saddened by their moulting pelts and mournful eyes. And as for love, well! Had she not once felt herself to be rich with it? Had she not once ruled her world like a queen with palaces? It angered her that John had created a version of herself which she could somehow never imitate afterwards. Try as she might to accommodate them, her subsequent lovers had stood in her life like Ming vases in a council flat.

Agnes sat slumped in her pew for some time. It seemed that she could no longer shelter in the conviction of her own sanctity. Once he had wanted her, but that didn't mean she was chosen. There was, however, she saw, a certain liberation to be found in ordinariness. Without John, without the myth of his faith in her, the cursed claim it made for her own exceptionalness, she was free to be as miserable as she liked.

Chapter Twenty-one

IN daydreams Agnes had construed her future as a career woman with elaborations which at the time had not seemed particularly fantastical: herself at the frantic centre of office life, fielding calls and making deals, jittery with caffeine and wearing a suit perhaps. The reality was at once more demanding and more pedestrian.

On Monday morning she sat alone at her desk with an interminable set of galleys for the new issue. A wet stain from a cup of coffee spilled moments before over her leg was beginning to cool, and her trousers adhered damply to the flesh of her thigh. It was eleven thirty and Greta had not yet appeared. The office was overheated, although outside the winter air was unusually damp and sticky. Agnes leafed disconsolately through the pages and grew tearful. She could sit here and weep and no one would notice. This realisation alone was enough to make her cry. Instead she stamped her foot and, in a fit of daring, brought back her hand in order to sweep the pile from the desk and send it flying, disordered, to the floor.

'Not in yet?' said Jean, putting her head round the door before Agnes could follow through her sabotaging blow.

'Not yet.' Agnes replaced her hand on the desk and suddenly found herself strangely absorbed in her work. She creased her forehead at the page in front of her and scribbled something in the margin. 'Is that hotel feature ready for layout?'

'I'm sure I don't know,' replied Jean, with the ineffable certainty of her position. She hovered in the doorway. 'When you have a moment, dear,' she continued presently, 'perhaps you could give her a little ring on the telephone. Make sure all is well.'

Jean disappeared from view, leaving Agnes to nurture feelings of resentment that Greta's failure to come to work should be met with a tender concern somewhat lacking in the admonishments she received for her own shortcomings. In the spirit of defiance she loitered over her proof-reading for a further half-hour before making the call. She was sure Greta would not be at home in any case. Her lapses tended to occur in transit. She would emerge from the grey area of hazard and adventure which was the transport system with the triumphant aspect of one who had overcome great odds and gambled with death to do so.

To Agnes's surprise, however, the phone was picked up after several rings, albeit without any of the usual pleasantries.

'Greta?' she ventured into the silence. 'Is that you?'

'Who is this?'

The voice sounded so unfamiliar that Agnes thought she must have dialled a wrong number; but while her feelings on such occasions were normally a mixture of horror and fascination as she landed with the arbitrariness of a falling meteor on the house of a complete stranger, her prevailing sense of Greta's essential oddness led her to persevere.

'It's me. Agnes. From the office,' she added stupidly.

'Oh,' said Greta (for it was indeed she), apparently enlightened by this latest addition. 'What do you want?'

'Well – nothing really. It's just that you didn't come to work and we wondered what had happened to you. We thought you might have overslept so we decided to give you a wake-up call!'

'Just leave me alone.'

Greta's voice had at least the effect of distracting Agnes from uncomfortable ruminations about her own tone of asinine plural jollity. Greta put the phone down. Agnes stared at the receiver in her hand and felt unutterably wounded. How could she speak to her like that, she who was only trying to help? As if she, Agnes, were in the wrong, sitting here alone in the office at twelve o'clock with no one to help or comfort her! Worse still, as if Agnes were not a friend or a sharer of confidences! As if she didn't have her own cross to bear on this muggy Monday morning, with Finchley Central loitering on her doorstep like a persistent beggar and a stack of work dull as a telephone directory on her desk!

The receiver in her hand began to emit an alarmist noise. She recognised within its unrelenting blare the possibility that Greta had come to some harm which she was not prepared to divulge over the telephone. She wondered what she should do. To phone again would be futile; to raise the alarm somehow presumptuous. To do nothing would assist neither of them, for she would surely not be able to concentrate on her work with such a conversation so recently in her memory? The only remaining option appeared to be an impulsive act. She must go to Greta's house herself and offer succour.

'I'm going out!' she cried, barrelling into Jean in the corridor, who wisely stood back as if from the path of a wailing ambulance.

She left the building and headed for the tube station. As if sensing her new-found command, a train came immediately. She boarded it and the crowds seemed to part like water before her, affording her a choice of seats. As the train was set in motion, Agnes felt the very tracks reverberating with her intent. Her face reflected in the window opposite looked severe but heroic, and the other passengers maintained a respectful distance. She drew herself up, ruminating upon the defence a sense of self-importance could provide against the importunate presence of the general public.

As the train rattled downhill towards Camden, however, the mysterious nature of her crusade began to nudge against her consciousness. What manner of thing could it be that had laid Greta, normally blithe and buoyant in adversity, so low? Perhaps she had received bad news from Mrs Sankowitz, her voice leaking through the interference from Saskatchewan to relay the particulars of death or destitution. Or something closer to home, a burglary or even an attempt upon her life. Perhaps she was unwell. Agnes disembarked at Camden with less composure than she had set out. What help was she, who knew so little of the world? What comfort could she offer, what unconventional wisdom, that she did not herself require? She trudged disconsolately over the lock and turned into Greta's road. Perhaps, worst of all, Greta was merely suffering from world-weariness and angst; and for that, Agnes knew, there was no cure.

She knocked softly at Greta's door, half-hoping not to be heard. Within seconds, however, the door flew open and Greta was before her. Her eyes were red and her cheeks puffy, but otherwise she seemed unharmed. She stood back to allow Agnes through.

'What do you want?' she said when they were in the sitting-room. Before Agnes could take steps to defend herself, she added: 'I've got tea, decaff, or juice.'

'What kind of juice?' said Agnes, playing for time.

'Mango.'

'I'll take tea.'

The preliminaries over with, they sat down in two facing armchairs. Greta's flat was small but light. Being on the ground floor, Agnes could observe passers-by on the pavement outside. That combined with the comfort of her chair and the steaming cup of tea could have served to make the ensuing silence quite pleasant, had Agnes not found herself becoming rather annoyed. It was her job to comfort and reassure, but she could surely not begin it until Greta had completed her own task of confessing, weeping even, and most importantly requiring her assistance. She began thinking about the more straightforward work she had left behind at the office.

'You'd better go,' said Greta. 'I'm sure you're busy.'

'Not at all,' replied Agnes politely. 'How are you, anyway?'

'Fine, fine,' mused Greta vaguely. 'The proofs are due back tomorrow and since I didn't show up there must be heaps to do.'

'Jean's taking care of it,' said Agnes, abandoning her only

means of escape. 'It's almost finished, anyway. What's wrong with you, actually?'

Greta gazed at her. She seemed to have no intention of replying. Agnes found something quite unsettling in her bearing, as if she had left her body to go through the motions while her mind hid somewhere dark and quiet.

'I've been thinking about my father,' Greta volunteered. 'Normally I don't think about him, but today he's been on my mind.'

'Oh.'

'I really hate him, you know.'

Interesting though this was, Agnes could not help but wonder nervously where it was all leading.

'Why?' she said, hoping for something specific. 'What makes you hate him?'

Greta gave an explosive snort of laughter.

'Well, what particularly?' Agnes persevered. 'I mean, why has he been on your mind?'

'Well, I was thinking about the last time he spanked me, actually,' Greta replied. 'He pulled down my pants, you know, and did it with his bare hand.'

'How old were you?' said Agnes. She couldn't think of what else to say.

'About sixteen. What a sleaze, huh?' Greta folded her arms over her chest. 'Not that it was anything unusual. It was just kind of part of the scenery in our house. He used to beat all us girls, and my brother too until he got too big to hit. The first time I remember him doing it was when my parents came back from this trip to Toronto. My dad used to go there sometimes for work and Mom would go to shop. Anyhow, they left the others in charge which was pretty dumb, seeing as they were into some weird stuff in those days. When my folks were away they could get pretty wild.'

'How old were you?' said Agnes. It sounded even less interesting second time around.

'About six, I guess. What they used to do was, they would smoke a lot of pot and then they would make me smoke some. Then they used to dress me up in funny clothes, like my sisters' lingerie, you know, suspender belts and things. Then they would put this big fat joint in my mouth and take pictures of me. Like that. Weird. Anyway, I remember my dad coming in the room and everyone stood up because they were so surprised. They didn't hear the car or anything. I was kind of lying on this sofa in this dumb underwear and I couldn't get up because I was so stoned, and he just stared at me, like stared without saying anything. Then he threw the others out and he came over to me and spanked me. You little tart, he said. Thwack.' Agnes flinched. 'That's what he called me, a little tart. I was, like, six!'

Agnes sat in silence. She wished she had never asked Greta about her father. She was unequal to such revelations. There had been a time, a while ago, when she had felt embarrassed by Greta's candour and somehow superior to it. Now, however, she felt embarrassed by her own inadequacy. Greta had shown her a secret wound, and Agnes had merely driven slowly by like a prurient motorist past a pile-up. She remembered the first night her lover had come back to her house, when they had sat on the bed exchanging pleasantries while the unspoken thrashed and flailed between them. She wondered when exactly in her life she had ceased to act, had ceased to be effective. Every time she came to the brink of another person, their borders lapping, she would draw back, afraid to jump across.

'Has something happened?' she said then, rather stiffly.

Greta nodded. Tears began to roll down her cheeks.

'I was raped!' she cried, shaking her head. 'I – he raped me!'

'Who?' said Agnes, horrified. 'Your father?'

'What? No, not him. That guy, the one – the guy I met on the tube. London Transport.'

She began to sob uncontrollably. Agnes got out of her chair and knelt awkwardly beside her.

'Do you want to talk about it?' she said. This was a line borrowed from innumerable television dramas which Agnes had hoped to pass off as her own.

'Not really,' gasped Greta, her chest heaving.

Agnes regarded her in agony of uncertainty. The television dramas had never dealt with rebuffal. She put a tentative arm around her, and felt Greta sag heavily against it.

'He came here last night,' she said thickly. 'He said he wanted to talk so I let him in. I let him in!' she cried, turning her shiny face incredulously to Agnes. 'And he wouldn't leave, so I said I was going to call the police and then he just kind of came up behind me. And there was nothing I could do. Nothing! He was really strong, you know? I didn't know people were that strong. I just – I just screamed and screamed.' A strangled laugh escaped from her throat. 'And then I hit him with that hat-stand over there. I guess I must have drawn blood. And then he left.'

Agnes felt Greta's body shake, and then realised that she herself was shaking. She felt sick to her stomach. Her heart felt strangely as if it were actually bleeding. She also felt something else, something rather like anger or disappointment; a blind, enraged surge of bitterness that the world should turn out to be so cruel and inferior a place, when all they had ever done was believe in its authority.

Down at the police station, Greta sat on a bench while Agnes attempted to attract the attention of one of the officials on duty. The station was bleak and neon-lit, and the air was heavy with misdemeanour. A man with wild nest of grey hair was striding up and down the waiting area, ranting at those who entered.

'It's black against white,' he informed Agnes. 'The forces of evil are rising up, all around! They come by night – they come by night, in the darkness, when we can't see them. They prowl through the streets!'

'Go home, then,' said Agnes curtly. 'That way you won't have to worry about it.'

The man strode off, muttering. A few minutes later, Agnes secured a policewoman and related Greta's misfortune. The woman went to make her a cup of tea. When she returned, she informed Greta that she would have to go to hospital, but that first she would have to give details of the incident. Greta assented quite cheerfully. She seemed to have recovered some of her composure.

'And then I whacked him over the head with a hat-stand,' she informed the balding policeman who was taking notes.

'A hat-stand.'

'Yeah. Victorian mahogany with these kind of curly bits at the top. Oh, yeah, and when he was leaving I yelled after him, "You bastard, you could at least have worn a condom."'

The policeman's face twitched.

'Is that all?' he said.

'Well, what did you expect me to do?' Greta demanded. 'Invite him back for goddamned elevenses?'

Finally Agnes got Greta home. She put her to bed, and stood for a moment watching her sleep. Her face was open and vulnerable. It alerted Agnes to the presence of something new in herself, something small and hard like a marble. By the time she left, it was growing dark.

Agnes was stalking the streets which once had stalked her. The elegant Georgian façades of Camden, which by day showed daring glimpses of adventurous curtain and flashes of brave scrubbed pine, by night glimmered palely behind shutters in streets which now seemed empty and afraid. Another city had taken charge, crawling down from trees and out of sewers, roosting in doorways among overstuffed garbage bags and trawling the littered pavements of the high street like antithetical shoppers. It was doubtlessly the latter's aspect of ownership which nightly sent the management scuttling back to their terraces to ponder the insuperables of social injustice over dinner and wine, and there were many occasions on which Agnes would have joined them. For tonight, however her loyalties lay with those whose hearts were hard. They were not emasculated, as she had been, by sympathy. Their cold nights and hungry days had lent them a certain menace. She had seen their misery eulogised in various artistic black and white photographs, a Brueghel glow of quirky despair in their faces as their souls shone beneath the skin for want of better lodging. Well, tonight she too lived in her own skin, homeless. Tonight she was a predator, sly as a guttersnipe.

She reached the lock and paused on the bridge for a moment looking out over the canal. The water looked dark and thick as blood. There was no moon overhead and the sky was black, like an empty space. A car passed behind her and someone shouted, 'Don't jump!' through the window as it sped away. People were so careless with one another, she thought as she turned and continued walking. They should be taught a lesson, and who better to teach it than they, the underclass, those who had been wronged?

A man walked past her on the pavement. He had been eyeing her uncertainly as he approached, as if trying to discern whether she was an object of admiration or studied avoidance. It was a look she had been getting a lot lately. Her signals had been growing dimmer and harder to read. She stared at him rudely, which at least had the effect of resolving his own dilemma. He looked away and dug his hands in his pockets.

'Hi, sexy!' she said loudly as he walked by her.

She heard him stop on the pavement behind her. She could feel his shock without even looking back at him.

'*What?*' he said, as if to himself.

She walked on unperturbed and eventually heard his diminishing footfalls as he walked away. Agnes smiled to herself. Weakness, she thought then, was, after all, nothing more than fear. Strength, consequently, must be becoming that which you feared. She began to laugh. Soon she was laughing so hard that she had to sit down in a doorway and clutch at her sides.

'Keep laughing, love. They say it stops ye crying. That's what they say, eh?' said a woman next to her.

'I suppose so,' replied Agnes, getting a grip on herself. She had thought she was alone.

'What's so bloody funny anyway?' said the woman.

She had a high-pitched voice and a Scottish accent. She was so tiny that Agnes would have mistaken her for a child had she not already seen the handbag face clenched tight as a withered fist. She wore a red coat and was sitting with her knees drawn up and her feet in a plastic bag.

'Tell us, Miss Tee-Hee, what's the joke?'

'Oh, it's only an old joke,' said Agnes. 'The one about the man and the woman. It's not really very funny.'

'La-de-da! Well, tell us it anyway, hen. I could do with a laugh.'

Agnes began to make something up. She had never been very good at telling jokes. Halfway through her rambling narrative, the woman began to cough. Her whole frame shook with the effort of trying to contain the bronchitic explosions within her bony chest. Presently the attack receded and she leaned back against the wall.

'Ha' ye got a cigarette for me, hen?' she whispered, peering up at Agnes with chastened watery eyes.

'No,' said Agnes. 'I could buy you some if you like, but I don't think they'd make you feel any better.'

The woman closed her eyes and leaned against her. She appeared to be asleep. Through her coat Agnes could feel she was as brittle as a bird. Her breath rattled and wheezed its way out of her pursed lips. A few minutes later she awoke.

'I'll tell you a secret, hen,' she said. Her face brightened. 'I'll tell you something no one else knows. Can I trust ye? Can I?'

'Of course.'

'Look at tha'!' The woman thrust out a skinny arm from within the folds of her coat, her spidery hand fluttering as she turned her arm about for Agnes to see. 'What d'ye make of tha'?'

'It's very thin,' ventured Agnes.

'Well, I can see tha'! You don't need glasses to see tha'.' She clenched up her face and nodded. 'I'm just bones, me. I don't need you to tell me tha'.'

'Sorry,' said Agnes.

'What's sorry? I'm the one should be sorry.' Her eyes closed again and she swayed unsteadily back and forth. 'Ha bloody ha. Tee-hee-hee. What's so bloody funny anyway? Eh?'

'Nothing. I'm not laughing.'

'I'll tell ye something.' Her eyes snapped open. 'I'm dying, that's what. Nae much more o' this for me.' She laughed a little and began to hum 'It's a Long Way to Tipperary'. 'No more Leicester Square for me. Goodbye to the high life.'

'Are you sure?' said Agnes.

'Course I am! Who else would be, eh? Am I sure, she says. Did ye nae look at this arm?' Her mouth chewed drily on air. *'It's a long way—'*

'Is there anything I can do? Would you like me to take you to the hospital or – or maybe you have someone I could call?'

The woman stopped singing and scrutinised her closely.

'Good thing my Jacky's not here,' she said firmly, nodding her head.

'Who's Jacky? Is she a friend? Maybe we should call her.'

Another seizure, however, prevented the woman from replying. She shook silently. When she raised her head, Agnes saw that in fact she was laughing.

'Ay,' she gasped. 'Good thing Jacky's away. Aye, it's a good thing.'

'Who is Jacky?'

'He's my boy, hen. Who else but my lovely boy? "Is she a friend?" ' she mimicked. 'Good thing Jacky did nae hear tha' – he's a great big thing, that he is.'

'Well, where is he?'

'He'd want to be here, though. Pretty thing like yourself, ye'd have your hands full.' She laughed, rocking herself.

'Why isn't he helping you?' she burst out.

'Aye, you'd not get a moment's peace. That's a fact, that is.' She closed her eyes and leaned back. 'I believe it's my bedtime.'

'Where are you going to sleep? You can come and stay at my house if you like. We can take the tube. It's not that far.'

She opened her eyes.

'Have ye got any clothes?'

'Yes, of course. I can give you some.'

'It's a bit worn.' She plucked at the sleeve of her coat. 'That it is. A bit worn. But it's a lovely red. A lovely colour, that red. Just ask for Annie and they'll tell ye where to find me. Ask anyone here.' She indicated the barren sweep of the dark high street.

'But what about tonight?'

'I've got me bed right here.'

She patted the doorstep and closed her eyes. Agnes removed a note from her wallet and crumpled it into the tiny fist. As she did so, the eyes opened.

'Dunnae forget,' she said. 'Just ask for Annie. Ye can put them in a bag and ask for Annie.'

'I won't forget. It was nice to meet you.'

'The pleasure's all mine, I'm sure,' said Annie demurely.

Agnes got up. She had other business to attend to. As she turned to leave the thin arm scuttled out from beneath the coat and grabbed her hand.

'Dunnae forget,' she said. 'Or I'll haunt ye. I will. I'll haunt ye.'

In the tube station everyone was transient except the transients, who hovered by the barriers like vultures waiting to swoop. The escalator trundled around like a mobile tongue disgorging diminishing gobs of passengers out into the cold night. It was getting late. People wrapped their coats around them and eyed those in the foyer suspiciously. They hurried out to the street, anxious suddenly to be home.

Agnes did not look at them as they passed. She was looking instead at the two guards who were hanging around the wooden booth by the ticket barrier. One of them spat at the wall. The other one had his hands in his pockets and was whistling.

'Oi, Wayne,' said the one who had spat. 'What do you reckon to this lot, then?'

He nodded in Agnes's direction. She felt sure Greta's assailant hadn't been called Wayne.

'Dunno, mate,' said Wayne. He grinned nastily. 'We could send 'em down the tunnels for the night, I suppose. They won't know they're living.'

Wayne's mate found this hypothesis hilarious and guffawed loudly. One or two of the tramps by the door sidled surreptitiously out into the street.

An attractive woman emerged from the escalator, and both guards followed her with their eyes as she passed through the barriers.

'I could fancy that,' said Wayne's mate. 'Fancy a bit of rough, my dear?' he yelled after her in a plummy voice.

The girl passed close to Agnes as she left the station. Her face was burning. Back inside, the guards had forgotten her already and were laughing about something else. Scum, Agnes thought. Absolute scum. She wanted to run after the girl and offer her something: friendship, loyalty, invisibility, whatever she wanted. We should stick together, she would say. She would tell her about Annie. That was what happened to you in the end. You had to stick together.

More people hurried through the barriers. Agnes craned her neck to see beyond them. She wanted to get a better look at Wayne's mate.

'Last train!' he shouted just then. 'Ten minutes till the last train!'

He turned his back and leaned against the booth. Agnes looked at her watch. She had not realised it was so late. She would have to come back tomorrow. The tramps began pulling blankets out of plastic bags and unfurling them against the wall at the back of the station. They were bedding down, and would remain there till morning if Wayne's mate did not succeed in luring them to the tunnels. Agnes knew she had to go home. She had no choice, any more than they did. It was who she was. Even so, with the alternatives lined up against the wall like convicts, she was fascinated by the opportunity of change. She could lose it all just by doing nothing. Just by staying here, she could become someone else. There would be a certain freedom in having nothing. The possibilities were endless.

She went over to the ticket machine and got out her purse. It was empty. She had given the last of her money to Annie. A knot of panic began to grow in her stomach. It was all right, she could go back to Greta's house and maybe spend the night there. It was several seconds before she remembered telling Greta not to answer the phone or the doorbell. She could phone home and ask Merlin to meet her at the door to pay for a taxi. That was the answer. She found a telephone and reversed the charges. There was nobody at home. Agnes stood in the cold neon-lit station and felt a wave of desperation rise up in her throat. A middle-aged man in a camel-hair coat was coming through the ticket barriers.

'Excuse me,' she said politely, approaching him. 'I'm trying to get home and I don't seem to have any money. I wonder if you could help me.'

He hesitated momentarily, surprised. She could see him trying to work her out. He looked away and walked past her. The outrage! She stared after him, dumbfounded. As if it wasn't obvious what kind of person she was! She caught her reflection dimly in one of the steel plates fixed to the wall and was surprised. She looked scruffy and old. It had been a long day. A woman came off the escalator and approached the barriers. Agnes felt her heart swell with relief. She looked kind and would surely be sympathetic.

'Excuse me—' she began, before remembering how far this approach had got her last time. The woman had stopped and was looking at her expectantly. 'Can you spare me some change?' Agnes blurted out.

The woman immediately looked embarrassed. She sighed and put a hand in her pocket.

'Oh, all right,' she said, holding out a ten-pence piece. 'Although why you people can't get jobs like everyone else escapes me.'

She clicked smartly off before Agnes had time to respond.

So much for change, she thought. Ten pence indeed. Wayne's mate had been observing her progress and now sauntered over to the ticket barrier.

'Oi, you,' he said. 'Clear off.'

Agnes looked at him with barely disguised distaste. The badge on his lapel read 'Kevin'.

'Kevin!' she said. 'I might have guessed. How incredibly original.'

A man was approaching from the escalator. He was about her age. He looked like he might understand.

'I said clear off, you old tart!' said Kevin.

'I assure you,' Agnes replied, 'there is nothing I would like better. But first I must draw your attention to a certain matter.' She smiled winningly and pointed at his trousers. 'Your flies are undone.'

As he looked down, she walked over to the man and stood purposefully in front of him.

'Excuse me,' she began.

He looked at her and her heart almost stopped. It was John. His hair a bit longer, perhaps, his clothes different. Something was pounding in her chest.

'Can I help you?' he said presently.

Agnes felt faint. He didn't recognise her, then. She stared at him in silence.

'Do you need money?' he said. He delved into a pocket and took out some coins. 'There. I hope that helps.'

He smiled at her and began walking away. Agnes looked in her hand. He had given her two pounds.

'Thank you,' she said.

He stopped and turned around. He looked almost ashamed.

'It's the least I can do,' he said.

Chapter Twenty-two

AGNES sat at the wooden table in the kitchen of her family home. It was late evening. Outside, against the dark sky, the darker shadows of bats swooped and spun like falling leaves. Agnes's mother, bare-faced and dressing-gowned, made tea with the air of one rallying round.

'It's funny that you're here,' she said presently. Agnes did not attempt to deny it. 'Tom's coming home tomorrow. You must have smelled trouble with your sixth sense. You always were good at that.'

'What on earth do you mean?' said Agnes, aiming for a specific rather than a general explanation of her parent's meaning. 'What sort of trouble? What's happened?'

The house had seemed quiet and strangely unfamiliar when she arrived. They hadn't been expecting her, and their unpreparedness made her feel as if she had happened unawares upon a secret behind-the-scenes existence; like a restaurant in the early morning, the chairs on tables, the smell of disinfectant, someone pushing a mop around perhaps.

'He's lost his job,' said her mother. 'They told him a few days ago. For some reason, I thought he'd have told you himself.'

She looked rather flushed with the unexpected responsibility of relaying information of such newsworthiness.

'Lost his job?' Agnes was incredulous. 'But – but how could he? How?'

'He didn't just drop it in the street, dear. There is a recession on, after all.'

Agnes's mother had grown up during the war, and found the vocabulary of that harrowing period indelibly fixed in her memory.

'Poor Tom. I wonder what he'll do. God, it seems so unfair.'

'Life is unfair!' replied her mother rather shrilly. 'We've always tried to protect you children from disappointment, but I'm afraid we just can't any more. You have to find out for yourselves what it's like. Your father and I can't pick up the pieces whenever things go wrong, you know!' She went to the sink and turned on a tap. 'We're too old.'

She began washing up a teapot. Agnes stared at her dumbfounded.

'You're not old,' she said. 'And besides, no one's asking you to pick up the pieces.' She thought of adding 'don't be so melodramatic' for old times' sake, but decided against it.

'Aren't they?' sighed her mother. She dried the teapot with a towel which Agnes recognised as one she used to take to the swimming-pool. 'Well, I don't know, in that case. I really don't,' she insisted. 'First Tom calls up in a state. Then you arrive on our doorstep looking like death warmed up with heaven knows what problems. What are we expected to do? It's hard to – to readjust to all this.'

Agnes found this speech rather wounding. While in moments of happiness and high confidence she would not have minded in the least her mother's retirement from parental services, and indeed would probably have actively encouraged her liberation, her current state of despondency cast a somewhat different light on things. She did not want to hear that her primal protector had been replaced by someone offering tea and limited sympathy. It was not a fair exchange.

'Well, what did you expect?' she said crossly. 'Did you think we'd both be safely ensconced in nice country houses by now having babies?'

'*I* was,' her mother replied; somewhat cruelly, Agnes thought.

'Well, I'm sorry we can't all be like you, then. The fact is, we can't just stop being your children.' Such logic, if nothing else, was certainly a throw-back to the old days. 'You'd hate it if we didn't run to you with all our problems, Mother,' she continued with a semblance of maturity. 'You know you would.'

Her mother smiled wanly and sat down at the table.

'Yes, you're probably right. But I must say, it makes a pleasant change to have the temper tantrums oneself occasionally.'

'That was nothing,' Agnes returned. 'You missed out the bit about not asking to be born.'

She grinned edgily. The times when she had sought exemption, immunity – perhaps even grace! – with such claims to innocence were still too fresh in her memory to regard with more than passing irony.

They had to collect Tom from the local station because his company car had been rescinded. Such seizures made Agnes fearful of the brutal arena of office politics. As they swung round the corner to find Tom sitting forlornly on his suitcase in the deserted forecourt, Agnes saw in his destitution evidence of a cruelty she had long suspected lurked behind the civilised façade of corporate life. He had ceased to please them, and they had ejected him from their circle without a thought to loyalty or love. One had to watch one's back these days, she reminded herself. There were a lot of funny people about.

The car stopped and positions were shifted by silent consensus. Agnes's father vacated the driver's seat and removed to the back, where Agnes soon joined him from her earlier place in the front passenger seat, now occupied by her mother. Tom, afforded the rare opportunity to assert himself unchallenged in the family hierarchy behind the driving wheel, now however chose this moment to demur.

'Come on, Dad,' he said. 'You can't sit in the back seat like someone's old granny. You drive.'

'Not at all,' declined their father politely. 'I'm quite happy being chauffeured about. I've got Agnes here to keep me company. You sit up there with your mother.'

'Oh, all right,' grumbled Tom, getting in. 'But I hope you realise this is playing havoc with my masculine role-models.'

Agnes was becoming increasingly aware that her father was happy to take the back seat not just in the most literal of senses. She looked at him as the car pulled out on to the road, and saw in the harsh daylight that his hair had now turned completely white.

'Dad, you're so old!' she almost said; but managed 'I'm so cold!' instead.

'No stamina,' he replied, fumbling about behind him for a rug. 'There, that should fix it.'

He had, she saw, long since substituted kindness for authority. Leaning against him with the gentle pull of the car, her mother's grey head bobbing serenely in front of her, Agnes saw in the cycles of all their ageing new evidence of compatibility. They too, she realised, had once been children. They didn't ask to be born either.

'Shall we have a fire?' said Agnes's mother when they got home. The wind had grown fiercer overnight and was whining over the sill of the door and round the window-panes.

'Good idea,' said her father. 'I'll chop some wood.' He waited hopefully for someone to relieve him of the burden of his offer. 'Unless Tom feels like hefting an axe,' he added, when no one did.

'Do I have to?' said Tom, whose masculine role-models were evidently once more intact.

Agnes offered to assist him, and the two of them made their way out to the old shed where their father had used to breed rabbits. Their community had long since become extinct, and the ruins of old hutches were stacked against one wall to make room for the woodpile, which, Agnes's father had found, required less upkeep and could be consumed without undue sentiment.

The shed smelt mouldy and dank. It was a country smell, strong and not altogether unpleasant. It summoned equally strong memories. She could not recall having smelt anything so pungent in her years away from home. The odour gave her a strange sense of those years being effortlessly wiped away. The life she had left behind only yesterday seemed already indistinct.

'This won't be enough,' said Tom, examining the small pieces he had gathered from the floor of the shed and thrown into the large basket they had brought with them.

He picked up an axe and began chopping more wood. The pieces cleaved cleanly from the gnarled blocks, as if they had always had within them the seeds of separateness. A fresh smell of pencil shavings wafted through the shed.

'Can I have a go?' said Agnes.

'Okay.' Tom looked at her doubtfully. 'Be careful, though. You could cut yourself. It's sharp.'

Agnes reined in a remark concerning the contrasting bluntness of his views on gender stereotypes.

'Put your hands lower down,' said Tom, observing her critically. 'No, not like that. You have to bring it down harder. Put your foot on it, woman. That way it doesn't roll.'

She hefted the axe and brought it down on the block of wood. It split into two with a sharp crack.

'Bull's-eye!' she said gleefully.

'Now cut those into two. They're too big.'

'They are not! Leave them alone. They're perfect.'

'They're too bloody big.' Tom sat down on the woodpile. 'Go on, let's see you do it again.'

'Okay.' Agnes raised the axe above her head. 'Watch this.'

The block of wood toppled over on impact and was sent spinning away to the other side of the shed. Tom began clapping sarcastically.

'Shut up!' Agnes went to retrieve it. 'I was just practising.'

Her next blow was more successful. She threw the logs in the basket and picked up another block. She had begun to work up quite a sweat.

'Let's have a go,' said Tom.

'No.' Agnes wielded the axe. 'I'm enjoying myself. Besides, I'm armed and dangerous.'

'It was only a matter of time,' mumbled Tom.

They picked up the basket and carried it by the handles back to the house.

'I did more than you,' said Agnes.

'Well, that's not my fault. You wouldn't let me do any. Anyway, mine are better than yours.'

'They are not!'

'They bloody well are. Mine are art.'

They staggered into the kitchen and put down the basket.

'Oh, well done,' said their mother, beaming at her united offspring hopefully. 'So, did you have a nice chat?'

'Agnes is too macho to chat.'

'Tom's a male supremacist. He couldn't chat to a woman unless she was gagged and tied to a chair.'

'Really, Agnes! Do you have to be so vulgar?'

'Who's vulgar?' inquired their father, looking up from the paper.

'Never mind, Alex.'

'I must say, I do object to what they show on the television. I can hardly understand what they're saying these days. All they seem to do is jump in and out of bed, as if that was all anybody did!'

'Lunch is ready,' said their mother firmly.

'How's your love life, Agnes?' persisted her father; a question he had put with increasing frequency over the years, as he realised that something in his general bearing safeguarded him from receiving any kind of detailed answer.

'I don't have a love life, Dad. I'm too busy.'

'She has a kind of love time-share,' interjected Tom.

'Besides,' Agnes confessed, 'there's no one around these days – no one that I like, anyway.'

'Don't know what's got into chaps these days,' said her father. 'Pretty girl like you. In my day they would have been queuing up at your door. These days they queue up for social security.'

There was a moment's silence in honour of the death of romantic England.

'I can't think why they call it security,' opined her mother, putting dishes on the table. 'Tom feels very insecure without a job, don't you, dear?'

Agnes and Tom glanced at each other across the table. Tom raised one eyebrow and began passing plates around in silence. A few minutes later, however, a loud guffaw escaped from their father's lips. He leaned over and patted his wife's arm fondly.

'That was very good, dear,' he said. 'Very good.'

'They're both completely bonkers,' said Tom. He turned around and looked at the house, from which they had just emerged to go for a walk. 'Good thing they live out here, at any rate.'

'What do you mean?' said Agnes.

'Well, if they lived anywhere else they'd probably have been locked up by now. I suppose it's one of the privileges of wealth. You can go nuts in your own secluded home.'

Agnes thought she detected something untoward in his tone, as if he meant it seriously. She did not respond. They were approaching the very spot where they had argued several weeks before, the ill-feeling of which occasion was still fresh enough in her memory to make her not want to resuscitate it.

'So what's wrong with you?' said Tom suddenly.

'Nothing.' Agnes opened the small gate at the bottom of their garden and strode out into the field beyond. 'Why do you ask?'

'Dunno. I just thought you only came home when you had something to moan about.'

'You should know by now,' retorted Agnes, becoming riled, 'that I like to have the occasional luxury break from my spartan socialist existence. And I really don't see why you're trying to wind me up.'

Agnes delivered this speech with the dawning consciousness that Tom was, rather than attempting to detect dark motives for her own presence here, probably merely trying subtly to illuminate a conversational path towards his own. He had just lost his job, for goodness' sake, thought Agnes. She resolved to be more patient.

'I wasn't,' said Tom. 'It's just the truth, that's all.'

'Look, just because you've got a bloody axe to grind about getting the sack doesn't give you the right to have a go at me! Much good your conservative claptrap has done you now. You can take your stupid principles and flog them for pin money for all I care. You're going to need it, as I assume you won't be accepting help from the welfare state!'

To her surprise, Tom flopped down on the grass and started laughing. The dogs lumbered over and began mournfully to lick his face.

'I thought you were supposed to be depressed,' snapped Agnes.

Tom tickled the dogs' bellies.

'Whatever gave you that idea?' he said. 'I'm not depressed at all.' He shut his eyes and crinkled up his face towards the sky as if it were sun-filled rather than a cloudy iron-grey. 'I feel – I feel free!'

'What do you mean?' said Agnes. For one so recently initiated into the working world, such claims to liberation outside it were hard to bear.

'Well, it's not exactly living, is it?' Tom stretched languorously. 'Cooped up in an office all day long with people you don't really like. At someone else's beck and call from morning till night. And what's it all for?'

He sat up and glared expectantly at Agnes, who found herself without a reply immediately to hand.

'Money,' he revealed finally.

'Well, of course it is,' she replied. 'What else did you think it would be for?'

'But don't you see?' cried Tom exasperatedly. 'It doesn't mean anything! There's no meaning!'

Agnes stared at him.

'Look,' he continued. 'I've spent most of my life thinking that it didn't really matter what happened to the rest of the

world as long as I was all right. And I thought I was all right!
But now I realise I was just – half-asleep, dreaming, and now
I've woken up and really started to see things. I was living a
lie, but I was so involved in it I thought it was the truth. My
life was a kind of imprisonment, Agnes. I've set myself free.'

'You didn't exactly have much choice,' Agnes reminded
him. 'You were sacked, after all.'

'Yes!' said Tom. 'Being sacked was just the beginning. It
was like a sign. It opened my eyes!'

'A sign,' said Agnes.

'And shall I tell you what I see? I see that the world is
dying, destroying itself with greed. All my life I've taken,
without a thought to the consequences. So, now I reckon it's
time for me to give something back!'

'You're going to save the world?' said Agnes. 'Well, thank
heavens for that. We were all getting a bit worried there.
Good thing you had a change of heart.'

'I understand it might take time for you to get used to it,'
said Tom. 'After all, I used to give you a pretty hard time
about things like this. But I hope that sooner or later you'll
be pleased. I remember something you said to me, last time
we were home. It's kept coming back to me the last few days.
You said something about my making money out of other
people's misfortune. I'll never forget that. That's what started
me thinking. I thought, is that really what I want to do? When
I die, do I want people to say, Oh, Tom, yes, of course, he
made his money screwing people who'd already screwed up
their own lives. It was the way you said it, you make it sound
so – so *evil*. Making money out of other people's misfortune.'

'I was probably just jealous,' said Agnes. 'I couldn't make
money out of my own misfortune, let alone anyone else's.'

'But I admire that, Agnes. You do your job for the love of
it. That takes character, and guts.'

'So what exactly are you going to do?' inquired Agnes,
moving hastily on from this undeserved eulogy. It disturbed
her even more than his plans for global salvation, although
she was reassured by her certainty that Tom's creative views

on unemployment would evaporate with the first whiff of a lucrative job opportunity.

'I thought I might try and find something in conservation, actually,' he replied. 'There's these companies which are like environmental hired guns. They keep an eye on industry and big business. I know the field, so I thought I may as well put it to good use. I've been writing letters.'

'Do you mean to say you're serious about this?'

'Of course I am.' He looked surprised. 'I thought you'd be pleased. You've certainly changed your tune these days.'

He got up and began brushing grass from his trousers. Agnes suddenly became aware of how cold it was. She rose from the hard November ground and followed him slowly back to the house.

Agnes went up to her room that night to find her mother sitting on the bed.

'I brought you up a blanket,' she said as Agnes appeared in the doorway. 'It seemed rather cold.'

Agnes sat down beside her on the bed and waited to be afforded the real purpose of her visit. She knew her mother to be no handmaiden of domestic drudgery. She was not a bringer of blankets or provider of packed lunches. While this deficiency had certainly been a source of grief in the past, when Agnes had seen the dotingly cut sandwiches and fond crisp-packets of others of proof of a somehow superior love, these days she would not have suffered being the progeny of an unpaid servant. Now she would rather see herself descended from a harbourer of ulterior motives.

'How did you find Tom?' asked her mother. Years of suffering at the hands of over-smart children had not apparently taught her to avoid questions which could beg such precocious answers as 'I just looked up and there he was.'

'Oh, Tom's fine,' Agnes replied bitterly. 'Tom's found the meaning of life. Apparently it has to do with shooting people who drop litter.'

She waited for the torrent of uncomprehending concern which her over-literal reply would undoubtedly provoke. She did not want to talk about Tom. She did not want to discuss the worrying proclivities of others. Right now, she wanted to be warm and hidden, nursed and held like something precious; taken back inside the body beside her, for example, to float and hum wordlessly. For a while, her mother said nothing.

'What about you?' she volunteered presently. 'You don't seem quite yourself, if you don't mind my saying so. Is there anything wrong?'

'Everything!' burst out Agnes, who had not really thought anything was. 'Everything's wrong! I hate myself! I hate my life, I do!'

She began noisily to cry. Her mother, although slightly taken aback by this outburst, nevertheless held out her arms and enfolded Agnes within them. Agnes howled. Soon she had clambered on to her mother's lap, still weeping, and the two of them effected an embrace which their various ages and sizes might have rended improbable.

'There, there,' soothed her mother. 'Now what's this all about, hmm? What's it all about? Agnes, dear, you may have to get off my lap. It's a bit of a strain on my silly old knees. You know what they're like in cold weather.'

This instruction precipitated a fresh overture of grief.

'I'm too big!' Agnes cried.

'Oh, really, darling!' sighed her mother. 'I agree you are a bit plumper, but it's just my arthritis. There's absolutely no need to take it personally.'

'No, not like that!' Agnes hid her face in her mother's arm. 'I want to be a child again. I don't know what's wrong with me. I just want to be small and have someone protect me and look after me!'

'Well, we all feel like that,' said her mother firmly.

'Do we?' Agnes peered at her through watery eyes.

'Of course. Life can be very frightening sometimes, darling. Everyone finds it so, no matter what impression they might give to the contrary. Of course we all want to be children again. Why do you think people love routine and security so much? It makes them feel safe. It reminds them of when they were children. But it's most important to take life by the horns and not let it push you around. Things will come right in the end.'

'But when is the end?' Agnes wiped her nose on the back of her hand. 'I mean, what's to say things have to come right? I always believed there would be a point where I would definitely know if I was happy – when I would become myself, if you see what I mean, instead of just impersonating what I thought I should be. And now I feel as if I've suddenly woken up and things have gone by without me seeing them. They've just gone by in the night!'

'That's life,' nodded her mother uncertainly.

'But there must be more!' she cried. 'There must be more to this than *life*. There must be a point where things are infinite – where something is just infinitely sad, or where you've definitely failed, and who's to say things will get better? Why should we be so sure of life, if we don't even know what it is? Half of us are afraid to live, the other half are afraid to die! You're right, we're like children – we think we have to come top at life. But what happens if we just fail? Do we get expelled? Do we have to do detention?'

'I felt as if I'd failed,' interjected her mother, evidently recognising something of her own in the jumble of her daughter's philosophical yard-sale. 'When I had my miscarriage, before you were born, I felt as if I'd failed dreadfully.'

'Did you?' said Agnes, her tirade ambushed by the arrival of incontrovertable fact. 'Why?'

Her mother's face bore within its lines the imprint of other times, of feelings mapped out and revisited secretly, perhaps, by night. She was suddenly aware that she wanted her mother to have cared deeply, to have darkly nurtured a private grief. It might change things, like a magic trick. She would become a stranger with wounds. She might be able to shed new light on the situation.

'We wanted that baby so much, you see. That little girl.

It's like that, you invest them with personality.' She hugged her arms around herself. 'It used to amaze me, feeling her move about. I would think, this tiny creature needs me like no one else does. You'll know when it happens to you, it's an extraordinary kind of love in those first months. So when she died I felt unimaginably guilty. She was so tiny and vulnerable and there was nothing I could do to help her. It seems ridiculous now, but I really blamed myself.'

'But it wasn't your fault!' said Agnes.

'That's what I mean, dear. Things rarely are. And what I've been trying to say to you is that you have to go on, because as much as life knocks you down, really life is the only thing that can pick you up again. I couldn't have known it then, but now I think, well, if that hadn't happened, there wouldn't have been room for Agnes. It all turned out for the best, because here you are.'

Agnes knew her debts were being called in. She could not but read an element of accusation in the tale. Things – indeed, whole lives! – had been sacrificed to bring her here, and what was she doing but criticising everything in sight? One could take nothing for granted. Even the ambiguous gift of her birth depended upon a miscarriage of justice. Her mother patted her hand comfortingly. Agnes felt as if she had drifted off to sleep halfway through a film, and had jolted back to consciousness, bleary-eyed, to find the plot had lurched forward and the characters taken on an unsettling air of mystery.

In the village churchyard, headstones jutted unevenly out of overgrown winter grass like mouldering, superfluous teeth. Agnes examined a few empty plots in the diffident manner of one comparing hotel rooms, noting their situation and aspect. One had to make provision for the future.

Perusing some of the grimier tablets, she found that they dated back as far as a hundred years or more. She wondered if anyone visited them now: people in bright tracksuits and shiny cars proudly displaying their ancestors to indifferent children, as if forbearance were something unusual. She lingered, sharing their silence. Patience was probably *de rigueur* for those under ground.

'In Memory of Our Son Mark,' read a newer one. 'Who Died at the Age of Twenty-One.' The implied tragedy drew her like a tabloid headline. Who was this Mark, cut down in his prime? Agnes leaned closer to examine the inscription. He had left loving memories, apparently; all his ends tied, his bills paid, his laundry clean and folded. What had he known to make him so prepared, leaving the neat equation of himself to be applied later to the incomprehensible fact of his absence? She could see them using it, those who had known him, figuring out the arithmetic of his imaginary life. Mark would be twenty-three by now, for instance; by now, Mark would perhaps be getting his first job; now Mark would say this and do that.

It couldn't have been easy for him, remembering his future as well as his past. She herself would have botched the job, with the muddled, sprawling sum of her parts. If, for example, a piece of masonry from the church's crumbling roof were now to fall upon her, her disappearance would leave an uncertain taste in the mouth. They would find dirty underwear, rent demands, unfinished arguments. People would come to the door asking for that ten pounds they had lent her, that apology she never gave, that explanation for herself she had promised. Things would come up. Her parents would grow terse and resentful. She would boil beneath their surface, spoiling things. Before long, her death would begin to lend life a guilty ease. There would be more room in the car. They could watch what they liked on television. Eventually they would murder the memory of her, scratching the uncomfortable itch of her lingering absence. Mark was unscratchable, it seemed; a bunch of burning nerve ends projecting himself like an amputated leg. He was good at it. She was half in love with him already.

Agnes ambled around the hard, mud-rutted path to the door of the church. It looked shut. She had used to go in sometimes when she was a child, loving its sanctuary, the dark womb and whale-belly. She loved its mouldy smell and dank air. It was the smell of history. It told her there had been other times; that these times, too, would pass. Now she was unsure about things. She wondered if it had a door policy, or opening hours, like a pub. She leaned on the weatherbeaten wooden slab, and found that it opened easily.

Inside, the church was cold and empty, and seemed somehow frozen in an attitude of suspended action; as if, a moment before, the wooden pews had been jiggling in the aisles, the candlesticks hopping on the altar, the stained-glass saints quaffing communion wine. There was about it an aspect of unsupervision which should have provoked anarchy.

Agnes's feet echoed on the stone slabs of the floor as she approached the altar. It was covered with a cloth like something in a morgue. Before, when she was younger, she had come here to pray; or to complain, rather, presenting a list of woes and requests to the management as if there were some kind of democratic machinery in place to deal with them. Compensation! She had wanted compensation for daily disappointments and injustices. She had believed justice would be done! Agnes almost laughed aloud at the very thought of it. She would never have guessed that growing older was merely the process through which certainties became doubts. The grey areas grew larger, more amorphous. It showed around the eyes and over the hips: a gradual yielding to disappointment, a comfortable acceptance of pain. One acquired a glazed look. Indeed, had she not begun to see in herself the re-routed wires of fear, the concealed pipes and drains of desolation? She had hovered over bottles of shampoo in supermarkets, not knowing which one to buy, something fluttering in her eye like a tic, like an absence of want, like a malfunction of greed; wondered why she didn't know, why she couldn't choose, what else there could be if this wasn't important!

At moments like these something seemed to open up vastly beneath her and she would lurch, gasping, towards its vacancy. Once, ages ago, Merlin had said that he thought she was lucky to have been born into a ready-made set of religious beliefs. This had, he claimed, imbued her from childhood with an instinctive relation to the Other, which others spent lifetimes trying to achieve. At the time she had sneered at his Otherisms; she knew the grandees of her creed by name, had its hierarchies graven upon her heart. That particularly nasty strain of belief that was mysticism, to which she assumed he was referring when he spoke of the wasted lifetimes of the agnostic world, had nothing whatsoever to do with her own high-pedigree catechism; and appeared to her to consist mainly of the desire to explain phenomena such as spectral activity, telepathy and alien spacecraft.

Now, however, she too was beginning to detect something querulous within herself; doubtful yearnings which could not, it seemed, be answered by her story-book religion with its sacraments and sacrifices. The sun came out behind the stained-glass windows, illuminating their peopled mosaic with colour as if through chromatic aberration. She needed something bigger, less constricting, something more applicable to the modern world, of which, after all, she was a part. She gazed at the bright pieces of glass. Their colours were luminous, gorgeous lozenges with dark rheumatic joints. She found herself becoming so hypnotised by them that she could no longer see the figures which arose out of their union. They floated blurrily in and out of her field of vision, quaint and heraldic: the glass ghosts of a divine fiction, a land neither dead nor living; a whole world of human hope caught worshipping the sun.

The visitors' book had been there ever since she could remember. She flicked through it, reading the comments. 'V. Good', someone had written, as though marking an essay. Others picked up adjectives and passed them on like an unimaginative virus: 'lovely and peaceful'; 'peaceful and beautiful'; 'beautiful and quiet'; 'quiet and lovely'. She turned back to the comments which predated this verbal epidemic. Most of them were from children, gleefully seizing the rare opportunity to give their small opinions. 'A good place to sit and think', wrote Tim, aged five. Agnes wondered what a five-year-old had to think about. She went to the beginning of the book, where the writing, dated from 1975, had begun to fade. Her eye lighted on one childish script. 'It's good to quietly hide', it read. She looked along the line for the name of this splitter of infinitives, this timorous asylum-seeker, this petrified wisp who saw so little in the world to reassure her. Agnes Day, aged six and a half.

As she walked home, Agnes passed a tree which had been struck by lightning. Its demise was not recent. In fact, Agnes had never known it to be any other way. She and Tom had used to play there, climbing up into its truncated top where there had formed a high, hollowed dish lined with soft moss. It had stumpy arms which the climber could easily grasp, scorched smooth with few scratchy twigs. They had delighted in its useful deformity and would spend hours there while the wheat-fields planed flatly around them to the horizon, muddy-brown and stark in winter, waving golden in summer.

Agnes jumped over the small ditch beside the road and began to climb the tree. It was much easier than she remembered. In less than a minute she was at the top of the crippled trunk. She heaved herself over the side and sat down in the bowl of its distended open neck. Almost immediately she was suffused with warmth. It had always been mysteriously warm in that tree, she remembered. This was probably owing to the shelter it provided against the biting East Anglian winds, but Agnes and Tom had entertained the theory that the fire which smote it still coursed, ghost-like, around its blackened remains.

She drew up her knees and hugged them against her chest, rocking back and forth. In such historic locations, one could allow the years to roll back unabated. She thought of all the time she had seen pass and felt sad; not for its irretrievability, for she was haunted by its taste and tincture still; but for herself, helpless as she had so often been before the things which befell her, bewildered and credulous and afraid. And for the fact that all along she had been there, always there, trailing along in the wake of her aspirations, driving through her days with eyes fixed in a rear-view mirror on the road behind; always there, popping up in every memory like coincidence, the reluctant and culpable star of her own recollections.

The dark furrows striating the iron-hard winter fields fanned out around her to the horizon. She had been here many times before. She knew them by heart. Their familiarity struck her just then as rather menacing, as if she had come to the end of something. Only yesterday, had she not demanded of her mother to know when it would be, this defining moment, this 'in the end' that everybody spoke of? Well, perhaps it was here. She knew this place. The connection crackled round her like an electric circuit, bleakly synchronising things. Perhaps she had no more time to start again. Perhaps she would not be saved. Indeed, there was an apocalypse at hand and it was perhaps no more than this: that she had been here before!

Her history welled up in her: things burned, frozen, buried alive, a whole disordered catalogue of stories told or hidden. She alone could make sense of them. She alone could tell it as it was, for who else would remember? She must begin! She would begin, with the seeds of a starting place planted here in her revisiting, to tell of the mysterious normality of things, of their unexceptional symmetry, of the uninterrupted rise and fall of days; of how one could wait, could waste as much time as there was between birth and burial waiting for things that never came!

The low plain of the darkening sky cupped over her like a giant hand, creased with clouds. She felt herself growing smaller before it, until finally she was tiny and the years had gone back and it was summer, and she was tasting once again the loveliness of unknowing, the certainty of belief, the delicious prospect of a future as yet untold. She had been in no hurry – she had had all the time in the world; and yet still she had thought then that it would be better than this. She raised herself on her knees and peered over the top of the tree. A sudden blast of icy wind slapped her cheeks. In dreams, she had perched in its withered breast as if at the prow of a ship: the wind coming off the fields into her hair, the sun nipple-warm and magnetic, the wheat a dragonfly ocean of swaying stalks over which they appeared to be sailing.

Chapter Twenty-three

AGNES came back from her parents' house to a London cloaked with the promise of a storm. Although it was still early evening King's Cross was deserted, as if a nuclear alert had sounded moments before her arrival. The air smelled oddly grassy and fresh. A strong wind whipped down the Gray's Inn Road, causing litter to scuttle and fly along the pavements. Agnes got on the underground, scenting change.

When she got home, Nina was lounging around the house as if she lived there. By now the wind was bellowing through the empty streets and as Agnes entered the hall a sudden gust slammed the door ferociously shut behind her. Nina jumped up nervously from the sofa at the sound and Agnes saw her make a dash for the staircase. She herself, however, had had precisely that exigent means of escape in mind, and the two of them encountered one another at the foot of the stairs like embarrassed acquaintances caught in a chemist's buying condoms.

'I thought you were away,' accused Nina.

'I was,' replied Agnes.

She surrendered the stairs by stepping back to allow her through. Nina nodded curtly and began to proceed up them. Agnes watched her legs disappearing from view, and for what seemed like the first time, felt a physical ache of regret for the sad demise of their friendship.

'Nina!' she called up the stairs. 'Nina, can we talk? Please?'

There was silence on the upper floor. Agnes took comfort from the sound, deducing that if Nina had not exactly retracted her escape, she had at least suspended it in order to consider her offer. Presently, a long sigh was emitted from the top of the stairwell.

'Okay.' She began a suspicious descent. 'If you want.'

Agnes remained frozen at the foot of the stairs while Nina proceeded sullenly past her. She had not expected, after making her initial overture, to be afforded the lion's share of the work involved in drawing up some sort of armistice. She had assumed that her concession would immediately precipitate a warm and tearful reunion. Nina sat leadenly on the sofa and looked resentful. Agnes realised she had always been rather frightened of Nina, and this thought, combined with a sudden sensation of recklessness induced by the oddly comforting realisation that what was already lost could not be lost again, conspired to make her all at once quite brave.

'Don't do that!' she cried, marching into the sitting-room.

'What? Do what?'

'Slouch around like a – like a teenager!'

She stood in front of her and glared down. Nina, who had been caught unawares by her attack, now attempted to marshal her forces.

'Since when were you my mother?' she said, folding her arms and pinching up her face in a manner which somehow managed to give more truth to Agnes's accusation than she herself had been able to do.

'There you go again! You sound about fourteen! It's pathetic, it's—' Agnes felt weak with daring. She thought of sitting down, but decided her present stance afforded her a certain authority. 'It's beneath you,' she continued masterfully. 'We don't have to talk, okay? We don't *have* to do anything! We're grown up, in case you hadn't noticed, so don't give me all that grudging aquiescence.'

Nina observed a brief, dumbfounded silence.

'My mother would never say grudging acquiescence,' she pointed out finally.

'Your mother is a — a suburban android with furry seat covers on the loo!'

Nina considered this.

'How do you know that?' she said.

'I don't,' Agnes confessed.

'Well, actually, she doesn't have furry seat covers,' Nina said, quite amiably. 'That kind of thing is class war in East Sheen. Frilly valances, now that's another story.'

'I'm sorry,' Agnes replied, attempting to prolong this unexpected vein of good humour. 'I underestimated her. What is a valance, anyway?'

'Valance,' said Nina, getting up, 'is where old housewives go to die. Shall I make some coffee?'

Agnes wondered if she was asking for permission, and if so, whether this suggested a new and entirely unbargained-for respect.

'I'll help,' she said, leaving nothing to chance.

The strain of politeness lent things a certain awkwardness. In the kitchen, Nina filled the kettle while Agnes got mugs out of the cupboard. In the course of their duties they almost collided with one another, and found themselves engaging in a quickstep of embarrassed avoidance like strangers on a pavement.

'Sorry,' they said in unison.

Agnes wondered if this understated apology were sufficient to encompass the full range of their transgressions.

'How's Jack?' she nobly inquired, extending the hand of friendship still further. Nina visibly stiffened.

'Jack and I aren't seeing each other any more.'

'Oh. I'm sorry.'

'What for? It wasn't working. It was wrong. I was wrong,' she added, plugging in the kettle.

She turned around to face Agnes, as if expecting her to speak. Agnes, taken by surprise, could only emit a stunned silence.

'I got confused, I suppose,' Nina continued presently. She turned away again and busied herself with the coffee cups.

Her shaking hands rattled them against the counter-top. 'I thought I didn't need people, not really. But I started needing him. I don't know why.'

'You loved him,' Agnes interjected, feeling herself once more to be on known territory.

'Maybe,' shrugged Nina. 'But I didn't like him. Is that possible? I always thought that sort of talk was for people who didn't know their own minds, but there you go.'

Agnes found herself on the verge of agreeing whole-heartedly with the former part of this statement, but realised in time that to do so might merely provide evidence as to the truth of the latter.

'Why didn't you like him?' she inquired.

'Well, to begin with it was little things, I suppose. I found myself having to convince myself that he had reasons for doing this or that. It was as if I was making excuses for him. I just – pretended not to notice things.'

'What do you mean?'

'Haven't you ever done that? Wanted something so much that you'll do anything, tell yourself any kind of lie, just to keep believing in it? It's like – it's like some kind of addiction.'

'But you can't know everything!' Agnes cried. 'People are more – mysterious than that, aren't they? Perhaps he would have surprised you. How could you know?'

'That's the difference between you and me,' Nina replied. She smiled. 'You say mysterious, I say shifty. What's your idea of mystery, anyway? Your heart's desire ingesting hard drugs on the quiet while you wring your hands in the bedroom and wonder what you're doing wrong?'

Agnes gasped at the cruelty of this blow.

'But you knew,' she said. 'I may have been stupid, but you *knew*!'

'I know,' said Nina unhappily. 'All I'm saying is that none of us are innocent. I was looking for a way of holding on to Jack, and that was it. Like we had a secret and we were banding together.' She laughed strangely. 'I was in the boys' club for a while there. The truth is that I didn't want to admit

I was disappointed in him. I convinced myself it was in your best interests not to know – see, there's your mystery! I thought I was saving you.' She drew herself up. 'But I acted disloyally and I apologise.'

'That's okay,' Agnes replied, able to be generous now that her name had been cleared on at least one count. 'But I shouldn't be saved from things!' she added.

'What do you mean?' Nina looked rather startled.

'I don't really know,' Agnes confessed. 'I suppose I meant that I shouldn't *need* to be saved from things. It makes me sound so – naïve. But how else am I supposed to learn if I'm never told? How am I supposed to know?'

'Well—' Nina looked perplexed. 'Like I said, it isn't always a question of being told, is it? I mean, sometimes you just have to find things out for yourself.'

'But how?' Agnes cried. 'By telepathy? I mean, where did everyone else learn how the world works? Sometimes I feel as if I've missed something, some vital clue that would make everything clear.' She gazed out of the kitchen window, where the dark trees waved their long branches in the wind like frantic, keening arms. 'And then sometimes I think that I do know things, things that no one else knows.'

'Like what?' said Nina suspiciously.

'Oh, nothing useful! Things that aren't really there, at any rate. Metaphors, I suppose you'd call them. As if everything is actually something else.'

'Oh.'

'So really it's no surprise that I miss the obvious,' Agnes continued, 'when nothing is as it seems.'

Nina leaned against a cupboard and looked thoughtful.

'I've always thought it was more a question of your distorting the truth rather than not seeing it,' she said.

'Why would I do that?' said Agnes nervously. She stared at the floor. She was not accustomed to hearing herself so frankly discussed, although it did occur to her that this might simply be because she wasn't normally present when such discussions were held.

'How should I know? Maybe you don't like the way things are. Maybe you want to protect yourself. Everyone selects certain things from what's around them to conform with their idea of how they want life to be. Like I've always gone for outlandish, subversive things because I'm afraid of being normal.'

'Really?' Agnes was surprised.

'So would you,' said Nina, 'if you'd grown up in East Sheen.'

'I've always wanted to be normal,' Agnes confessed.

Nina raised her eyebrows. Agnes felt they were like two old women comparing varicose veins, each secretly marvelling at the other's worse defect beside their own known one.

'Like I said,' Nina continued. 'Everyone has their own way of dealing with things. Sometimes it's hard to admit the truth. Like with Jack. I was well on the way to hating myself, because it seemed easier than hating him. Do you see what I'm saying? Sometimes we'll ruin everything, sacrifice everything, just so that one thing can be perfect.'

'But nothing is perfect!' said Agnes. The truth of her words dawned on her only after she had said them. It seemed to her then the saddest thing she had ever known. 'Nothing is,' she repeated.

'No,' said Nina, putting a friendly arm around her. 'But some things are pretty good.'

Agnes was in Jean's office. Beyond the window a low sky darkened, threatening rain. A gust of wind rattled the glass against the stainless steel casing like something trying to get in. Agnes glanced at the clock on the wall and synchronised her watch with it to pass the time. Opposite her, Jean appeared to be recounting the story of her life.

'In those days I was doing your job, although the company was much smaller then, of course. There was something rather – cosy about it. Things were quite different then. Everyone knew everybody else.'

'Of course,' echoed Agnes belatedly. Even in this alien era in the history of *Diplomat's Week*, she knew everyone trapped within its portals and had effectively tired of the vast majority. Figures bent against the wind scurried past on the pavement outside.

'We were almost like a family,' Jean continued sighingly. 'That was our philosophy, sort of "keep it in the family". So when the editor, my boss, finally went – well, it seemed very natural.'

'Had he been ill for long?'

'Excuse me? Oh, no! Oh no, you misunderstand me! Goodness no, he didn't die. He retired.'

'Oh.'

'So it seemed natural that I would – you know—'

'Take over?'

'Exactly. But I hadn't expected it, not at all! You could have knocked me over with a feather when they told me. Once the first thrill had passed, of course, I became terribly nervous. What did I know about running a department? I was like you – a young girl with no real ambitions of my own. I didn't think I'd be able to keep up. All the cut and thrust, you know. But then the MD said to me, "Jean," he said, "what this place needs is the feminine touch." I felt much better after that.'

Agnes twitched nervously. She longed for Greta, who was taking a few days off. It was hard to laugh at things on one's own. One got sucked in.

'So what do you think, dear?' said Jean.

'About what?'

'Well – well, about everything.' She waved her hands distractedly in the air, a gesture apparently intended to encompass global concerns.

'What do you mean?' Agnes persisted.

'Agnes, dear, haven't you listened to a word I've been saying?'

'Yes, you told me about the old days and your boss leaving,' she obediently repeated. 'And then—'

'Oh dear,' Jean interjected. 'We don't seem to be understanding one another very well, do we?'

'It's not my fault!' Agnes cried impatiently. 'You won't tell me what you're trying to say! Just say it in a way I can understand.'

'I'm leaving,' Jean blurted out. 'And there's really no need—'

'You see, it wasn't so hard!' said Agnes. 'It's really very easy. You should try it more often.'

'I admit I might not have made things clear,' Jean conceded nobly. 'It's all been rather sudden, you see. These upheavals can be quite stressful, I've found.'

'I'm sure,' Agnes politely returned. 'But you'll be surprised how quickly one adapts.'

A spatter of rain hit the window with a gravelly sound. Old autumn leaves were hurled acrobatically into the air by a fierce gust of wind. The disturbance outside made the atmosphere within the office suddenly rather pleasant. They sat in companionable silence. Agnes thought of Jean leaving, and decided she might even miss her.

'So why are you leaving?' she inquired presently, as the still-mysterious fact of it occurred to her.

'I'm getting married.'

'To Dave?'

'To David, yes. We decided last week.'

'Congratulations,' said Agnes. An atmosphere of candour having now been established, she felt confident to continue: 'But – if you don't mind my saying so – that doesn't necessarily mean you have to leave, does it?'

Jean took some time to consider the question. Agnes was struck by the thought that her soon-to-be ex-boss might be harbouring some old-fashioned ideas about wifely duty from which she herself might be able to dissuade her. Further delay, however, forced upon her the idea that such concealments could only hint at the importunate presence of scandal and subterfuge. Perhaps Jean had become pregnant and was being driven by shame towards a hasty union. The thought of it filled her with horror: not so much for the fallen Jean, but for the thought that her inquiry might provoke tearful confessions. She wished she could recall her words. Under such circumstances, they were both prurient and inflammatory. Despite the currently civilised tone of their discussions, she felt sure her relationship with Jean would not bear up beneath the strain.

'I'm not just doing it for David,' Jean finally declared. She pronounced her words carefully. 'Although David certainly showed me the way and I am profoundly grateful to him for it. Our forthcoming marriage should make that gratitude adequately clear. But there are other, greater reasons for my resignation. I am dedicating my life to Jesus and all his works.' She fixed Agnes with a steely eye. 'And might I tell you, for me there could be no greater privilege.'

Agnes's horror doubled. Jean gave her a sinister smile. All at once, the thought of her leaving did not seem so very unfortunate. Agnes glanced at the door, calculating the time it would take to hurl herself through it should Jean decide to commence her ministry peremptorily with the doubter before her. Immediately, however, she repented her aversion. What business was it of hers if Jean found happiness in the employ of the Almighty? Was it, perhaps, her own recent sense of redundancy from that very realm that had brought from her such a response? Could she resent the certainty currently illuminating Jean's features, knowing that she herself no longer possessed it? Might she even be jealous?

'So,' she said hurriedly, before she could work upon herself the conversion which, so far, Jean had not attempted to perform. 'So, who's replacing you? That is, if you don't mind my asking. I mean, I don't want it to seem as if I want you to go or anything, but it would be helpful to know what we can expect.' She laughed shrilly. 'I suppose they'll be getting a real slavedriver. After a couple of months, we'll probably be begging you to come back.'

'As a matter of fact,' said Jean, who did not seem to find this idea particularly amusing, 'we were thinking of offering you the job.'

Her tone suggested that, based on the evidence of their conversation, this offer could at any moment be withdrawn. Agnes stared at her in amazement.

'*Me?*' she said.

A fierce wind tore round the corner of Elwood Street, hurdling the low garden walls like a greyhound. The trees groaned in the dark while empty tin cans rattled percussively on the pavements. Agnes sat in the house listening to the storm brewing. A draught was whistling through the crack in the wall and she felt its cold breath on the back of her neck. She moved from the sofa to the armchair. Now it was licking her leg like a fawning cat. It was hard to think amidst all this disturbance. She got up crossly and slammed out into the desolate garden.

A deckchair left over from the summer was leaning against the wall, its striped innards fluttering darkly in the wind. She unfolded it and sat down. All around her were the blazing square of windows from other houses, astonished eyes in the darkness. She leaned back and looked at the moonless sky.

'Agnes?'

Merlin clattered out of the back door and stumbled into the garden. He wrapped his coat around him and crumpled his face against the wind.

'Getting some air?' he said blithely, trying to get into the spirit of things.

'I'm trying to think.'

'Do you want some help?' He sat down cross-legged beside her. 'I'm very good on cosmic issues and I can throw in man trouble at a discount.'

'You sound very cheerful.' Agnes peered at him through the shadows of trees. 'What's happened?'

'Ah.' He smiled. 'Very perceptive of you. Well, let's just say that I'm no longer in bondage to the power-crazed lusts of the dominatrix.' He sighed contentedly. 'I seem once again to be my own man. Whatever that means.'

'So what happened? Did she catch you reading *Cosmopolitan*?'

'Nothing so tawdry.' Merlin laughed. 'I keep it well hidden beneath my desk. No, she has found a replacement, impossible though it may seem.'

'Who?'

'My male secretary, as it happens. He doesn't seem to mind. He's sleeping my way to the top.'

'Or his own.'

'Or his own. Anyway, now that I'm an expert in the fickleness of womankind,' he continued casually, 'I may as well put it to good use.'

'How?'

'Well, you know.' Merlin rubbed his face with embarrassment. 'Like, a girlfriend.'

'You mean you've got one? Who is she?'

'No, no, I don't mean I've got one. I'm just – well, open to offers.'

Agnes stared at him. She almost began to laugh, but the aspect of vulnerability in his face moved her instead to tenderness.

'You're right,' she said. 'We've monopolised you for too long.'

'Oh, it's not that! I've never really thought about it before, I suppose. I always assumed I was something of a late bloomer. Besides, I preferred having women as friends. Maybe it's to do with my upbringing. I've been well schooled in the effects of male iniquity.'

'So now you've had a close encounter with the effects of female iniquity, you reckon it's time to get your own back.'

'Not at all. It sounds quite strange, I know, but I think that what happened made me see myself in a different way. Not as a friend of women—' he cackled melodramatically – 'but as a seducer of them.'

Agnes thought about this. At first it made her sad, as she thought it must do watching a favourite child grow up and

hence away from those who had loved him first. And yet
Merlin was no child! She had never thought before about how
unusual he was. It seemed to her then that she never knew
she had things until she lost them.

'It won't change anything,' he said, watching her.

She wondered if he would become suspicious, defensive,
embittered; if he would watch her and Nina with new eyes,
understanding things about them, blaming them for a hurt
inflicted by someone else. For a moment she felt she would
have done anything to protect him from the course which
now opened out so temptingly before him. She could tell him,
as no one had told her, the perils that awaited him there, the
hidden traps and future pains to which innocence was blind.
She could save him from it, as she herself had wanted to be
saved!

'It will,' she said resignedly. 'But perhaps that's no bad
thing, after all.' She met his gaze. 'I suppose you have to find
out for yourself.'

He nodded and leaned against her chair. They sat for a
moment in silence. The storm appeared suddenly to abate and
in the stillness Agnes felt they could have stayed like that for
ever. Before long, however, a fresh gust of wind whipped
around them and Merlin sat up.

'So what's up?' He smiled cheerfully and added: 'Doc?'

'Well—' Agnes folded her arms across her chest and sighed.
'Jean's leaving. They've offered me her job.'

'But that's great! It's great, isn't it?'

'No!' she cried. 'Of course it isn't! Why do you think I'm
sitting out here, for heaven's sake? Because I'm pleased about
it?'

The door slammed and Nina stumbled out into the garden.

'What is this?' she yelled against the wind. 'A bloody earth
summit?'

'It's an open-air careers forum,' replied Merlin, patting the
space beside him. 'Come and sit down. You might learn
something.'

'You're mad,' said Nina. 'Both of you.'

'Not me,' Merlin innocently replied. He pointed at Agnes. 'Her.'

'Why? What's up?'

Agnes threw Merlin a murderous glance.

'I didn't say anything!' he protested.

'What's going on?' Nina demanded.

'Jean's leaving,' Agnes wearily repeated. 'And they've offered me her job.'

'Oh.' Nina wrapped her coat around her chest. 'Oh. What are you going to do?'

'What is this?' exclaimed Merlin. 'I don't understand. Somebody explain to me why I alone don't feel depressed by this news. I thought I was supposed to be the sensitive one around here.'

'Well,' explained Nina. 'It's a big commitment. And Agnes isn't even sure that she likes the company or the product. Am I right, Ag?'

Agnes nodded.

'I take it you two have patched things up,' commented Merlin despondently. 'My double-agent days are over.'

'Would you want to spend the rest of your life at *Diplomat's Week*?' burst out Agnes. 'I mean, I always thought it was something temporary – something to do while I was waiting for . . . for real life to begin, I suppose.' She looked at them both imploringly. 'If I accept, well, it will become real life.'

'Is that so bad?' said Merlin.

'I think that rather depends,' observed Nina, 'on what she was expecting.' She drew her knees up beneath her chin. 'Unfortunately, things have an annoying way of not becoming real until they're unpleasant.' She laughed. 'Do you remember how we were at college? We spent all our time drinking white wine and mock-identifying with the proletariat. Now I seem to spend all my time drinking bloody instant coffee and mock-identifying with students lounging around in sixteenth-century buildings.'

'It's a cross the middle classes have to bear,' opined Merlin.

'We come somewhere between hubris and entropy. Anyway, what was Agnes expecting?'

'How should I know?' Nina shrugged. 'Why don't you ask her?'

'Agnes,' said Merlin sonorously. 'Reveal to us your great expectations.'

'Well—' Agnes thought about it. 'Aren't everyone's the same? Something glamorous, interesting, exciting—'

'—utterly unobtainable,' continued Merlin.

A blast of wind roared around them.

'But won't you be in charge?' said Nina into the sudden quiet of its subsidence.

'I suppose so. Of the magazine, anyway.'

'Well, couldn't you make it exciting?'

'What do you mean?'

'Change it, you know. Make it what you want.'

'It's called *Diplomat's Week*, Nina,' said Merlin. 'I don't think the scope is exactly endless.'

'Whose side are you on?' demanded Nina.

'I'm not sure, but I seem to be being left behind,' said Merlin mildly.

'Why not?' said Nina, addressing Agnes. 'Diplomacy is quite interesting, actually. It's politics. Also, it's a weekly, so you could have a news section as well as features. You could give the magazine an opinion. That sort of thing makes you indispensable.'

'I'm not sure how that would go down,' said Agnes. 'All we offer at the moment are restaurant reviews and lists of executive nightclubs. Our readership would probably simultaneously keel over if we mentioned politics.'

'Get new readers!' Nina cried. 'Increase your circulation!'

Agnes's own circulation had already visibly increased. She felt her heart pounding against her ribcage.

'Do you think I could?' she said. 'I mean, do you honestly think so?'

'Try,' Nina replied. 'And find out.'

'How much would they pay you?' Merlin inquired.

Agnes mentioned the sum Jean had proposed.

'Well, for God's sake,' sighed Merlin exasperatedly. He slapped his forehead. 'Why don't you just do it for the money?'

'The weirdest thing happened to me on my way here,' said Greta, bounding into the office. 'This guy came up to me and told me he thought I was beautiful. Can you believe it?'

'What did you do?' said Agnes fearfully.

'Nothing. He just said it and then he walked away. I was kind of miffed, actually.'

She seated herself on Agnes's desk, giving Agnes the opportunity to view at close quarters the physiognomy so admired by her benign assailant.

'You do look well,' she commented. 'You obviously needed a rest.'

'I feel different,' Greta agreed. 'I feel – happy, I guess. I know it may sound stupid, but I'm beginning to think those bad feelings, the ones I told you about, well, that they might have gone away.'

'Oh!' said Agnes delightedly. 'Do you think so?'

'Yeah. Neat, huh? I wonder if I'm going to meet just nice people from now on. I'll feel like such a sleaze.'

'But what do you think caused it?'

'Who knows? Maybe I faced my fear, like in those encounter groups. Maybe that son of a bitch did me a favour after all. I feel exorcised.' She grinned. 'Born again, even. Talking of which, are you taking this goddamned job or not? Have you made up your dumb mind?'

'Well – yes.'

'Yes you've made up your dumb mind, or yes you—'

'I'm taking the job.' Agnes interjected, while Greta leapt and cheered around the office. 'Although what I'm going to do with all this power I can't imagine. Make everyone wear orange uniforms to work or something.'

'Shame,' said Greta. 'I look great in orange.'

'What do you mean?' Agnes stared at her in horror. 'Aren't you going to be here?'

'Well, no, I guess.'

'But – but, Greta, you can't! We'll do everything equally, I promise. Oh, please stay! I won't tell you what to do, I promise! Please!'

'It wouldn't be right,' said Greta firmly. 'Someone has to be boss. Besides, I've got other plans. I want to be a gardener.'

'A gardener?'

'Sure. I found this place in Highgate where I can learn. I start next month.'

'But why?'

'Well, it would be kind of peaceful, don't you think? All those pretty flowers, and you get to wear overalls, and being outside all day is really good for your complexion as well.'

'I suppose so.' Agnes looked at her miserably.

'Don't look so glum, honey! You can find some robot to do all the work, and you and me can have a great time going out and getting smashed. It'll be neat.'

'Actually,' Agnes confessed, cheering up, 'I can see you as a gardener.'

'I knew you would. And you'll do a better job here than that Bible-bashing hussy, and things will turn out just fine. Just you wait and see.'

'Oh, Greta.' Agnes found herself becoming quite tearful. 'What will I do without you? I'll be so lonely here.'

'You need to have some fun,' said Greta. 'You need to find yourself a honey and that way you'll feel fine.'

'Oh.' Agnes put a hand to her own face. 'Oh, I don't think so. Besides, I don't suppose anyone would be interested in me now.'

She felt a solitary tear roll down her cheek.

'Stop that sniffling,' said Greta. 'Let's go out and celebrate. Actually, I think I could stand a little action too, while we're on the subject. Something sensitive for a change. Someone with a little innocence.'

'Greta,' said Agnes, 'I have to introduce you to my friend Merlin.'

Chapter Twenty-four

AGNES Day packed some clothes in a bag and left the house like someone leading a double life. It was cold and already dark, though she had left the office early so as to complete the commission in hand before the hours of witch and rat approached. The darkness made time uncertain. It floundered about the craven streets of north London like an amateur detective, looking for clues.

She headed towards the Blackstock Road with a furtive air. Only that morning, she and Nina and Merlin had had their modest bid for the house in Elwood Street accepted, and as a newly inaugurated member of the property-owning classes she wondered if her currently charitable behaviour would be deemed appropriate by that mysterious breed. Their purchase of the house was in itself a moderately charitable act. They were, they were agreed, to save it from the jaws of death. They would seal the crack, support the outer wall, and thus prevent their warmth, friendship and security from leaking inadvertently out. Agnes's parents had been delighted by this news. It was, they assured her, the right time in her life to be making such a move.

She took the bus to Camden. On the high street, the yellow light overlaying the darkness gave it the look of an alien city. Beside the shuttered shop-fronts sacks of rubbish lurked lumpily in the shadows. A man rooted in a bin, tossing unwanted articles over his shoulder and putting others in his pockets. He dug out a half-eaten piece of pizza and raised it to his lips.

Agnes got off the bus and walked back to the doorway where she had loitered that evening several weeks ago, dragging the sack of clothes behind her. A group of smartly dressed people walked past her, laughing noisily. Their perfumes collided behind them like skidding cars, with disastrous results. One of the women's jewellery clanked as she walked, as if she were made of tin. Agnes saw something on the pavement and she bent down to pick it up. It was a black leather wallet. She opened it and saw it was full of money.

'Excuse me!' she cried to the retreating group.

They walked on obliviously. She realised she had reached the doorstep, and she went to inspect it. It was empty. Moments later she guiltily remembered the wallet in her hand.

'Excuse me!' she called again, running to catch them up.

One or two of the group heard her cries, and stopped.

'I think you dropped this,' she panted, thrusting the wallet into the hands of the bejewelled woman.

'Oh.' The woman examined it. 'No, it's not mine. Ted!' she called to one of the men standing ahead. 'Ted, is this yours?'

Agnes waited while Ted searched his pockets and shook his head. The other men began searching their pockets too. The woman was now holding the wallet as if it were contaminated.

'No, this is nothing to do with us,' she said, shaking her head. She held it out to Agnes.

'Keep it!' Agnes cried. She darted across the road and into a side street. After a while she heard them move on. They were discussing something in bemused voices. She wondered what they would do with it; whether they would hand it over to the police, perhaps, or give it away. Perhaps the woman would keep it, guiltily, in a drawer, while it burned a hole through her expensive lingerie. The thought of it made Agnes laugh, and the sound of her own laughter reminded her of her purpose.

She walked back on to the main road and headed for the

tube station. On her way, she discerned a figure huddling amongst a mountain of rubbish bags on the pavement. He had erected a shelter for himself out of cardboard and was lying on his side within it.

'Excuse me,' she said, approaching him. 'Do you know where I can find Annie?'

He appeared to be asleep. Halfway through her question, however, he opened one bloodshot eye and peered at her.

'Spare some change,' he said.

'Annie,' repeated Agnes. 'Do you know where I can find her?'

'Spare some change for an old man,' he said.

Agnes fumbled in her pockets. At this rate her quest was going to cost her a fortune. The man nodded as she gave him the money and promptly shut his eyes again. She gazed despairingly along the deserted road. Shortly ahead of her on the right was a small side street. She turned into it, hearing the noise of restaurants, and saw that it was full of people going in and out of cafés and standing on the pavements. Several passers-by had stopped and were observing a group of men on the other side of the road, who were arranged in various positions of repose between two skips. They were surrounded by plastic bags, on which some of them sat. One man remained standing in the centre, and spoke while the others listened.

'Blessed are the poor,' he announced. As she drew closer Agnes saw that he was reading from a book. 'For they shall get bleeding rich. They shall inherit the bleeding earth, lads.' He surveyed them imperiously. 'But not before bleeding time.'

The group laughed, and several coughing fits were precipitated.

'What's more,' he continued. 'Blessed are the hungry, 'n' all. They shall be satisfied. Satisfied!' he bellowed.

'Mine's sausage and chips, mate,' chirped one of them, a small bald man, looking at the sky. The group roared.

'That's enough of your wit, slaphead,' retorted the leader. 'Blessed are ye when people despise you and call you all sorts of names, except on this one occasion, right?'

A subdued wave of laughter rippled among them. Agnes approached from behind the skip.

'Excuse me,' she said.

A heavy silence descended. All eyes turned to her. One or two people murmured.

'Bugger off,' said the leader. 'Can't you see we're busy?'

'Yes,' said Agnes. 'But I'm trying to find someone – a friend, that is, and I wondered if you might know where she is.'

'Nice sort of friend, is she?' replied the man, to varying volumes of laughter. 'Live around these parts, does she?' He indicated the derelict lot behind him.

'She's called Annie,' continued Agnes hurriedly. 'She used to be in a doorway up there. She said people round here knew her. I've brought her some things, that's all. I thought—'

'Anyone 'ere know Annie?' announced the man, unnecessarily loudly. Several heads were shaken.

'She that Scottish bird?' volunteered one.

'Yes!' Agnes cried. 'Yes, that's her. Do you know her?'

'Not so's people would talk about it,' quipped the man.

'Well, do you know where she is?'

The man looked at her. He was bearded and wore a tattered tweed hat.

'She ain't here,' he said finally. 'And you ain't going to find her, neither. She's gone.'

'Where? Where has she gone?'

'Dunno. She's just gone, is all. Haven't seen her round for a couple of weeks.'

'She the Scottish one?' said the leader belatedly. 'I got you now. I know 'er.'

'Do you know where she is?' said Agnes.

'Skin and bone, that the one? Yeah, I got you. Used to be up by the river, up there? Yeah, she's gone.'

The sack in Agnes's hand was heavy and she put it down. She was too late. Annie had died, in the coldness of a London night with no one in all the city to comfort her.

'But where's she gone?' she said again.

Her mind could scarcely encompass the question. Where,

after all, was there to go? Did one just disappear, and then die again as gradually people forgot the particulars of one's life? She felt terror grip at her throat. She wondered if Annie would haunt her, her withered little ghost scuttling about the room while Agnes slept alone.

The group were regarding her now with some sympathy.

'Sorry, love,' said one of them.

''Er son come to find her,' said the leader suddenly. 'Took 'er off home with him, so I heard.'

'What?' Agnes stared at him. 'Her son?'

The faithless Jacky had returned, then! She felt her heart swell with relief.

''S right. Took 'er back to Scotch-land. Know 'er well, did you?'

'No,' Agnes cheerfully replied. 'No, I didn't really know her very well.'

She turned to go, leaving the bag with them. Perhaps they could find some use for its contents. The group of men watched her.

'By the way,' she said, turning back to them, 'what exactly are you all doing?'

'What does it look like?' said the leader. 'It's a bleeding Bible class, innit?'

On the bus to Highbury she sat at the top and looked out of the window. At this level, the pavement classes were all but obliterated. One sailed, ship-like, through a strange element of streetlamps and first-floor windows, a post-diluvian world. She thought of the strange congregation she had just stumbled upon. Really, they hadn't seemed mad at all. In fact, they were quite ordinary. For a moment the empty bus appeared to shift around her to accommodate them. It struck her that faith was a free element, like air. One could have it for nothing. One could have it when one had nothing else. It was one of the comforts of ordinariness. The bus shuddered to a halt and one or two people clomped up the stairs. A man in a long coat sat down in the adjacent seat. Out of the corner of her eye Agnes could see that he was young and rather handsome. He did not look at her. She returned despondently to her perusal of the window.

It was perhaps, after all, very simple, she thought as the bus turned into the Holloway Road. It was just a question of not looking too closely at things. Close up, the mad weave was bizarre and imageless, but from a distance a pattern could perhaps be discerned and somewhere within it all that she knew: her family, her friends and then herself, all of them busily plaiting and sewing, creating the small corner of life they would one day look back on, together or apart, as their own. She supposed one only found out how one compared by looking at the picture. It was the final result and she would wait for it, as those around her were now waiting.

The bus became entangled in a long rope of traffic. There was a unanimous sigh as the passengers settled back, resigned, into their seats. There was no hurry, after all. For ordinary people, such as herself, there was nothing to hasten towards, no defining moment. She too leaned back in her seat, succumbing to the journey's hiatus.

The bus lurched forward a few feet and then stopped. She thought of John, of his irreversible loss. Tears began to start up behind her eyes. She felt his name forming in her throat, swelling in her brain; the cipher of her desire, the word that lay between herself and the unthinkable! He was no longer perfect. In fact, he was irreparable. The worst of it was that she no longer needed him. He hadn't even left her that. For a moment her mind roared with grief for him; and then he was gone.

Agnes looked up, blinking. The light in the bus was exceptionally bright. Someone seemed to be speaking to her.

'Excuse me?' she said.

'I said, it gets boring, doesn't it?'

It was the man in the seat next to hers. He was smiling benignly at her. She wondered what she had been doing to make him so concerned.

'Only if you want to get there,' she replied.

He appeared to be considering her answer.

'That's true,' he said, nodding.

'I mean,' she explained, 'if you were going to the Odd Fellows' reunion party, you wouldn't be in such a hurry, would you?'

He looked at her bemusedly. She felt herself blushing. Suddenly he laughed.

'I suppose not,' he said. 'But I don't know if it would be worth it.'

'That depends on how odd a fellow you are,' she replied. 'You never know, it might open up a whole new world.'

He laughed again, this time more heartily.

'My name's Steven,' he said, extending his hand.

She looked at the hand and then at him. Perhaps things weren't so ordinary after all.

'Agnes,' she replied, shaking it. 'Agnes Day.'